FANTASY?

Nightmare, dream, horror, idyll? A strange excursion to the edge (at least) of reality and—surely?—beyond. For if not, the implications curdle the blood.

Mr. Machen's style is elliptical, crabwise, cheerful and totally deceptive. For at the root of his seemingly straightforward story of prosaic, indeed, rather stuffy Londoners, lies a deliberation of evil that sends one scurrying back through the pages to see if such things can really be.

And this is indeed, the burden of his tale —if, in fact, it can be so described. Respectability, he seems to say, is merely a screen for unimaginable horrors lurking right beneath the well-shined, sturdy shoes of your neighbor. But then, does that make this all *real*?

And that being so, *where do you fit in?*

THE THREE IMPOSTORS

Arthur Machen

Introduction by
Lin Carter

BALLANTINE BOOKS • NEW YORK
An Intext Publisher

Introduction copyright © 1972 by Lin Carter

All rights reserved.

SBN 345-02643-8-125

This edition published by arrangement with
Alfred A. Knopf, Inc.

First Printing: June, 1972

Printed in the United States of America

Cover art by Bob LoGrippo

BALLANTINE BOOKS, INC.
101 Fifth Avenue, New York, N.Y. 10003

About THE THREE IMPOSTORS
and Arthur Machen:

Baghdad-on-the Thames

Like everyone else who loves the kingdom of books, and whose life has been devoted to adventuring within the all-but-limitless borders of that kingdom, I have found my way to certain books which seem to have been written for my pleasure alone.

It is a common experience. I read about four hundred books every year; most of them are quite forgettable, but a few stay with me; and each year I discover a book or two, or maybe three, to which I find myself returning, year after year.

But then there is that rare, precious book that becomes a lifelong companion, a book to which I am constantly referring, a book which I will reread perhaps twenty times in my life, each time with the fresh feeling of discovery, and with new excitement, finding therein some sparkling new marvel I had never noticed before.

You do not find many such books, even in a lifetime devoted to reading—perhaps twenty, or, if you are very lucky, twenty-five. But they remain in your mind and supply you with a host of names and scenes and characters and symbols which form a sort of private mythology, a personal iconography wherewith to interpret the people and events in your life.

Every booklover will have a different, very personal list. My own list includes T. H. White's *The Sword in the Stone,* Gustave Flaubert's *Salammbô,* James Branch

Cabell's *The Cream of the Jest,* William Beckford's *Vathek,* Milton's *Paradise Lost,* the *Romances* of Voltaire, Thomas B. Costain's *The Black Rose,* A. Merritt's *The Face in the Abyss,* John Steinbeck's *Cannery Row,* the *Cantos* of Ezra Pound, Thackeray's *The Rose and the Ring,* Andrew Lang's *Prince Prigio,* and a few others.

The list, you will notice, is heterogeneous in the extreme. It includes a bestseller-type historical novel very popular in my teens and Flaubert's masterpiece, one of the most superb examples of sheer style ever crafted. The range extends from the noblest epic poem in the English language written a decade after the death of Oliver Cromwell to a modernist epic, quirky, elitist, dissociative, and largely incomprehensible to most readers. The list includes the work of a pulp magazine adventure story writer, and one of the lesser novels of a modern Pulitzer Prize winner. The list is hardly to be construed as my personal choice of the "best" novels ever written: it is, simply, those novels I have encountered along the way which speak to my own character and personality with an intimate voice.

Somewhere on that list belongs *The Three Impostors.* I can neither justify its position on my shelf of lifelong favorites, nor explain why the book appeals to me so powerfully. Indeed, I find myself floundering helplessly at the task of simply describing it.

The Three Impostors is a novel; then again, it is not a novel at all, but a string of episodes and short stories tied together by a very thin narrative thread. It is a work of fantasy; then again, it is a work of Gothic horror. Lastly, it is a picaresque and weirdly comic satire of London life.

Of all the books that come to my mind, *The Three Impostors* most completely defies description. Like *Don Quixote* or *Lolita,* it has almost everything in it: adventure, comedy, romance, horror, satire, dream, nightmare, and idyll. The book is an almost inexhaustible source of excitement and pleasure; perhaps that is why I find myself returning to it again and again, finding therein each time some new delight I had never before noticed.

Most readers will recognize the name of Arthur Machen as that of one of the finest modern craftsmen in the rich field of supernatural horror. Many will know him for such tales as *The Novel of the White Powder,* or *The Novel of the Black Seal*—gems of weird fiction very frequently anthologized, and both, oddly, found within the crowded pages of *The Three Impostors.* But Machen was very much more than just a writer of weird fiction: he was a poet, a journalist, a mystic, an essayist, a translator (of Casanova's *Memoirs* and of the *Heptameron* of Marguerite, Queen of Navarre), an occultist (belonging, with Yeats and Aleister Crowley, to the Hermetic Order of the Golden Dawn), a serious critic of literature (for which see his *Hieroglyphics,* a fascinating treatise on the theory of literature as "ecstacy"), and more.

He was one of the noblest stylistic masters of the English language in our century, and an internationally famous literary connoisseur who knew everyone from Oscar Wilde to James Branch Cabell.

Machen was born in Wales; to be precise, in Caerleon-on-Usk, a tiny, remote village that had once been the golden Isca of the Roman legions, and later one of the splendid capitols of King Arthur and a seat of the Round Table. He was born Arthur Llewelyn Jones on March 3, 1863. That was a very long time ago: George MacDonald was a young novelist of thirty-nine, and had published his first novel, *Phantastes,* only five years before; while the great William Morris, not yet thirty, was a decade or so away from writing his first fantasy romance, *The Wood Beyond the World.* Lord Dunsany, E. R. Eddison, Cabell, Lovecraft, and Merritt had not even been born.

Arthur Machen spent his early years as an only child in a country rectory; his family circle consisted of a clergyman father, an invalid mother, and a maiden aunt who had the task of raising the boy. Inured to loneliness from his earliest years, Machen turned to the wild, glorious, untamed nature of wooded Wales for solace, and to the world of books for companionship. He fed upon Dickens, Cervantes, De Quincey, Scott, Tennyson, and the Brontës. His formal schooling was got at the Hereford Cathedral School, which dates to the fourteenth century and which offered a sound classical education. He revolted against the compulsory athletics and the English public school tradition in general and quit school at seventeen.

He came to London that same year, taking with him a solid knowledge of French and Latin. Instead of schooling himself further, he turned to juvenile verse writing, producing reams of heroica inspired by Swinburne. His first book, published at his own expense in a limited edition of one hundred copies, was a long poem called *Eleusinia*. He later admitted that he had simply taken an article on the Eleusinian Mysteries from Smith's *Classical Dictionary* and turned it into verse—"some blank, some rhymed, but all bad"—as a recent biography, Wesley D. Sweetser's *Arthur Machen*, puts it. (Incidentally, with his *Eleusinia*, Machen invented a system which might be called the "do-it-yourself collector's item." Unhappy with the poem a while later, he destroyed all but two copies of the book, thus making it a rarity for collectors beyond the dreams of avarice.)

Machen became caught up in the raffish, slummy world of the Grub Street journalist, hacking out bits of newspaper copy, starving (and freezing) in a garret, taking odd jobs in literary fields, doing a bit of translating here and a book review there. He was calling himself "Arthur Machen" by this time (you will have to admit that Arthur L. Jones is not a very memorable name for an author). This pen-name came about in an amusing way: while Arthur was still a boy at school, his father took to calling himself Jones-Machen, thus adding his wife's maiden name to his own surname. He may have done this to give the illusion of family background, or perhaps he hoped to solicit some support for the boy's schooling by appealing to family-conscious wealthier relatives. At any rate, our author adopted the bifurcated surname while still at school, and later trimmed it down to just Machen.

His classical education, early reading, and the old authors he found himself translating all contributed to forming his style. It was one of the most remarkable of his achievements. As Philip Van Doren Stern describes it:

A taste for his work has to be acquired; the writing is polished and elaborate, the thinking is subtle, and the imagery is rich with the glowing color that is to be found in medieval church glass. His style does not belong to our period of stripped diction and fast-moving prose; it stems instead from the latter part of the nineteenth century, and preserves some of the formality of that age when authors were learned people who had to undergo long apprenticeships to master their profession.

Machen wrote *The Three Impostors* in 1890. He was a young man of twenty-seven, far from being famous, still grubbing in Grub Street for the wherewithal to keep body and soul together. It was, more or less, his first novel. By this slight bit of hedging I mean that it was the first actual novel he had written (if you want to call it a novel, and some of you won't), although he had at twenty-one composed something called *The Chronicles of Clemendy*. Now, you can call *Clemendy* a novel, if you like, but to my taste its claims to that classification are even slenderer than those of *The Three Impostors*. *Clemendy* reads like a horribly inept and ill-advised attempt to re-write Rabelais. If you have ever read Rabelais—and I have, grimly plodding every foot of the way—you will probably have decided (as I did) that whatever the excellences of Rabelais may be, they are largely invisible to the ordinary reader; and thus the notion of someone sitting down deliberately to *imitate* Rabelais may strike you as mildly incredible. Anyway, *Clemendy* seems to me almost unreadable, and whether something no more novelistic than Chaucer's *Canterbury Tales* is to be considered a novel remains highly questionable. But *The Three Impostors* is closer to the formal novel than anything Machen had previously attempted, and thus it may be called his first. He did not write many.

My title for this introduction is "Baghdad-on-the-Thames." I wonder if you will agree and interpret *The Three Impostors* as I do. To me it reads rather as if Machen were trying to look at London as Scheherezade looked at Baghdad—through eyes that saw everyday life as a tangle of incredible coincidences, chance meetings, overheard anecdotes, and marvelous encounters. The book teems with adventure and romance, but the exotic coloring and bizarre ornament are mostly a matter of point of view and personal interpretation. At any rate, through the eyes of Arthur Machen, London becomes a fantastic metropolis, filled with intrigue and mystery and marvels.

Most commentators on *The Three Impostors* consider it an imitation of Robert Louis Stevenson's *The New Arabian Nights.* This may be so—I must confess to never having read this book of Stevenson's. I know that Machen once was asked the source or sources of *The Three Impostors* and replied that it had come entirely from his head—and Stevenson's; but I can't see that it really matters very much where the book came from, so long as we have it to enjoy. Some of the best books in the world are imitations of other books (in fact, speaking of Rabelais, his *Gargantua and Pantagruel* just happens to be laid in that same Utopia invented by Sir Thomas More, while Stevenson's *New Arabian Nights* is, of course, an imitation of the *old* Arabian Nights).

Like many of the best books I know, *The Three Impostors* was a dismal flop when it first came out. It had a bit of trouble getting published in the first place, come to think of it; Machen began it in 1890, but John Lane did not publish it until five years later. By then Machen was becoming established. He had already published his most famous tale, *The Great God Pan,* and Lane's famous publishing house, The Bodley Head, had issued it with illustrations by the spectacular Aubrey Beardsley, which had not harmed the sales any.

But 1895 was the year of the stormy public scandal centering around Oscar Wilde and his rather sensational *amours.* Anything remotely connected with Wilde—such as *The Three Impostors,* written by an acquaintance, and illustrated by Wilde's own illustrator—was to be shunned as a tainted thing. Thus the reviews of *The Three Impostors* either denounced or dismissed the novel, and it was a very long time before people could look at the book with clear, unprejudiced eyes and see its remarkable beauties.

Arthur Machen was eighty-four when he died on December 15, 1947. Most of his major work was done when he was quite young, and he was largely forgotten before his demise. But a few American Machen enthusiasts of excellent literary taste, Vincent Starrett and Carl Van Vechten most importantly, introduced him to the readers in this country during the 1920s, and thus he came in for quite a renaissance on this side of the Atlantic although he had faded into limbo in the country of his birth long before.

The 1920s, you will recall, saw a rebirth of interest in belles-lettres. Beautifully written books, especially if they were tinged with delicate eroticism or were even faintly perverse, touched with obscure lore, occult learning, were being imported and actually read in the United States. These were the days when James Branch Cabell (a great Machen admirer, by the way) and J.-K. Huysmans and Edgar Saltus rose to fame in a republic which had generally reserved its laurels for writers of the general ilk of Lew Wallace and (at the other end of a narrow spectrum) James Fenimore Cooper.

It was Alfred A. Knopf, that famed publisher of amazingly good taste and not inconsiderable daring, who brought Machen into print on this side of the Atlantic. H. P. Lovecraft read Machen, learned much from him, and praised him highly in his brilliant study of the weird story, *Supernatural Horror in Literature*. Thus given a new lease on life, *The Three Impostors* began to accumulate the good reviews it had deserved from the beginning, ran through several printings, and became in fact just about Machen's best-known and most popular book.

From this position it has since declined a bit. The 1920s, of course, are long over—who reads Cabell or Huysmans or even Edgar Saltus today?—and Machen is primarily remembered for several very brilliant examples of short weird fiction. Oddly enough, it is in the world of the mystery writers which *The Three Impostors* is remembered, and it has been reprinted in recent years under the guise of a mystery story. But it is intrinsic in the ambiguous, all-encompassing style and nature of *The Three Impostors* that it can pass as almost any kind of fiction. Even adult fantasy!

—LIN CARTER
Editorial Consultant:
Ballantine Adult Fantasy Series

Hollis, Long Island, New York

The Three
Impostors

A Note on The Three Impostors

Most editions of *The Three Impostors* omit for some reason "The Decorative Imagination" and the "Novel of the Iron Maid."

I have no idea why this is. Perhaps it may have been done by Mr. Machen himself; few authors can resist the temptation offered by a new edition of one of their older books to tinker and tamper with the text yet once again. (I have been guilty of this sort of thing myself.)

At any rate, there are pleasant things in "The Decorative Imagination," and the "Novel of the Iron Maid" deserves a place beside the "Novel of the Dark Valley," the "Novel of the Black Seal," and the "Novel of the White Powder." So I have returned both of these brief sections to the text.

I include this note of explanation in case my readers already closely familiar with the text of *The Three Impostors* who may not have seen "The Decorative Imagination" or the "Novel of the Iron Maid" before are wondering where in the world these two unfamiliar items come from.

And I trust Mr. Machen, from whatever literary Valhalla he now inhabits, will smile down approvingly on an editor so fond of his book that he is willing to overrule even its author in restoring to the text a few lost pages.

—LIN CARTER

Prologue

'And Mr. Joseph Walters is going to stay the night?' said the smooth, clean-shaven man to his companion, an individual not of the most charming appearance, who had chosen to make his ginger-coloured moustache merge into a pair of short chin-whiskers.

The two stood at the hall door, grinning evilly at each other; and presently a girl ran quickly down the stairs and joined them. She was quite young, with a quaint and piquant rather than a beautiful face, and her eyes were of a shining hazel. She held a neat paper parcel in one hand, and laughed with her friends.

'Leave the door open,' said the smooth man to the other, as they were going out. 'Yes, by——,' he went on with an ugly oath, 'we'll leave the front door on the jar. He may like to see company, you know.'

The other man looked doubtfully about him.

'Is it quite prudent, do you think, Davies,' he said, pausing with his hand on the mouldering knocker. 'I don't think Lipsius would like it. What do you say, Helen?'

'I agree with Davies. Davies is an artist, and you are commonplace, Richmond, and a bit of a coward. Let the door stand open, of course. But what a pity Lipsius had to go away! He would have enjoyed himself.'

'Yes,' replied the smooth Mr. Davies, 'that summons to the west was very hard on the doctor.'

The three passed out, leaving the hall door, cracked and

riven with frost and wet, half open, and they stood silent
for a moment under the ruinous shelter of the porch.

'Well,' said the girl, 'it is done at last. We shall hurry
no more on the track of the young man with spectacles.'

'We owe a great deal to you,' said Mr. Davies politely;
'the doctor said so before he left. But have we not all three
some farewells to make? I, for my part, propose to say
good-bye here, before this picturesque but mouldy resi-
dence, to my friend, Mr. Burton, dealer in the antique and
curious,' and the man lifted his hat with an exaggerated
bow.

'And I,' said Richmond, 'bid adieu to Mr. Wilkins, the
private secretary, whose company has, I confess, become
a little tedious.'

'Farewell to Miss Lally, and to Miss Leicester also,'
said the girl, making as she spoke a delicious curtsy.
'Farewell to all occult adventure; the farce is played.'

Mr. Davies and the lady seemed full of grim enjoyment, but Richmond tugged at his whiskers nervously.

'I feel a bit shaken up,' he said. 'I've seen rougher
things in the States, but that crying noise he made gave
me a sickish feeling.'

The three friends moved away from the door, and began to walk slowly up and down what had been a gravel
path, but now lay green and pulpy with damp mosses. It
was a fine autumn evening, and a faint sunlight shone on
the yellow walls of the old deserted house, and showed
the patches of gangrenous decay, the black drift of rain
from the broken pipes, the scabrous blots where the bare
bricks were exposed, the green weeping of a gaunt laburnum that stood beside the porch, and ragged marks near
the ground where the reeking clay was gaining on the
worn foundations. It was a queer, rambling old place, the
centre perhaps two hundred years old, with dormer windows sloping from the tiled roof, and on each side there
were Georgian wings; bow windows had been carried up
to the first floor, and two dome-like cupolas that had once
been painted a bright green were now grey and neutral.
Broken urns lay upon the path, and a heavy mist seemed
to rise from the unctuous clay; the neglected shrubberies,

grown all tangled and unshapen, smelt dank and evil, and there was an atmosphere all about the deserted mansion that proposed thoughts of an open grave. The three friends looked dismally at the rough grasses and the nettles that grew thick over lawn and flower-beds; and at the sad water-pool in the midst of the weeds. There, above green and oily scum instead of lilies, stood a rusting Triton on the rocks, sounding a dirge through a shattered horn; and beyond, beyond the sunk fence and the far meadows, the sun slid down and shone red through the bars of the elm trees.

Richmond shivered and stamped his foot.

'We had better be going soon,' he said; 'there is nothing else to be done here.'

'No,' said Davies; 'it is finished at last. I thought for some time we should never get hold of the gentleman with the spectacles. He was a clever fellow, but, Lord! he broke up badly at last. I can tell you, he looked white at me when I touched him on the arm in the bar. But where could he have hidden the thing? We can all swear it was not on him.'

The girl laughed, and they turned away, when Richmond gave a violent start.

'Ah!' he cried, turning to the girl, 'what have you got there? Look, Davies, look; it's all oozing and dripping?'

The young woman glanced down at the little parcel she was carrying, and partially unfolded the paper.

'Yes, look, both of you,' she said; 'it's my own idea. Don't you think it will do nicely for the doctor's museum? It comes from the right hand, the hand that took the Gold Tiberius.'

Mr. Davies nodded with a good deal of approbation, and Richmond lifted his ugly high-crowned bowler, and wiped his forehead with a dingy handkerchief.

'I'm going,' he said, 'you two can stay if you like.'

The three went round by the stable-path, past the withered wilderness of the old kitchen-garden, and struck off by a hedge at the back, making for a particular point in the road. About five minutes later two gentlemen, whom idleness had led to explore these forgotten outskirts

of London, came sauntering up the shadowy carriage-drive.
They had spied the deserted house from the road, and
as they observed all the heavy desolation of the place, they
began to moralize in the great style, with considerable
debts to Jeremy Taylor.

'Look, Dyson,' said the one, as they drew nearer; 'look
at those upper windows; the sun is setting, and, though
the panes are dusty, yet—

> "The grimy sash an oriel burns."

'Phillipps,' replied the elder and (it must be said) the
more pompous of the two, 'I yield to fantasy; I cannot
withstand the influence of the grotesque. Here, where all
is falling into dimness and dissolution, and we walk in
cedarn gloom, and the very air of heaven goes mouldering to the lungs, I cannot remain commonplace. I look
at that deep glow on the panes, and the house lies all enchanted; that very room, I tell you, is within all blood and
fire.'

Adventure of the
Gold Tiberius

The acquaintance between Mr. Dyson and Mr. Charles Phillipps arose from one of those myriad chances which are every day doing their work in the streets of London. Mr. Dyson was a man of letters, and an unhappy instance of talents misapplied. With gifts that might have placed him in the flower of his youth among the most favoured of Bentley's favourite novelists, he had chosen to be perverse; he was, it is true, familiar with scholastic logic, but he knew nothing of the logic of life, and he flattered himself with the title of artist, when he was in fact but an idle and curious spectator of other men's endeavours. Amongst many delusions, he cherished one most fondly, that he was a strenuous worker; and it was with a gesture of supreme weariness that he would enter his favourite resort, a small tobacco-shop in Great Queen Street, and proclaim to any one who cared to listen that he had seen the rising and setting of two successive suns. The proprietor of the shop, a middle-aged man of singular civility, tolerated Dyson partly out of good nature, and partly because he was a regular customer. He was allowed to sit on an empty cask, and to express his sentiments on literary and artistic matters till he was tired, or the time for closing came; and if no fresh customers were attracted, it is believed that none was turned away by his eloquence. Dyson was addicted to wild experiments in tobacco; he never wearied of trying new combinations; and one eve-

7

ning he had just entered the shop, and given utterance to his last preposterous formula, when a young fellow of about his own age, who had come in a moment later, asked the shopman to duplicate the order on his account, smiling politely, as he spoke, to Mr. Dyson's address. Dyson felt profoundly flattered, and after a few phrases the two entered into conversation, and in an hour's time the tobacconist saw the new friends sitting side by side on a couple of casks, deep in talk.

'My dear sir,' said Dyson, 'I will give you the task of the literary man in a phrase. He has got to do simply this —to invent a wonderful story, and to tell it in a wonderful manner.'

'I will grant you that,' said Mr. Phillipps, 'but you will allow me to insist that in the hands of the true artist in words all stories are marvellous and every circumstance has its peculiar wonder. The matter is of little consequence; the manner is everything. Indeed, the highest skill is shown in taking matter apparently commonplace and transmuting it by the high alchemy of style into the pure gold of art.'

'That is indeed a proof of great skill, but it is great skill exerted foolishly, or at least unadvisedly. It is as if a great violinist were to show us what marvellous harmonies he could draw from a child's banjo.'

'No, no, you are really wrong. I see you take a radically mistaken view of life. But we must thresh this out. Come to my rooms; I live not far from here.'

It was thus that Mr. Dyson became the associate of Mr. Charles Phillipps, who lived in a quiet square not far from Holborn. Thenceforth they haunted each other's rooms at intervals, sometimes regular, and occasionally the reverse, and made appointments to meet at the shop in Queen Street, where their talk robbed the tobacconist's profit of half its charm. There was a constant jarring of literary formulas, Dyson exalting the claims of the pure imagination; while Phillipps, who was a student of physical science and something of an ethnologist, insisted that all literature ought to have a scientific basis. By the mistaken benevolence of deceased relatives both young men were placed out of reach of hunger, and so, meditating high achievements, idled their time pleasantly away, and revelled in the careless joys of a Bohemianism devoid of the sharp seasoning of adversity.

One night in June Mr. Phillipps was sitting in his room in the calm retirement of Red Lion Square. He had opened the window, and was smoking placidly, while he watched the movement of life below. The sky was clear, and the afterglow of sunset had lingered long about it. The flushing twilight of a summer evening vied with the gas-lamps in the square, and fashioned a chiaroscuro that had in it something unearthly; and the children, racing to and fro upon the pavement, the lounging idlers by the public-house, and the casual passers-by rather flickered and hovered in the play of lights than stood out substantial things. By degrees in the houses opposite one window after another leapt out a square of light; now and again a figure would shape itself against a blind and vanish, and to all this semi-theatrical magic the runs and flourishes of brave Italian opera played a little distance off on a piano-organ seemed an appropriate accompaniment, while the deep-muttered bass of the traffic of Holborn never ceased. Phillipps enjoyed the scene and its effects; the light in the sky faded and turned to darkness, and the square gradually grew silent, and still he sat dreaming at the window, till the sharp peal of the house-bell roused him, and looking at his watch, he found that it was past ten o'clock. There was a knock at the door, and his friend Mr. Dyson entered, and, according to his custom, sat down in an arm-chair and began to smoke in silence.

'You know Phillipps,' he said at length, 'that I have always battled for the marvellous. I remember your maintaining in that chair that one has no business to make use of the wonderful, the improbable, the odd coincidence in literature, and you took the ground that it was wrong to do so, because as a matter of fact the wonderful and the improbable don't happen, and men's lives are not really shaped by odd coincidence. Now, mind you, if that were so, I would not grant your conclusion, because I think the "criticism-of-life" theory is all nonsense; but I deny your premiss. A most singular thing has happened to me tonight.'

'Really, Dyson, I am very glad to hear it. Of course, I oppose your argument, whatever it may be; but if you would be good enough to tell me of your adventure, I should be delighted.'

'Well, it came about like this. I have had a very hard day's work; indeed I have scarcely moved from my old bureau since seven o'clock last night. I wanted to work out that idea we discussed last Tuesday, you know, the notion of the fetish-worshipper?'

'Yes, I remember. Have you been able to do anything with it?'

'Yes; it came out better than I expected; but there were great difficulties, the usual agonies between the conception and the execution. Anyhow, I got it done about seven o'clock to-night, and I thought I should like a little of the fresh air. I went out and wandered rather aimlessly about the streets; my head was full of my tale, and I didn't much notice where I was going. I got into those quiet places to the north of Oxford Street as you go west, the genteel residential neighbourhood of stucco and prosperity. I turned east again without knowing it, and it was quite dark when I passed along a sombre little by-street, ill-lighted and empty. I did not know at the time in the least where I was, but I found out afterwards that it was not very far from Tottenham Court Road. I strolled idly along, enjoying the stillness; on one side there seemed to be the back premises of some great shop; tier after tier of dusty windows lifted up into the night, with gibbet-like contrivances for raising heavy goods, and below large doors, fast closed and bolted, all dark and desolate. Then there came a huge pantechnicon warehouse; and over the way a grim blank wall, as forbidding as the wall of a gaol, and then the headquarters of some volunteer regiment, and afterwards a passage leading to a court where waggons were standing to be hired; it was, one might almost say, a street devoid of inhabitants, and scarce a window showed the glimmer of a light. I was wondering at the strange peace and dimness there, where it must be close to some roaring main artery of London life, when suddenly I heard the noise of dashing feet tearing along the pavement at full speed, and from a narrow passage, a news or something of that kind, a man was discharged as from a catapult under my very nose, and rushed past me, flinging something from him as he ran. He was gone, and down another street in an instant, almost before I knew what had happened; but I didn't much bother about him, I was watching something else. I told you he had thrown something away; well, I watched what seemed a line of flame flash through the air and fly quivering over the pavement, and in spite of myself I could not help tearing after it. The impetus lessened, and I saw something like a bright halfpenny roll slower and slower, and then deflect towards the gutter, hover for a moment on the edge, and dance down into a drain. I believe I cried out in positive despair, though I hadn't the least notion what I was hunting; and then, to my joy, I saw that, instead of dropping into a sewer, it had fallen flat across two bars. I stooped down and picked it up and whipped it into my pocket, and I was just about to walk on when I heard again that sound of dashing footsteps. I don't know why I did it, but as a matter of fact I dived down into the mews, or whatever it was, and stood as much in the shadow as possible. A man went by with a rush a few paces from where I was standing, and I felt uncommonly pleased that I was hiding. I couldn't make out much feature, but I saw his eyes gleaming and his teeth showing, and he had an ugly-looking knife in one hand, and I thought things would be very unpleasant for gentleman number one if the second robber, or robbed, or what you like, caught him up. I can tell you, Phillipps, a fox-hunt is exciting enough, when the horn blows clear on a winter morning, and the hounds give tongue, and the red-coats charge away, but it's nothing to a man-hunt, and that's what I had a slight glimpse of to-night. There was murder in the fellow's eyes as he went by, and I don't think there was much more than fifty seconds between the two. I only hope it was enough.'

Dyson leant back in his arm-chair, relit his pipe, and

puffed thoughtfully. Phillipps began to walk up and down the room, musing over the story of violent death fleeting in chase along the pavement, the knife shining in the lamplight, the fury of the pursuer, and the terror of the pursued.

'Well,' he said at last, 'and what was it, after all, that you rescued from the gutter?'

Dyson jumped up, evidently quite startled. 'I really haven't a notion. I didn't think of looking. But we shall see.'

He fumbled in his waistcoat pocket, drew out a small and shining object, and laid it on the table. It glowed there beneath the lamp with the radiant glory of rare old gold; and the image and the letters stood out in high relief, clear and sharp, as if it had but left the mint a month before. The two men bent over it, and Phillipps took it up and examined it closely.

'Imp. Tiberius Cæsar Augustus,' he read the legend, and then looking at the reverse of the coin, he stared in amazement, and at last turned to Dyson with a look of exultation.

'Do you know what you have found?' he said.

'Apparently a gold coin of some antiquity,' said Dyson coolly.

'Quite so, a gold Tiberius. No, that is wrong. You have found *the* gold Tiberius. Look at the reverse.'

Dyson looked and saw the coin was stamped with the figure of a faun standing amidst reeds and flowing water. The features, minute as they were, stood out in delicate outline; it was a face lovely and yet terrible, and Dyson thought of the well-known passage of the lad's playmate, gradually growing with his growth and increasing with his stature till the air was filled with the rank fume of the goat.

'Yes,' he said; 'it is a curious coin. Do you know it?'

'I know about it. It is one of the comparatively few historical objects in existence; it is all storied like those jewels we have read of. A whole cycle of legend has gathered round the thing; the tale goes that it formed part of an issue struck by Tiberius to commemorate an infamous excess. You see the legend on the reverse: "Victoria." It is said that by an extraordinary accident the whole issue was thrown into the melting-pot, and that only this one coin escaped. It glints through history and legend, appearing and disappearing, with intervals of a hundred years in time, and continents in place. It was "discovered" by an Italian humanist, and lost and rediscovered. It has not been heard of since 1727, when Sir Joshua Byrde, a Turkey merchant, brought it home from Aleppo, and vanished with it a month after he had shown it to the virtuosi, no man knew or knows where. And here it is!'

'Put it in your pocket, Dyson,' he said, after a pause. 'I would not let any one have a glimpse of the thing if I were you. I would not talk about it. Did either of the men you saw see you?'

'Well, I think not. I don't think the first man, the man who was vomited out of the dark passage, saw anything at all; and I am sure that he could not have seen me.'

'And you didn't really see them. You couldn't recognize either the one or the other if you met him in the street to-morrow?'

'No, I don't think I could. The street, as I said, was dimly lighted, and they ran like mad men.'

The two men sat silent for some time, each weaving his own fancies of the story; but the lust of the marvellous was slowly overpowering Dyson's more sober thoughts.

'It is all more strange than I fancied,' he said at last. 'It is queer enough what I saw; a man is sauntering along a quiet, sober, everyday London street, a street of grey houses and blank walls, and there, for a moment, a veil seems drawn aside, and the very fume of the pit steams up through the flagstones, the ground glows, red-hot, beneath his feet, and he seems to hear the hiss of the infernal caldron. A man flying in mad terror for his life, and furious hate pressing hot on his steps with knife drawn ready; here, indeed, is horror; but what is all that to what you have told me? I tell you, Phillipps, I see the plot thicken; our steps will henceforth be dogged with mystery, and the most ordinary incidents will teem with significance. You may stand out against it, and shut your eyes, but they

will be forced open; mark my words, you will have to
yield to the inevitable. A clue, tangled if you like, has
been placed by chance in our hands; it will be our business to follow it up. As for the guilty person or persons
in this strange case, they will be unable to escape us, our
nets will be spread far and wide over this great city, and
suddenly, in the streets and places of public resort, we
shall in some way or other be made aware that we are in
touch with the unknown criminal. Indeed I almost fancy
I see him slowly approaching this quiet square of yours;
he is loitering at street corners, wandering, apparently
without aim, down far-reaching thoroughfares, but all the
while coming nearer and nearer, drawn by an irresistible
magnetism, as ships were drawn to the Loadstone Rock
in the Eastern tale.'

'I certainly think,' replied Phillipps, 'that if you pull
out that coin and flourish it under people's noses as you
are doing at the present moment, you will very probably
find yourself in touch with the criminal, or a criminal.
You will undoubtedly be robbed with violence. Other-
wise, I see no reason why either of us should be troubled.
No one saw you secure the coin, and no one knows you
have it. I, for my part, shall sleep peacefully, and go
about my business with a sense of security and a firm
dependence on the natural order of things. The events of
the evening, the adventure in the street, have been odd, I
grant you, but I resolutely decline to have any more to do
with the matter, and, if necessary, I shall consult the
police. I will not be enslaved by a gold Tiberius, even
though it swims into my ken in a manner which is somewhat melodramatic.'

'And I, for my part,' said Dyson, 'go forth like a knight-
errant in search of adventure. Not that I shall need to
seek; rather adventure will seek me; I shall be like a
spider in the midst of his web, responsive to every movement, and ever on the alert.'

Shortly afterwards Dyson took his leave, and Mr.
Phillipps spent the rest of the night in examining some
flint arrow-heads which he had purchased. He had every
reason to believe that they were the work of a modern

and not a palæolithic man; still he was far from gratified when a close scrutiny showed him that his suspicions were well founded. In his anger at the turpitude which would impose on an ethnologist, he completely forgot Dyson and the gold Tiberius; and when he went to bed at first sunlight, the whole tale had faded utterly from his thoughts.

The Encounter
of the Pavement

Mr. Dyson, walking leisurely along Oxford Street, and
staring with bland inquiry at whatever caught his attention,
enjoyed in all its rare flavours the sensation that he was
really very hard at work. His observation of mankind, the
traffic, and the shop windows tickled his faculties with an
exquisite bouquet; he looked serious, as one looks on
whom charges of weight and moment are laid; and he was
attentive in his glances to right and left, for fear lest he
should miss some circumstances of more acute significance.
He had narrowly escaped being run over at a crossing by
a charging van, for he hated to hurry his steps, and indeed
the afternoon was warm; and he had just halted by a place
of popular refreshment, when the astounding gestures of
a well-dressed individual on the opposite pavement held
him enchanted and gasping like a fish. A treble line of
hansoms, carriages, vans, cabs, and omnibuses was tearing
east and west, and not the most daring adventurer of the
crossings would have cared to try his fortune; but the person who had attracted Dyson's attention seemed to rage
on the very edge of the pavement, now and then darting
forward at the hazard of instant death, and at each
repulse absolutely dancing with excitement, to the rich
amusement of the passers-by. At last a gap that would have
tried the courage of a street-boy appeared between the
serried lines of vehicles, and the man rushed across in a
frenzy, and escaping by a hair's-breadth, pounced upon

16

Dyson as a tiger pounces on her prey. 'I saw you looking about you,' he said, sputtering out his words in his intense eagerness; 'would you mind telling me this! Was the man who came out of the Aerated Bread Shop and jumped into the hansom three minutes ago a youngish-looking man with dark whiskers and spectacles? Can't you speak, man? For heaven's sake, can't you speak? Answer me; it's a matter of life and death.'

The words bubbled and boiled out of the man's mouth in the fury of his emotion, his face went from red to white, and the beads of sweat stood out on his forehead; he stamped his feet as he spoke, and tore with his hand at his coat, as if something swelled and choked him, stopping the passage of his breath.

'My dear sir,' said Dyson, 'I always like to be accurate. Your observation was perfectly correct. As you say, a youngish man—a man, I should say, of somewhat timid bearing—ran rapidly out of the shop here, and bounced into a hansom that must have been waiting for him, as it went eastwards at once. Your friend also wore spectacles, as you say. Perhaps you would like me to call a hansom for you to follow the gentleman?'

'No, thank you; it would be a waste of time.' The man gulped down something which appeared to rise in his throat, and Dyson was alarmed to see him shaking with hysterical laughter; he clung hard to a lamp-post, and swayed and staggered like a ship in a heavy gale.

'How shall I face the doctor?' he murmured to himself. 'It is too hard to fail at the last moment.' Then he seemed to recollect himself; he stood straight again, and looked quietly at Dyson.

'I owe you an apology for my violence,' he said at last. 'Many men would not be so patient as you have been. Would you mind adding to your kindness by walking with me a little way? I feel a little sick; I think it's the sun.'

Dyson nodded assent, and devoted himself to a quiet scrutiny of this strange personage as they moved on together. The man was dressed in quiet taste, and the most scrupulous observer could find nothing amiss with the fashion or make of his clothes; yet, from his hat to his boots, everything seemed inappropriate. His silk hat, Dyson thought, should have been a high bowler of odious pattern, worn with a baggy morning-coat, and an instinct told him that the fellow did not commonly carry a clean pocket-handkerchief. The face was not of the most agreeable pattern, and was in no way improved by a pair of bulbous chin-whiskers of a ginger hue, into which moustaches of like colour merged imperceptibly. Yet, in spite of these signals hung out by nature, Dyson felt that the individual beside him was something more than compact of vulgarity. He was struggling with himself, holding his feelings in check; but now and again passion would mount black to his face, and it was evidently by a supreme effort that he kept himself from raging like a madman. Dyson found something curious, and a little terrible, in the spectacle of an occult emotion thus striving for the mastery, and threatening to break out at every instant with violence; and they had gone some distance before the person whom he had met by so odd a hazard was able to speak quietly.

'You are really very good,' he said. 'I apologize again; my rudeness was really most unjustifiable. I feel my conduct demands an explanation, and I shall be happy to give it to you. Do you happen to know of any place near here where one could sit down? I should really be very glad.'

'My dear sir,' said Dyson solemnly, 'the only café in London is close by. Pray do not consider yourself as bound to offer me any explanation, but at the same time I should be most happy to listen to you. Let us turn down here.'

They walked down a sober street and turned into what seemed a narrow passage past an iron-barred gate thrown back. The passage was paved with flagstones, and decorated with handsome shrubs in pots on either side, and the shadow of the high walls made a coolness which was very agreeable after the hot breath of the sunny street. Presently the passage opened out into a tiny square, a charming place, a morsel of France transplanted into the heart of London. High walls rose on either side, covered with glossy creepers, flower-beds beneath were gay with nasturtiums, and marigolds, and odorous mignonette, and in the centre of the square a fountain, hidden by greenery, sent a cool shower continually plashing into the basin beneath. Chairs and tables were disposed at convenient intervals, and at the other end of the court broad doors had been thrown back; beyond was a long, dark room, and the turmoil of traffic had become a distant murmur. Within the room one or two men were sitting at the tables, writing and sipping, but the courtyard was empty.

'You see, we shall be quiet,' said Dyson. 'Pray sit down here, Mr.——?'

'Wilkins. My name is Henry Wilkins.'

'Sit here, Mr. Wilkins. I think you will find that a comfortable seat. I suppose you have not been here before? This is the quiet time; the place will be like a hive at six o'clock, and the chairs and tables will overflow into that little alley there.'

A waiter came in response to the bell; and after Dyson had politely inquired after the health of M. Annibault, the proprietor, he ordered a bottle of the wine of Champigny.

'The wine of Champigny,' he observed to Mr. Wilkins, who was evidently a good deal composed by the influence of the place, 'is a Tourainian wine of great merit. Ah, here it is; let me fill your glass. How do you find it?'

'Indeed,' said Mr. Wilkins, 'I should have pronounced it fine Burgundy. The bouquet is very exquisite. I am fortunate in lighting upon such a good Samaritan as yourself: I wonder you did not think me mad. But if you knew the terrors that assailed me, I am sure you would no longer be surprised at conduct which was certainly most unjustifiable.'

He sipped his wine, and leant back in his chair, relishing the drip and trickle of the fountain, and the cool greenness that hedged in this little port of refuge.

'Yes,' he said at last, 'that is indeed an admirable wine. Thank you; you will allow me to offer you another bottle?'

The waiter was summoned, and descended through a trap-door in the floor of the dark apartment and brought up the wine. Mr. Wilkins lit a cigarette, and Dyson pulled out his pipe.

'Now,' said Mr. Wilkins, 'I promised to give you an explanation of my strange behaviour. It is rather a long story, but I see, sir, that you are no mere cold observer of the ebb and flow of life. You take, I think, a warm and an intelligent interest in the chances of your fellow-creatures, and I believe you will find what I have to tell not devoid of interest.'

Mr. Dyson signified his assent to these propositions; and though he thought Mr. Wilkins's diction a little pompous, prepared to interest himself in his tale. The other, who had so raged with passion half an hour before, was now perfectly cool, and when he had smoked out his cigarette, he began in an even voice to relate the

NOVEL OF THE DARK VALLEY

I am the son of a poor but learned clergyman in the west of England—but I am forgetting, these details are not of special interest. I will briefly state, then, that my father, who was, as I have said, a learned man, had never learnt the specious arts by which the great are flattered, and would never condescend to the despicable pursuit of self-advertisement. Though his fondness for ancient ceremonies and quaint customs, combined with a kindness of heart that was unequalled and a primitive and fervent piety, endeared him to his moorland parishioners, such were not the steps by which clergy then rose in the Church, and at sixty my father was still incumbent of the little benefice he had accepted in his thirtieth year. The income of the living was barely sufficient to support life in the decencies which are expected of the Anglican parson; and when my father died a few years ago, I, his only child, found myself thrown upon the world with a slender capital of less than a hundred pounds, and all the problem of existence before me. I felt that there was nothing for me to do in the country, and as usually happens in such cases, London drew me like a magnet. One day in August, in the early morning, while the dew still glittered on the turf, and on the high green banks of the lane, a neighbour drove me to the railway station, and I bade good-bye to the land of the broad moors and unearthly battlements of the wild tors. It was six o'clock as we neared London; the faint, sickly fume of the brickfields about Acton came in puffs through the open window, and a mist was rising from the ground. Presently the brief view of successive streets, prim and uniform, struck me with a sense of monotony; the hot air seemed to grow hotter; and when we had rolled beneath the dismal and squalid houses, whose dirty and neglected backyards border the line near Paddington, I felt as if I should be stifled in this fainting breath of London. I got a hansom and drove off, and every street increased my gloom; grey houses with blinds drawn down, whole thoroughfares almost desolate, and the foot-passengers who seemed to stagger wearily along rather than walk, all made me feel a sinking at heart. I put up for the night at a small hotel in a street leading from the Strand, where my father had stayed on his few brief visits to the town; and when I went out after dinner, the real gaiety and bustle of the Strand and Fleet Street could cheer me but little, for in all this great city there was no single human being whom I could claim even as an acquaintance. I will not weary you with the history of the next year, for the adventures of a man who sinks are too trite to be worth recalling. My money did not last me long; I found that I must be neatly dressed, or no one to whom I applied would so much as listen to me; and I must live in a street of decent reputation if I wished to be treated with common civility. I applied for various posts, for which, as I now see, I was completely devoid of qualification; I tried to become a clerk without having the smallest notion of business habits; and I found, to my cost, that a general knowledge of literature and an execrable style of penmanship are far from being looked upon with favour in commercial circles. I had read one of the most charming of the works of a famous novelist of the present day, and I frequented the Fleet Street taverns in the hope of making literary friends, and so getting the introductions which I understood were indispensable in the career of letters. I was disappointed; I once or twice ventured to address gentlemen who were sitting in adjoining boxes, and I was answered, politely indeed, but in a manner that told me my advances were unusual. Pound by pound, my small resources melted; I could no longer think of appearances; I migrated to a shy quarter, and my meals became mere observances. I went out at one and returned to my room at two, but nothing but a mere milk-cake had occurred in the interval. In short, I became acquainted with misfortune; and as I sat amidst slush and ice on a seat in Hyde Park, munching a piece of bread, I realized the bitterness of poverty, and the feelings of a gentleman reduced to something far below the condition of a vagrant. In spite of all discouragement I did not desist in my efforts to earn a living. I consulted advertisement columns, I kept my eyes open for a chance, I looked in at the windows of stationers' shops, but all in vain. One evening I was sitting in a Free Library, and I saw an advertisement in one of the papers. It was something like this: 'Wanted by a gentleman a person of literary tastes and abilities as secretary and amanuensis. Must not object to travel.' Of course I knew that such an advertisement would have answers by the hundred, and I thought my own chances of securing the post extremely small; however I applied at the address given, and wrote to Mr. Smith, who was staying at the West End. I must confess that my heart gave a jump when I received a note a couple of days later, asking me to call at the Cosmopole at my earliest convenience. I do not know, sir, what your experiences of life may have been, and so I cannot tell you whether you have known such moments. A slight sickness, my heart beating rather more rapidly than usual, a choking in the throat, and a difficulty of utterance; such were my sensations as I walked to the Cosmopole; I had to mention the name twice before the hall porter could understand me, and as I went upstairs my hands were wet. I was a good deal struck by Mr. Smith's appearance; he looked younger than I did, and there was something mild and hesitating about his expression. He was reading when I came in, and he looked up when I gave my name. 'My dear sir,' he said, 'I am really delighted to see you. I have read very carefully the letter you were good enough to send me. Am I to understand that this document is in your own handwriting?' He showed me the letter I had written, and I told him I was not so fortunate as to be able to keep a secretary myself. 'Then, sir,' he went on, 'the post I advertised is at your service. You have no objection to travel, I presume?' As you may imagine, I closed pretty eagerly with the offer he made, and thus I entered the service of Mr. Smith. For the first few weeks I had no special duties; I had received a quarter's salary, and a handsome allowance was made me in lieu of board and lodging. One morning, however, when I called at the hotel according to instructions, my master informed me that I must hold myself in readiness for a sea-voyage, and, to spare unnecessary detail, in the course of a fortnight we had landed at New York. Mr. Smith told me that he was engaged on a work of a special nature, in the compilation of which some peculiar researches had to be made; in short, I was given to understand that we were to travel to the far West.

After about a week had been spent in New York we took our seats in the cars, and began a journey tedious beyond all conception. Day after day, and night after night, the great train rolled on, threading its way through cities the very names of which were strange to me, passing at slow speed over perilous viaducts, skirting mountain ranges and pine forests, and plunging into dense tracts of wood, where mile after mile and hour after hour the same monotonous growth of brushwood met the eye, and all along the continual clatter and rattle of the wheels upon the ill-laid lines made it difficult to hear the voices of our fellow-passengers. We were a heterogeneous and ever-changing company; often I woke up in the dead of night with a sudden grinding jar of the breaks, and looking out found that we had stopped in the shabby street of some frame-built town, lighted chiefly by the flaring windows of the saloon. A few rough-looking fellows would often come out to stare at the cars, and sometimes passengers got down, and sometimes there was a party of two or three waiting on the wooden sidewalk to get on board. Many of the passengers were English; humble households torn up from the moorings of a thousand years, and bound for some problematical paradise in the alkali desert or the Rockies. I heard the men talking to one another of the great profits to be made on the virgin soil of America, and two or three, who were mechanics, expatiated on the wonderful wages given to skilled labour on the railways and in the factories of the States. This talk usually fell dead after a few minutes, and I could see a sickness and dismay in the faces of these men as they looked at the ugly brush or at the desolate expanse of the prairie, dotted here and there with frame houses, devoid of garden or flowers or trees, standing all alone in what might have been a great sea frozen into stillness. Day after day the waving sky-line, and the desolation of a land without form or colour or variety, appalled the hearts of such of us as were Englishmen, and once in the night as I lay awake I heard a woman sobbing and asking what she had done to come to such a place. Her husband tried to comfort her in the broad speech of Gloucestershire, telling her the ground was so rich that one had only to plough it up and it would grow sunflowers of itself, but she cried for her mother and their old cottage and the bee-hives like a little child. The sadness of it all overwhelmed me, and I had no heart to think of other matters; the question of what Mr. Smith could have to do in such a country, and of what manner of literary research could be carried on in the wilderness, hardly troubled me. Now and again my situation struck me as peculiar; I had been engaged as a literary assistant at a handsome salary, and yet my master was still almost a stranger to me; sometimes he would come to where I was sitting in the cars and make a few banal remarks about the country, but for the most part of the journey he sat by himself, not speaking to any one, and so far as I could judge, deep in his thoughts. It was, I think, on the fifth day from New York when I received the intimation that we should shortly leave the cars; I had been watching some distant mountains which rose wild and savage before us, and I was wondering if there were human beings so unhappy as to speak of home in connection with those piles of lumbered rock, when Mr. Smith touched me lightly on the shoulder. 'You will be glad to be done with the cars, I have no doubt, Mr. Wilkins,' he said. 'You were looking at the mountains, I think? Well, I hope we shall be there to-night. The train stops at Reading, and I dare say we shall manage to find our way.'

A few hours later the breaksman brought the train to a standstill at the Reading depôt, and we got out. I noticed that the town, though of course built almost entirely of frame-houses, was larger and busier than any we had passed for the last two days. The depôt was crowded; and as the bell and whistle sounded, I saw that a number of persons were preparing to leave the cars, while an even greater number were waiting to get on board. Besides the passengers, there was a pretty dense crowd of people, some of whom had come to meet or to see off their friends and relatives, while others were merely loafers. Several of our English fellow-passengers got down at Reading, but the confusion was so great that they were lost to my sight almost immediately. Mr. Smith beckoned me to follow him, and we were soon in the thick of the mass; and the continual ringing of bells, and hubbub of voices, the shrieking of whistles, and the hiss of escaping steam, confused my senses, and I wondered dimly, as I struggled after my employer, where we were going, and how we should be able to find our way through an unknown country. Mr. Smith had put on a wide-brimmed hat, which he had sloped over his eyes, and as all the men wore hats of the same pattern, it was with some difficulty that I distinguished him in the crowd. We got free at last, and he struck down a side street, and made one or two sharp turns to right and left. It was getting dusk, and we seemed to be passing through a shy portion of the town; there were few people about in the ill-lighted streets, and these few were men of the unprepossessing pattern. Suddenly we stopped before a corner house. A man was standing at the door, apparently on the look-out for some one, and

I noticed that he and Smith gave sharp glances one to the other.

'From New York City, I expect, mister?'

'From New York.'

'All right; they're ready, and you can have 'em when you choose. I know my orders, you see, and I mean to run this business through.'

'Very well, Mr. Evans, that is what we want. Our money is good, you know. Bring them round.'

I had stood silent, listening to this dialogue and wondering what it meant. Smith began to walk impatiently up and down the street, and the man Evans was still standing at his door. He had given a sharp whistle, and I saw him looking me over in a quiet, leisurely way, as if to make sure of my face for another time. I was thinking what all this could mean, when an ugly slouching lad came up a side passage, leading two raw-boned horses.

'Get up, Mr. Wilkins, and be quick about it,' said Smith; 'we ought to be on our way.'

We rode off together into the gathering darkness, and before long I looked back and saw the far plain behind us, with the lights of the town glimmering faintly; and in front rose the mountains. Smith guided his horse on the rough track as surely as if he had been riding along Piccadilly, and I followed as well as I could. I was weary and exhausted, and scarcely took note of anything; I felt that the track was a gradual ascent, and here and there I saw great boulders by the road. The ride made but little impression on me. I have a faint recollection of passing through a dense black pine forest, where our horses had to pick their way among the rocks, and I remember the peculiar effect of the rarefied air as we kept still mounting higher and higher. I think I must have been half asleep for the latter half of the ride, and it was with a shock that I heard Smith saying—

'Here we are Wilkins. This is Blue Rock Park. You will enjoy the view to-morrow. Tonight we will have something to eat, and then go to bed.'

A man came out of a rough-looking house and took the horses, and we found some fried steak and coarse whiskey awaiting us inside. I had come to a strange place. There were three rooms—the room in which we had supper, Smith's room, and my own. The deaf old man who did the work slept in a sort of shed, and when I woke up the next morning and walked out I found that the house stood in a sort of hollow amongst the mountains; the clumps of pines and some enormous bluish-grey rocks that stood here and there between the trees had given the place the name of Blue Rock Park. On every side the snow-covered mountains surrounded us, the breath of the air was as wine, and when I climbed the slope and looked down, I could see that, so far as any human fellowship was concerned, I might as well have been wrecked on some small island in mid-Pacific. The only trace of man I could see was the rough log-house where I had slept, and in my ignorance I did not know that there were similar houses within comparatively easy distance, as distance is reckoned in the Rockies. But at the moment, the utter, dreadful loneliness rushed upon me, and the thought of the great plain and the great sea that parted me from the world I knew caught me by the throat, and I wondered if I should die there in that mountain hollow. It was a terrible instant, and I have not yet forgotten it. Of course, I managed to conquer my horror; I said I should be all the stronger for the experience, and I made up my mind to make the best of everything. It was a rough life enough, and rough enough board and lodging. I was left entirely to myself. Smith I scarcely ever saw, nor did I know when he was in the house. I have often thought he was far away, and have been surprised to see him walking out of his room, locking the door behind him, and putting the key in his pocket; and on several occasions, when I fancied he was busy in his room, I have seen him come in with his boots covered with dust and dirt. So far as work went I enjoyed a complete sinecure; I had nothing to do but to walk about the valley, to eat and to sleep. With one thing and another I grew accustomed to the life, and managed to make myself pretty comfortable, and by degrees I began to venture farther away from the house, and to explore the country. One day I had contrived to

get into the neighbouring valley, and suddenly I came
upon a group of men sawing timber. I went up to them,
hoping that perhaps some of them might be Englishmen;
at all events, they were human beings, and I should hear
articulate speech; for the old man I have mentioned, besides being half blind and stone deaf, was wholly dumb
so far as I was concerned. I was prepared to be welcomed
in rough and ready fashion, without much of the forms of
politeness, but the grim glances and the short, gruff
answers I received astonished me. I saw the men glance
oddly at each other; and one of them, who had stopped
work, began fingering a gun, and I was obliged to return
on my path uttering curses on the fate which had brought
me into a land where men were more brutish than the
very brutes. The solitude of the life began to oppress me
as with a nightmare, and a few days later I determined
to walk to a kind of station some miles distant, where a
rough inn was kept for the accommodation of hunters and
tourists. English gentlemen occasionally stopped there for
the night, and I thought I might perhaps fall in with some
one of better manners than the inhabitants of the country.
I found, as I had expected, a group of men lounging about
the door of the log-house that served as a hotel, and as I
came nearer I could see that heads were put together and
looks interchanged, and when I walked up the six or seven
trappers stared at me in stony ferocity, and with something of the disgust that one eyes a loathsome and venomous snake. I felt that I could bear it no longer, and I called
out—

'Is there such a thing as an Englishman here, or any
one with a little civilization?'

One of the men put his hand to his belt, but his
neighbour checked him, and answered me—

'You'll find we've got some of the resources of civilization before very long, mister, and I expect you'll not
fancy them extremely. But, anyway, there's an Englishman tarrying here, and I've no doubt he'll be glad to see
you. There you are; that's Mr. D'Aubernoun.'

A young man, dressed like an English country squire,

came and stood at the door, and looked at me. One of
the men pointed to me and said—

'That's the individual we were talking about last night.
Thought you might like to have a look at him, squire, and
here he is.'

The young fellow's good-natured English face clouded
over, and he glanced sternly at me, and turned away with
a gesture of contempt and aversion.

'Sir,' I cried, 'I do not know what I have done to be
treated in this manner. You are my fellow-countryman,
and I expected some courtesy.'

He gave me a black look and made as if he would go
in, but he changed his mind and faced me.

'You are rather imprudent, I think, to behave in this
manner. You must be counting on a forbearance which
cannot last very long, which may last a very short time
indeed. And let me tell you this, sir, you may call yourself an Englishman, and drag the name of England through
the dirt, but you need not count on any English influence
to help you. If I were you, I would not stay here much
longer.'

He went into the inn, and the men quietly watched my
face as I stood there, wondering whether I was going mad.
The woman of the house came out and stared at me as if
I were a wild beast or a savage, and I turned to her, and
spoke quietly—

'I am very hungry and thirsty. I have walked a long
way. I have plenty of money. Will you give me something
to eat and drink?'

'No, I won't,' she said. 'You had better quit this.'

I crawled home like a wounded beast, and lay down on
my bed. It was all a hopeless puzzle to me; I knew nothing
but rage, and shame, and terror, and I suffered little more
when I passed by a house in an adjacent valley, and some
children who were playing outside ran from me shrieking.
I was forced to walk to find some occupation; I should
have died if I had sat down quietly in Blue Rock Park
and looked all day at the mountains; but wherever I saw
a human being I saw the same glance of hatred and

aversion, and once as I was crossing a thick brake I heard a shot and the venomous hiss of a bullet close to my ear.

One day I heard a conversation which astounded me; I was sitting behind a rock resting, and two men came along the track and halted. One of them had got his feet entangled in some wild vines, and swore fiercely, but the other laughed, and said they were useful things sometimes.

'What the hell do you mean?'

'Oh, nothing much. But they're uncommon tough, these here vines, and sometimes rope is skerse and dear.'

The man who had sworn chuckled at this, and I heard them sit down and light their pipes.

'Have you seen him lately?' asked the humorist.

'I sighted him the other day, but the darned bullet went high. He's got his master's luck, I expect, sir, but it can't last much longer. You heard about him going to Jinks's and trying his brass, but the young Britisher downed him pretty considerable, I can tell you.'

'What the devil is the meaning of it?'

'I don't know, but I believe it'll have to be finished, and done in the old style too. You know how they fix the niggers?'

'Yes, sir, I've seen a little of that. A couple of gallons of kerosene 'll cost a dollar at Brown's store, but I should say it's cheap anyway.'

They moved off after this, and I lay still behind the rock, the sweat pouring down my face. I was so sick that I could barely stand, and I walked home as slowly as an old man, leaning on my stick. I knew that the two men had been talking about me, and I knew that some terrible death was in store for me. That night I could not sleep; I tossed on the rough bed and tortured myself to find out the meaning of it all. At last, in the very dead of night, I rose from the bed and put on my clothes, and went out. I did not care where I went, but I felt that I must walk till I had tired myself out. It was a clear moonlight night, and in a couple of hours I found I was approaching a place of dismal reputation in the mountains, a deep cleft in the rocks, known as Black Gulf Cañon. Many years before an unfortunate party of Englishmen and English women had camped here and had been surrounded by Indians. They were captured, outraged, and put to death with almost inconceivable tortures, and the roughest of the trappers or woodsmen gave the cañon a wide berth even in the daytime. As I crushed through the dense brushwood which grew above the cañon I heard voices; and wondering who could be in such a place at such a time, I went on, walking more carefully, and making as little noise as possible. There was a great tree growing on the very edge of the rocks, and I lay down and looked out from behind the trunk. Black Gulf Cañon was below me, the moonlight shining bright into its very depths from midheaven, and casting shadows as black as death from the pointed rock, and all the sheer rock on the other side, overhanging the cañon, was in darkness. At intervals a light veil obscured the moonlight, as a filmy cloud fleeted across the moon, and a bitter wind blew shrill across the gulf. I looked down, as I have said, and saw twenty men standing in a semicircle round a rock; I counted them one by one, and knew most of them. They were the vilest of the vile, more vile than any den in London could show, and there was murder, worse than murder, on the heads of not a few. Facing them and me stood Mr. Smith, with the rock before him, and on the rock was a great pair of scales, such as are used in the stores. I heard his voice ringing down the cañon as I lay beside the tree, and my heart turned cold as I heard it.

'Life for gold,' he cried, 'a life for gold. The blood and the life of an enemy for every pound of gold.'

A man stepped and raised one hand, and with the other flung a bright lump of something into the pan of the scales, which clanged down, and Smith muttered something in his ear. Then he cried again—

'Blood for gold, for a pound of gold, the life of an enemy. For every pound of gold upon the scales, a life.'

One by one the men came forward, each lifting up his right hand; and the gold was weighed in the scales, and each time Smith leant forward and spoke to each man in his ear. Then he cried again—

'Desire and lust for gold on the scales. For every pound of gold enjoyment of desire.'

I saw the same thing happen as before; the uplifted hand and the metal weighed, and the mouth whispering, and black passion on every face.

Then, one by one, I saw the men again step up to Smith. A muttered conversation seemed to take place. I could see that Smith was explaining and directing, and I noticed that he gesticulated a little as one who points out the way, and once or twice he moved his hands quickly as if he would show that the path was clear and could not be missed. I kept my eyes so intently on his figure that I noted little else, and at last it was with a start that I realized the cañon was empty. A moment before I thought I had seen the group of villainous faces, and the two standing, a little apart, by the rock; I had looked down a moment, and when I glanced again into the cañon there was no one there. In dumb terror I made my way home, and I fell asleep in an instant from exhaustion. No doubt I should have slept on for many hours, but when I woke up the sun was only rising, and the light shone in on my bed. I had started up from sleep with the sensation of having received a violent shock; and as I looked in confusion about me, I saw, to my amazement, that there were three men in the room. One of them had his hand on my shoulder and spoke to me—

'Come, mister, wake up. Your time's up now, I reckon, and the boys are waiting for you outside, and they're in a big hurry. Come on; you can put on your clothes; it's kind of chilly this morning.'

I saw the other two men smiling sourly at each other, but I understood nothing. I simply pulled on my clothes and said I was ready.

'All right; come on, then. You go first, Nichols, and Jim and I will give the gentleman an arm.'

They took me out into the sunlight, and then I understood the meaning of the dull murmur that had vaguely perplexed me while I was dressing. There were about two hundred men waiting outside, and some women too, and when they saw me there was a low muttering growl. I did not know what I had done, but that noise made my heart beat and the sweat come out on my face. I saw confusedly, as through a veil, the tumult and tossing of the crowd, discordant voices were speaking, and amongst all those faces there was not one glance of mercy, but a fury of lust that I did not understand. I found myself presently walking in a sort of procession up the slope of the valley, and on every side of me there were men with revolvers in their hands. Now and then a voice struck me, and I heard words as sentences of which I could form no connected story. But I understood that there was one sentence of execration; I heard scraps of stories that seemed strange and improbable. Some one was talking of men, lured by cunning devices from their homes and murdered with hideous tortures, found writhing like wounded snakes in dark and lonely places, only crying for some one to stab them to the heart, and so end their anguish; and I heard another voice speaking of innocent girls who had vanished for a day or two, and then come back and died, blushing red with shame even in the agonies of death. I wondered what it all meant, and what was to happen; but I was so weary that I walked on in a dream, scarcely longing for anything but sleep. At last we stopped. We had reached the summit of the hill overlooking Blue Rock Valley, and I saw that I was standing beneath a clump of trees where I had often sat. I was in the midst of a ring of armed men, and I saw that two or three men were very busy with piles of wood, while others were fingering a rope. Then there was a stir in the crowd, and a man was pushed forward. His hands and feet were tightly bound with cord; and though his face was unutterably villainous, I pitied him for the agony that worked his features and twisted his lips. I knew him; he was amongst those that had gathered round Smith in Black Gulf Cañon. In an instant he was unbound and stripped naked, borne beneath one of the trees, and his neck encircled by a noose that went around the trunk. A hoarse voice gave some kind of order; there was a rush of feet, and the rope tightened; and there before me I saw the blackened face and the writhing limbs and the shameful agony of death.

One after another half a dozen men, all of whom I had seen in the cañon the night before, were strangled before me, and their bodies were flung forth on the ground. Then there was a pause, and the man who had roused me a short while before came up to me, and said—

'Now, mister, it's your turn. We give you five minutes to cast up your accounts, and when that's clocked, by the living God, we will burn you alive at that tree.'

It was then I awoke and understood. I cried out—

'Why, what have I done? Why should you hurt me? I am a harmless man; I never did you any wrong.' I covered my face with my hands; it seemed so pitiful, and it was such a terrible death.

'What have I done?' I cried again. 'You must take me for some other man. You cannot know me.'

'You black-hearted devil,' said the man at my side, 'we know you well enough. There's not a man within thirty miles of this that won't curse Jack Smith when you are burning in hell.'

'My name is not Smith,' I said, with some hope left in me. 'My name is Wilkins. I was Mr. Smith's secretary, but I knew nothing of him.'

'Hark at the black liar,' said the man. 'Secretary be damned! You were clever enough, I dare say, to slink out at night and keep your face in the dark, but we've tracked you out at last. But your time's up. Come along.'

I was dragged to the tree and bound to it with chains; I saw the piles of wood heaped all about me, and shut my eyes. Then I felt myself drenched all over with some liquid, and looked again, and a woman grinned at me. She had just emptied a great can of petroleum over me and over the wood. A voice shouted, 'Fire away!' and I fainted, and knew nothing more.

When I opened my eyes I was lying on a bed in a bare, comfortless room. A doctor was holding some strong salts to my nostrils, and a gentleman standing by the bed, whom I afterwards found to be the sheriff, addressed me.

'Say, mister,' he began, 'you've had an uncommon narrow squeak for it. The boys were just about lighting up when I came along with the posse, and I had as much as I could do to bring you off, I can tell you. And, mind you, I don't blame them; they had made up their minds, you see, that you were the head of the Black Gulf gang, and at first nothing I could say would persuade them you weren't Jack Smith. Luckily, a man from here named Evans, that came along with us, allowed he had seen you with Jack Smith, and that you were yourself. So we brought you along and gaoled you, but you can go if you like when you're through with this faint turn.'

I got on the cars next day, and in three weeks I was in London; again almost penniless. But from that time my fortune seemed to change; I made influential friends in all directions; bank directors courted my company, and editors positively flung themselves into my arms. I had only to choose my career, and after a while I determined that I was meant by nature for a life of comparative leisure. With an ease that seemed almost ridiculous, I obtained a well-paid position in connection with a prosperous political club. I have charming chambers in a central neighbourhood, close to the parks, the club chef exerts himself when I lunch or dine, and the rarest vintages in the cellar are always at my disposal. Yet, since my return to London, I have never known a day's security or peace; I tremble when I awake lest Smith should be standing at my bed, and every step I take seems to bring me nearer to the edge of the precipice. Smith, I knew, had escaped free from the raid of the Vigilantes, and I grew faint at the thought that he would in all probability return to London, and that suddenly and unprepared I should meet him face to face. Every morning as I left my house I would peer up and down the street, expecting to see that dreaded figure awaiting me; I have delayed at street-corners, my heart in my mouth, sickening at the thought that a few quick steps might bring us together; I could not bear to frequent the theatres or music-halls, lest by some bizarre chance he should prove to be my neighbour. Sometimes I have been forced, against my will, to walk out at night, and then in silent squares the shadows have made me shudder, and in the medley of meetings in the crowded thoroughfares I have said to myself, 'It must come sooner or later; he will surely return to London, and I shall see him when I feel most secure.' I scanned the newspapers for hint or intimation of approaching danger, and no small type nor report of trivial interest was allowed to pass unread. Especially I read and re-read the advertisement columns, but without result; months passed by, and I was undisturbed till, though I felt far from safe, I no longer suffered from the intolerable oppression of instant and ever-present terror. This afternoon, as I was walking quietly along Oxford Street, I raised my eyes and looked across the road, and then at last I saw the man who had so long haunted my thoughts.'

Mr. Wilkins finished his wine, and leant back in his chair, looking sadly at Dyson; and then, as if a thought struck him, fished out of an inner pocket a leather letter-case, and handed a newspaper cutting across the table.

Dyson glanced closely at the slip, and saw that it had been extracted from the columns of an evening paper. It ran as follows:—

WHOLESALE LYNCHING

SHOCKING STORY

'A Dalziel telegram from Reading (Colorado) states that advices received there from Blue Rock Park report a frightful instance of popular vengeance. For some time the neighbourhood has been terrorized by the crimes of a gang of desperadoes, who, under the cover of a carefully planned organization, have perpertrated the most infamous cruelties on men and women. A Vigilance Committee was formed, and it was found that the leader of the gang was a person named Smith, living in Blue Rock Park. Action was taken, and six of the worst in the band were summarily strangled in the presence of two or three hundred men and women. Smith is said to have escaped.'

'This is a terrible story,' said Dyson; 'I can well believe that your days and nights are haunted by such fearful scenes as you have described. But surely you have no need to fear Smith? He has much more cause to fear you. Consider: you have only to lay your information before the police, and a warrant would be immediately issued for his arrest. Besides, you will, I am sure, excuse me for what I am going to say.'

'My dear sir,' said Mr. Wilkins, 'I hope you will speak to me with perfect freedom.'

'Well, then, I must confess that my impression was that you were rather disappointed at not being able to stop the man before he drove off. I thought you seemed annoyed that you could not get across the street.'

'Sir, I did not know what I was about. I caught sight of the man, but it was only for a moment, and the agony you witnessed was the agony of suspense. I was not perfectly certain of the face, and the horrible thought that Smith was again in London overwhelmed me. I shuddered at the idea of this incarnate fiend, whose soul is black with shocking crimes, mingling free and unobserved amongst the harmless crowds, meditating perhaps a new and more fearful cycle of infamies. I tell you, sir, that an awful being stalks through the streets, a being before whom the sunlight itself should blacken, and the summer air grow chill and dank. Such thoughts as these rushed upon me with the force of a whirlwind; I lost my senses.'

'I see. I partly understand your feelings, but I would impress on you that you have nothing really to fear. Depend upon it, Smith will not molest you in any way. You must remember he himself has had a warning; and indeed, from the brief glance I had of him, he seemed to me to be a frightened-looking man. However, I see it is getting late, and if you will excuse me, Mr. Wilkins, I think I will be going. I dare say we shall often meet here.'

Dyson walked off smartly, pondering the strange story chance had brought him, and finding on cool reflection that there was something a little strange in Mr. Wilkins's manner, for which not even so weird a catalogue of experiences could altogether account.

Adventure of the
Missing Brother

Mr. Charles Phillipps was, as has been hinted, a gentleman of pronounced scientific tastes. In his early days he had devoted himself with fond enthusiasm to the agreeable study of biology, and a brief monograph on the Embryology of the Microscopic Holothuria had formed his first contribution to the *belles lettres*. Later he had somewhat relaxed the severity of his pursuits, and had dabbled in the more frivolous subjects of palæontology and ethnology; he had a cabinet in his sitting-room whose drawers were stuffed with rude flint implements, and a charming fetish from the South Seas was the dominant note in the decorative scheme of the apartment. Flattering himself with the title of materialist, he was in truth one of the most credulous of men, but he required a marvel to be neatly draped in the robes of Science before he would give it any credit, and the wildest dreams took solid shape to him if only the nomenclature were severe and irreproachable. He laughed at the witch, but quailed before the powers of the hypnotist, lifting his eyebrows when Christianity was mentioned, but adoring protyle and the ether. For the rest, he prided himself on a boundless scepticism; the average tale of wonder he heard with nothing but contempt, and he would certainly not have credited a word or syllable of Dyson's story of the pursuer and pursued, unless the gold coin had been produced as visible and tangible evidence. As it was, he half suspected

38

that Dyson had imposed upon him; he knew his friend's disordered fancies, and his habit of conjuring up the marvellous to account for the entirely commonplace; and, on the whole, he was inclined to think that the so-called facts in the odd adventure had been gravely distorted in the telling. Since the evening on which he had listened to the tale he paid Dyson a visit, and had delivered himself of some serious talk on the necessity of accurate observation, and the folly, as he put it, of using a kaleidoscope instead of a telescope in the view of things, to which remarks his friend had listened with a smile that was extremely sardonic. 'My dear fellow,' Dyson had remarked at last, 'you will allow me to tell you that I see your drift perfectly. However, you will be astonished to hear that I consider you to be the visionary, while I am the sober and serious spectator of human life. You have gone round the circle; and while you fancy yourself far in the golden land of new philosophies, you are in reality a dweller in a metaphorical Clapham; your scepticism has defeated itself and become a monstrous credulity; you are, in fact, in the position of the bat or owl, I forget which it was, who denied the existence of the sun at noonday, and I shall be astonished if you do not one day come to me full of contrition for your manifold intellectual errors, with a humble resolution to see things in their true light for the future.' This tirade had left Mr. Phillipps unimpressed; he considered Dyson as hopeless, and he went home to gloat over some primitive stone implements that a friend had sent him from India. He found that his landlady, seeing them displayed in all their rude formlessness upon the table, had removed the collection to the dustbin, and had replaced it by lunch; and the afternoon was spent in malodorous research. Mrs. Brown, hearing these stones spoken of as very valuable knives, had called him in his hearing 'poor Mr. Phillipps,' and between rage and evil odours he spent a sorry afternoon. It was four o'clock before he had completed his work of rescue; and overpowered with the flavours of decaying cabbage leaves, Phillipps felt that he must have a walk to gain an appetite for the evening meal. Unlike Dyson he walked fast, with his eyes on the pavement, absorbed in his thoughts, and oblivious of the life around him; and he could not have told by what streets he had passed, when he suddenly lifted up his eyes and found himself in Leicester Square. The grass and flowers pleased him, and he welcomed the opportunity of resting for a few minutes, and glancing round, he saw a bench which had only one occupant, a lady, and as she was seated at one end, Phillipps took up a position at the other extremity, and began to pass in angry review the events of the afternoon. He had noticed as he came up to the bench that the person already there was neatly dressed, and to all appearance young; her face he could not see, as it was turned away in apparent contemplation of the shrubs, and, moreover, shielded with her hand; but it would be doing wrong to Mr. Phillipps to imagine that his choice of seat was dictated by any hopes of an affair of the heart, he had simply preferred the company of one lady to that of five dirty children, and having seated himself, was immersed directly in thoughts of his misfortunes. He had meditated changing his lodgings; but now, on a judicial review of the case in all its bearings, his calmer judgment told him that the race of landladies is like to the race of the leaves, and that there was but little to choose between them. He resolved, however, to talk to Mrs. Brown, the offender, very coolly and yet severely, to point out the extreme indiscretion of her conduct, and to express a hope for better things in the future. With this decision registered in his mind, Phillipps was about to get up from the seat and move off, when he was intensely annoyed to hear a stifled sob, evidently from the lady, who still continued her contemplation of the shrubs and flower-beds. He clutched his stick desperately, and in a moment would have been in full retreat, when the lady turned her face towards him, and with mute entreaty bespoke his attention. She was a young girl with a quaint and piquant rather than a beautiful face, and she was evidently in the bitterest distress. Mr. Phillipps sat down again, and cursed his chances heartily. The young lady looked at him with a pair of charming eyes of a shining hazel, which showed no trace of tears, though a handkerchief was in her hand; she bit her lip, and seemed to struggle with some overpowering grief, and her whole attitude was all-beseeching and imploring. Phillipps sat on the edge of the bench gazing awkwardly at her, and wondering what was to come next, and she looked at him still without speaking.

'Well, madam,' he said at last, 'I understood from your gesture that you wished to speak to me. Is there anything I can do for you? Though, if you will pardon me, I cannot help saying that that seems highly improbable.'

'Ah, sir,' she said in a low, murmuring voice, 'do not speak harshly to me. I am in sore straits, and I thought from your face that I could safely ask your sympathy, if not your help.'

'Would you kindly tell me what is the matter?' said Phillipps. 'Perhaps you would like some tea?'

'I knew I could not be mistaken,' the lady replied. 'That offer of refreshment bespeaks a generous mind. But tea, alas! is powerless to console me. If you will let me, I shall endeavour to explain my trouble.'

'I should be glad if you would.'

'I shall do so, and I shall try to be brief, in spite of the numerous complications which have made me, young as I am, tremble before what seems the profound and terrible mystery of existence. Yet the grief which now racks my very soul is but too simple; I have lost my brother.'

'Lost your brother! How on earth can that be?'

'I see I must trouble you with a few particulars. My brother, then, who is by some years my elder, is a tutor in a private school in the extreme north of London. The want of means deprived him of the advantages of a University education; and lacking the stamp of a degree, he could not hope for that position which his scholarship and his talents entitled him to claim. He was thus forced to accept the post of classical master at Dr. Saunderson's Highgate Academy for the Sons of Gentlemen, and he has performed his duties with perfect satisfaction to his principal for some years. My personal history need not trouble you; it will be enough if I tell you that for the last month I have been governess in a family residing at Tooting. My brother and I have always cherished the warmest mutual affection; and though circumstances into which I need not enter have kept us apart for some time, yet we have never lost sight of one another. We made up our minds that unless one of us was absolutely unable to rise from a bed of sickness, we should never let a week pass by without meeting, and some time ago we chose this square as our rendezvous on account of its central position and its convenience of access. And indeed, after a week of distasteful toil, my brother felt little inclination for much walking, and we have often spent two or three hours on this bench, speaking of our prospects and of happier days, when we were children. In the early spring it was cold and chilly; still we enjoyed the short respite, and I think that we were often taken for a pair of lovers as we sat close together, eagerly talking. Saturday after Saturday we have met each other here; and though the doctor told him it was madness, my brother would not allow the influenza to break the appointment. That was some time ago; last Saturday we had a long and happy afternoon, and separated more cheerfully than usual, feel- ing that the coming week would be bearable, and resolv- ing that our next meeting should be if possible still more pleasant. I arrived here at the time agreed upon, four o'clock, and sat down and watched for my brother, ex- pecting every moment to see him advancing towards me from the gate at the north side of the square. Five min- utes passed by, and he had not arrived; I thought he must have missed his train, and the idea that our interview would be cut short by twenty minutes, or perhaps half an hour, saddened me; I had hoped we should be so happy together to-day. Suddenly, moved by I know not what impulse, I turned abruptly round, and how can I describe to you my astonishment when I saw my brother advancing slowly towards me from the southern side of the square, accompanied by another person? My first thought, I remember, had in it something of resentment that this man, whoever he was, should intrude himself into our meeting; I wondered who it could possibly be, for my brother had, I may say, no intimate friends. Then as I looked still at the advancing figures, another feeling took possession of me; it was a sensation of bristling fear, the fear of the child in the dark, unreasonable and unreasoning, but terrible, clutching at my heart as with the cold grip of a dead man's hands. Yet I overcame the feeling, and looked steadily at my brother, waiting for him to speak, and more closely at his companion. Then I noticed that this man was leading my brother rather than walking arm-in-arm with him; he was a tall man, dressed in quite ordinary fashion. He wore a high bowler hat, and, in spite of the warmth of the day, a plain black overcoat, tightly buttoned, and I noticed his trousers, of a quiet black and grey stripe. The face was commonplace too, and indeed I cannot recall any special features, or any trick of expression; for though I looked at him as he came near, curiously enough his face made no impression on me—it was as though I had seen a well-made mask. They passed in front of me, and to my unutterable astonishment, I heard my brother's voice speaking to me, though his lips did not move, nor his eyes look into mine. It was a voice I cannot describe, though I knew it, but the words came to my ears as if mingled with splashing water and the sound of a shallow brook flowing amidst stones. I heard, then, the words, "I cannot stay," and for a moment the heavens and the earth seemed to rush together with the sound of thunder, and I was thrust forth from the world into a black void without beginning and without end. For, as my brother passed me, I saw the hand that held him by the arm, and seemed to guide him, and in one moment of horror I realized that it was a formless thing that has mouldered for many years in the grave. The flesh was peeled in strips from the bones, and hung apart dry and granulated, and the fingers that encircled my brother's arm were all unshapen, claw-like things, and one was but a stump from which the end had rotted off. When I recovered my senses I saw the two passing out by the gate. I paused for a moment, and then with a rush of fire to my heart I knew that no horror could stay me, but that I must follow my brother and save him, even though all hell rose up against me. I ran out, and looked up the pavement, and saw the two figures walking amidst the crowd. I ran across the road, and saw them turn up that side street, and I reached the corner a moment later. In vain I looked to right and left, for neither my brother nor his strange guardian was in sight; two elderly men were coming down arm-in-arm, and a telegraph boy was walking lustily along whistling. I remained there a moment horror-struck, and then I bowed my head and returned to this seat, where you found me. Now, sir, do you wonder at my grief? Oh, tell me what has happened to my brother, or I feel I shall go mad!'

Mr. Phillipps, who had listened with exemplary patience to this tale, hesitated a moment before he spoke.

'My dear madam,' he said at length, 'you have known how to engage me in your service, not only as a man, but as a student of science. As a fellow-creature I pity you most profoundly; you must have suffered extremely from what you saw, or rather from what you fancied you saw. For, as a scientific observer, it is my duty to tell you the plain truth, which, indeed, besides being true, must also console you. Allow me to ask you then to describe your brother.'

'Certainly,' said the lady eagerly; 'I can describe him accurately. My brother is a somewhat young-looking man; he is pale, has small black whiskers, and wears spectacles. He has rather a timid, almost a frightened expression, and looks about him nervously from side to side. Think, think! Surely you must have seen him. Perhaps you are an habitué of this engaging quarter; you may have met him on some previous Saturday. I may have been mistaken in supposing that he turned up that side street; he may have gone on, and you may have passed each other. Oh, tell me, sir, whether you have not seen him!'

'I am afraid I do not keep a very sharp lookout when I am walking,' said Phillipps, who would have passed his mother unnoticed; 'but I am sure your description is admirable. And now will you describe the person who, you say, held your brother by the arm?'

'I cannot do so. I told you his face seemed devoid of expression or salient feature. It was like a mask.'

'Exactly; you cannot describe what you have never seen. I need hardly point out to you the conclusion to be drawn; you have been the victim of an hallucination. You expected to see your brother, you were alarmed because you did not see him, and unconsciously, no doubt, your brain went to work, and finally you saw a mere projection of your own morbid thoughts—a vision of your absent brother, and a mere confusion of terrors incorporated in a figure which you can't describe. Of course your brother has been in some way prevented from coming to meet you as usual. I expect you will hear from him in a day or two.'

The lady looked seriously at Mr. Phillipps, and then for a second there seemed almost a twinkling as of mirth about here eyes, but her face clouded sadly at the dogmatic conclusions to which the scientist was led so irresistibly.

'Ah!' she said, 'you do no know. I cannot doubt the evidence of my waking senses. Besides, perhaps I have had experiences even more terrible. I acknowledge the force of your arguments, but a woman has intuitions which never deceive her. Believe me, I am not hysterical; feel my pulse, it is quite regular.'

She stretched out her hand with a dainty gesture, and a glance that enraptured Phillipps in spite of himself. The hand held out to him was soft and white and warm, and as, in some confusion, he placed his fingers on the purple vein, he felt profoundly touched by the spectacle of love and grief before him.

'No,' he said, as he released her wrist, 'as you say, you are evidently quite yourself. Still, you must be aware that living men do not possess dead hands. That sort of thing doesn't happen. It is, of course, barely possible that you did see your brother with another gentleman, and that important business prevented him from stopping. As for the wonderful hand, there may have been some deformity, a finger shot off by accident, or something of that sort.'

The lady shook her head mournfully.

'I see you are a determined rationalist,' she said. 'Did

you not hear me say that I have had experience even more terrible? I too was once a sceptic, but after what I have known I can no longer doubt.'

'Madam,' replied Mr. Phillipps, 'no one shall make me deny my faith. I will never believe, nor will pretend to believe that two and two make five, nor will I on any pretences admit the existence of two-sided triangles.'

'You are a little hasty,' rejoined the lady. 'But may I ask you if you ever heard the name of Professor Gregg, the authority on ethnology and kindred subjects?'

'I have done much more than merely hear of Professor Gregg,' said Phillipps. 'I always regarded him as one of our most acute and clearheaded observers; and his last publication, the "Textbook of Ethnology," struck me as being admirable in its kind. Indeed, the book had but come into my hands when I heard of the terrible accident which cut short Gregg's career. He had, I think, taken a country house in the West of England for the summer, and is supposed to have fallen into a river. So far as I remember, his body was never recovered.'

'Sir, I am sure that you are discreet. Your conversation seems to declare as much, and the very title of that little work of yours which you mentioned assures me that you are no empty trifler. In a word, I feel that I may depend on you. You appear to be under the impression that Professor Gregg is dead; I have no reason to believe that that is the case.'

'What?' cried Phillipps, astonished and perturbed. 'You do not hint that there was anything disgraceful? I cannot believe it. Gregg was a man of the clearest character; his private life was one of great benevolence; and though I myself am free from delusions, I believe him to have been a sincere and devout Christian. Surely you cannot mean to insinuate that some disreputable history forced him to flee the country?'

'Again you are in a hurry,' replied the lady. 'I said nothing of all this. Briefly, then, I must tell you that Professor Gregg left his house one morning in full health both of mind and body. He never returned, but his watch and chain, a purse containing three sovereigns in gold, and some loose silver, with a ring that he wore habitually, were found three days later on a wild and savage hillside, many miles from the river. These articles were placed beside a limestone rock of fantastic form; they had been wrapped into a parcel with a kind of rough parchment which was secured with gut. The parcel was opened, and the inner side of the parchment bore an inscription done with some red substance; the characters were undecipherable, but seemed to be a corrupt cuneiform.'

'You interest me intensely,' said Phillipps. 'Would you mind continuing your story? The circumstance you have mentioned seems to me of the most inexplicable character, and I thirst for elucidation.'

The young lady seemed to meditate for a moment, and she then proceeded to relate the

NOVEL OF THE BLACK SEAL

I must now give you some fuller particulars of my history. I am the daughter of a civil engineer, Steven Lally by name, who was so unfortunate as to die suddenly at the outset of his career, and before he had accumulated sufficient means to support his wife and her two children.

My mother contrived to keep the small household going on resources which must have been incredibly small; we lived in a remote country village, because most of the necessaries of life were cheaper than in a town, but even so we were brought up with the severest economy. My father was a clever and well-read man, and left behind him a small but select collection of books, containing the best Greek, Latin, and English classics, and these books were the only amusement we possessed. My brother, I remember, learnt Latin out of Descartes' 'Meditationes,' and I, in place of the little tales which children are usually told to read, had nothing more charming than a translation of the 'Gesta Romanorum.' We grew up thus, quiet, and studious children, and in course of time my brother provided for himself in the manner I have mentioned. I continued to live at home; my poor mother had become an invalid, and demanded my continual care, and about two years ago she died after many months of painful illness. My situation was a terrible one; the shabby furniture barely sufficed to pay the debts I had been forced to contract, and the books I dispatched to my brother, knowing how he would value them. I was absolutely alone; I was aware how poorly my brother was paid; and though I came up to London in the hope of finding employment, with the understanding that he would defray my expenses, I swore it should only be for a month, and that if I could not in that time find some work, I would starve rather than deprive him of the few miserable pounds he had laid by for his day of trouble. I took a little room in a distant suburb, the cheapest that I could find; I lived on bread and tea, and I spent my time in vain answering of advertisements, and vainer walks to addresses I had noted. Day followed on day, and week on week, and still I was unsuccessful, till at last the term I had appointed drew to a close, and I saw before me the grim prospect of slowly dying of starvation. My landlady was good-natured in her way; she knew the slenderness of my means, and I am sure that she would not have turned me out of doors; it remained for me then to go away, and to try to die in some quiet place. It was winter then and a thick white fog gathered in the early part of the afternoon, becoming more dense as the day wore on; it was a Sunday, I remember, and the people of the house were at chapel. At about three o'clock I crept out and walked away as quickly as I could, for I was weak from abstinence. The white mist wrapped all the streets in silence, a hard frost had gathered thick upon the bare branches of the trees, and frost crystals glittered on the wooden fences, and on the cold, cruel ground beneath my feet. I walked on, turning to right and left in utter haphazard, without caring to look up at the names of the streets, and all that I remember of my walk on that Sunday afternoon seems but the broken fragments of an evil dream. In a confused vision I stumbled on, through roads half town and half country, grey fields melting in to the cloudy world of mist on one side of me, and on the other comfortable villas with a glow of fire-light flickering on the walls, but all unreal; red brick walls and lighted windows, vague trees, and glimmering country, gas-lamps beginning to star the white shadows, the vanishing prespectives of the railway line beneath high embankments, the green and red of the signal lamps,—all these were but momentary pictures flashed on my tired brain and senses numbed by hunger. Now and then I would hear a quick step ringing on the iron road, and men would pass me well wrapped up, walking fast for the sake of warmth, and no doubt eagerly foretasting the pleasures of a growing hearth, with curtains tightly drawn about the frosted panes, and the welcomes of their friends; but as the early evening darkened and night approached, foot-passengers got fewer and fewer, and I passed through street after street alone. In the white silence I stumbled on as desolate as if I trod the streets of a buried city; and as I grew more weak and exhausted, something of the horror of death was folding thickly round my heart. Suddenly, as I turned a corner, some one accosted me courteously beneath the lamp-post, and I heard a voice asking if I could kindly point the way to Avon Road. At the sudden shock of human accents I was prostrated, and my strength gave way; I fell all huddled on the sidewalk, and wept and sobbed and laughed in violent hysteria. I had gone out prepared to die, and as I stepped across the threshold that had sheltered me, I consciously bade adieu to all hopes and all remembrances; the door clanged behind me with the noise of thunder, and I felt that an iron curtain had fallen on the brief passages of my life, that henceforth I was to walk a little way in a world of gloom and shadow; I entered on the stage of the first act of death. Then came my wandering in the mist, the whiteness wrapping all things, the void streets, and muffled silence, till when that voice spoke to me it was as if I had died and life returned to me. In a few minutes I was able to compose my feelings, and as I rose I saw that I was confronted by a middle-aged gentleman of pleasing appearance, neatly and correctly dressed. He looked at me with an expression of great pity, but before

I could stammer out my ignorance of the neighbourhood, for indeed I had not the slightest notion of where I had wandered, he spoke.

'My dear madam,' he said, 'you seem in some terrible distress. You cannot think how you alarmed me. But may I inquire the nature of your trouble? I assure you that you can safely confide in me.'

'You are very kind,' I replied, 'but I fear there is nothing to be done. My condition seems a hopeless one.'

'Oh, nonsense, nonsense! You are too young to talk like that. Come, let us walk down here, and you must tell me your difficulty. Perhaps I may be able to help you.'

There was something very soothing and persuasive in his manner, and as we walked together I gave him an outline of my story, and told of the despair that had oppressed me almost to death.

'You were wrong to give in so completely,' he said, when I was silent. 'A month is too short a time in which to feel one's way in London. London, let me tell you, Miss Lally, does not lie open and undefended; it is a fortified place, fossed and double-moated with curious intricacies. As must always happen in large towns, the conditions of life have become hugely artificial; no mere simple palisade is run up to oppose the man or woman who would take the place by storm, but serried lines of subtle contrivances, mines, and pitfalls which it needs a strange skill to overcome. You, in your simplicity, fancied you had only to shout for these walls to sink into nothingness, but the time is gone for such startling victories as these. Take courage; you will learn the secret of success before long.'

'Alas! sir,' I replied, 'I have no doubt your conclusions are correct, but at the present moment I seem to be in a fair way to die of starvation. You spoke of a secret; for heaven's sake tell it me, if you have any pity for my distress.'

He laughed genially. 'There lies the strangeness of it all. Those who know the secret cannot tell it if they would; it is positively as ineffable as the central doctrine of Freemasonry. But I may say this, that you yourself have penetrated at least the outer husk of the mystery,' and he laughed again.

'Pray do not jest with me,' I said. 'What have I done, *que sçais-je?* I am so far ignorant that I have not the slightest idea of how my next meal is to be provided.'

'Excuse me. You ask what you have done. You have met me. Come, we will fence no longer. I see you have self-education, the only education which is not infinitely pernicious, and I am in want of a governess for my two children. I have been a widower for some years; my name is Gregg. I offer you the post I have named, and shall we say a salary of a hundred a year?'

I could only stutter out my thanks, and slipping a card with his address, and a banknote by way of earnest into my hand, Mr. Gregg bade me good-bye, asking me to call in a day or two.

Such was my introduction to Professor Gregg, and can you wonder that the remembrance of despair and the cold blast that had blown from the gates of death upon me made me regard him as a second father? Before the close of the week I was installed in my new duties. The professor had leased an old brick manor-house in a western suburb of London, and here, surrounded by pleasant lawns and orchards, and soothed with the murmur of ancient elms that rocked their boughs above the roof, the new chapter of my life began. Knowing as you do the nature of the professor's occupations, you will not be surprised to hear that the house teemed with books, and cabinets full of strange, and even hideous, objects filled every available nook in the vast low rooms. Gregg was a man whose one thought was for knowledge, and I too before long caught something of his enthusiasm, and strove to enter into his passion for research. In a few months I was perhaps more his secretary than the governess of the two children, and many a night I have sat at the desk in the glow of the shaded lamp while he, pacing up and down in the rich gloom of the firelight, dictated to me the substance of his 'Textbook of Ethnology.' But amidst these more sober and accurate studies I always detected a something hidden, a longing and desire for some object to which he did not allude; and now and then he would break short in what he was saying and lapse into reverie, entranced, as it seemed to me, by some distant prospect of adventurous discovery. The textbook was at last finished, and we began to receive proofs from the printers, which were entrusted to me for a first reading, and then underwent the final revision of the professor. All the while his weariness of the actual business he was engaged on increased, and it was with the joyous laugh of a schoolboy when term is over that he one day handed me a copy of the book. 'There,' he said, 'I have kept my word; I promised to write it, and it is done with. Now I shall be free to live for stranger things; I confess it, Miss Lally, I covet the renown of Columbus; you will, I hope, see me play the part of an explorer.'

'Surely,' I said, 'there is little left to explore. You have been born a few hundred years too late for that.'

'I think you are wrong,' he replied; 'there are still, depend upon it, quaint, undiscovered countries and continents of strange extent. Ah, Miss Lally! believe me, we stand amidst sacraments and mysteries full of awe, and it doth not yet appear what we shall be. Life, believe me, is no simple thing, no mass of grey matter and congeries of veins and muscles to be laid naked by the surgeon's knife; man is the secret which I am about to explore, and before I can discover him I must cross over weltering seas indeed, and oceans and the mists of many thousand years. You know the myth of the lost Atlantis; what if it be true, and I am destined to be called the discoverer of that wonderful land?'

I could see the excitement boiling beneath his words, and in his face was the heat of the hunter; before me stood a man who believed himself summoned to tourney with the unknown. A pang of joy possessed me when I reflected that I was to be in a way associated with him in the adventure, and I too burned with the lust of the chase, not pausing to consider that I knew not what we were to unshadow.

The next morning Professor Gregg took me into his inner study, where, ranged against the wall, stood a nest

of pigeon-holes, every drawer neatly labelled, and the results of years of toil classified in a few feet of space.

'Here,' he said, 'is my life; here are all the facts which
I have gathered together with so much pains, and yet it
is all nothing. No, nothing to what I am about to attempt.
Look at this'; and he took me to an old bureau, a piece
fantastic and faded, which stood in a corner of the room.
He unlocked the front and opened one of the drawers.

'A few scraps of paper,' he went on, pointing to the
drawer, 'and a lump of black stone, rudely annotated with
queer marks and scratches—that is all that drawer holds.
Here you see is an old envelope with the dark red stamp
of twenty years ago, but I have pencilled a few lines at the
back; here is a sheet of manuscript, and here some cuttings
from obscure local journals. And if you ask me the
subject-matter of the collection, it will not seem extraordinary—a servant-girl at a farmhouse, who disappeared from
her place and has never been heard of, a child supposed
to have slipped down some old working on the mountains,
some queer scribbling on a limestone rock, a man murdered with a blow from a strange weapon; such is the
scent I have to go upon. Yes, as you say, there is a ready
explanation for all this; the girl may have run away to
London, or Liverpool, or New York; the child may be
at the bottom of the disused shaft; and the letters on the
rock may be the idle whims of some vagrant. Yes, yes,
I admit all that; but I know I hold the true key. Look!'
and he held out a slip of yellow paper.

*Characters found inscribed on a limestone rock on the
Grey Hills,* I read, and then there was a word erased,
presumably the name of a country, and a date some fifteen
years back. Beneath was traced a number of uncouth
characters, shaped somewhat like wedges or daggers, as
strange and outlandish as the Hebrew alphabet.

'Now the seal,' said Professor Gregg, and he handed
me the black stone, a thing about two inches long, and
something like an old-fashioned tobacco-stopper, much
enlarged.

I held it up to the light, and saw to my surprise the
characters on the paper repeated on the seal.

'Yes,' said the professor, 'they are the same. And the marks on the limestone rock were made fifteen years ago, with some red substance. And the characters on the seal are four thousand years old at least. Perhaps much more.'

'Is it a hoax?' I said.

'No, I anticipated that. I was not to be led to give my life to a practical joke. I have tested the matter very carefully. Only one person besides myself knows of the mere existence of that black seal. Besides, there are other reasons which I cannot enter into now.'

'But what does it all mean?' I said. 'I cannot understand to what conclusion all this leads.'

'My dear Miss Lally, that is a question I would rather leave unanswered for some little time. Perhaps I shall never be able to say what secrets are held here in solution; a few vague hints, the outlines of village tragedies, a few marks done with red earth upon a rock, and an ancient seal. A queer set of data to go upon? Half a dozen pieces of evidence, and twenty years before even so much could be got toegther; and who knows what mirage or *terra incognita* may be beyond all this? I look across deep waters, Miss Lally, and the land beyond may be but a haze after all. But still I believe it is not so, and a few months will show whether I am right or wrong.'

He left me, and alone I endeavoured to fathom the mystery, wondering to what goal such eccentric odds and ends of evidence could lead. I myself am not wholly devoid of imagination, and I had reason to respect the professor's solidity of intellect; yet I saw in the contents of the drawer but the materials of fantasy, and vainly tried to conceive what theory could be founded on the fragments that had been placed before me. Indeed, I could discover in what I had heard and seen but the first chapter of an extravagant romance; and yet deep in my heart I burned with curiosity, and day after day I looked eagerly in Professor Gregg's face for some hint of what was to happen.

It was one evening after dinner that the word came.

'I hope you can make your preparations without much trouble,' he said suddenly to me. 'We shall be leaving here in a week's time.'

'Really!' I said in astonishment. 'Where are we going?'

'I have taken a country house in the west of England, not far from Caermaen, a quiet little town, once a city, and the headquarters of a Roman legion. It is very dull there, but the country is pretty, and the air is wholesome.'

I detected a glint in his eyes, and guessed that this sudden move had some relation to our conversation of a few days before.

'I shall just take a few books with me,' said Professor Gregg, 'that is all. Everything else will remain here for our return. I have got a holiday,' he went on, smiling at me, 'and I shan't be sorry to be quit for a time of my old bones and stones and rubbish. Do you know,' he went on, 'I have been grinding away at facts for thirty years; it is time for fancies.'

The days passed quickly; I could see that the professor was all quivering with suppressed excitement, and I could scarce credit the eager appetence of his glance as we left the old manorhouse behind us and began our journey. We set out at midday, and it was in the dusk of the evening that we arrived at a little county station. I was tired and excited, and the drive through the lanes seems all a dream. First the deserted streets of a forgotten village, while I heard Professor Gregg's voice talking of the Augustan Legion and the clash of arms, and all the tremendous pomp that followed the eagles; then the broad river swimming to full tide with the last afterglow glimmering dustily in the yellow water, the wide meadows, the cornfields whitening, and the deep lane winding on the slope between the hills and the water. At last we began to ascend, and the air grew rarer. I looked down and saw the pure white mist tracking the outline of the river like a shroud, and a vague and shadowy country; imaginations and fantasy of swelling hills and hanging woods, and half-shaped outlines of hills beyond, and in the distance the glare of the furnace fire on the mountain, growing by turns a pillar of shining flame and fading to a dull point of red. We were slowly mounting a carriage drive, and then there came to me the cool breath and the secret of the great wood that was above us; I seemed to wander in its deepest depths, and there was the sound of trickling water, the scent of the green leaves, and the breath of the summer night. The carriage stopped at last, and I could scarcely distinguish the form of the house as I waited a moment at the pillared porch. The rest of the evening seemed a dream of strange things bounded by the great silence of the wood and the valley and the river.

The next morning, when I awoke and looked out of the bow window of the big, old-fashioned bedroom, I saw under a grey sky a country that was still all mystery. The long, lovely valley, with the river winding in and out below, crossed in mid-vision by a mediæval bridge of vaulted and buttressed stone, the clear presence of the rising ground beyond, and the woods that I had only seen in shadow the night before, seemed tinged with enchantment, and the soft breath of air that sighed in at the opened pane was like no other wind. I looked across the valley, and beyond, hill followed on hill as wave on wave, and here a faint blue pillar of smoke rose still in the morning air from the chimney of an ancient grey farmhouse, there was a rugged height crowned with dark firs, and in the distance I saw the white streak of a road that climbed and vanished into some unimagined country. But the boundary of all was a great wall of mountain, vast in the west, and ending like a fortress with a steep ascent and a domed tumulus clear against the sky.

I saw Professor Gregg walking up and down the terrace path below the windows, and it was evident that he was revelling in the sense of liberty, and the thought that he had for a while bidden good-bye to task-work. When I joined him there was exultation in his voice as he pointed out the sweep of valley and the river that wound beneath the lovely hills.

'Yes,' he said, 'it is a strangely beautiful country; and to me, at least, it seems full of mystery. You have not forgotten the drawer I showed you, Miss Lally? No; and you guessed that I have come here not merely for the sake of the children and the fresh air?'

'I think I have guessed as much as that,' I replied; 'but you must remember I do not know the mere nature of your investigations; and as for the connection between the search and this wonderful valley, it is past my guessing.'

He smiled queerly at me. 'You must not think I am making a mystery for the sake of a mystery,' he said. 'I do not speak out because, so far, there is nothing to be spoken, nothing definite, I mean, nothing that can be set down in hard black and white, as dull and sure and irreproachable as any blue-book. And then I have another reason: Many years ago a chance paragraph in a newspaper caught my attention, and focussed in an instant the vagrant thoughts and half-formed fancies of many idle and speculative hours into a certain hypothesis. I saw at once that I was treading on a thin crust; my theory was wild and fantastic in the extreme, and I would not for any consideration have written a hint of it for publication. But I thought that in the company of scientific men like myself, men who knew the course of discovery, and were aware that the gas that blazes and flares in the gin-palace was once a wild hypothesis—I thought that with such men as these I might hazard my dream—let us say Atlantis, or the philosopher's stone, or what you like—without danger of ridicule. I found I was grossly mistaken; my friends looked blankly at me and at one another, and I could see something of pity, and something also of insolent contempt, in the glances they exchanged. One of them called on me next day, and hinted that I must be suffering from overwork and brain exhaustion. "In plain terms," I said, "you think I am going mad. I think not"; and I showed him out with some little appearance of heat. Since that day I vowed that I would never whisper the nature of my theory to any living soul; to no one but yourself have I ever shown the contents of that drawer. After all, I may be following a rainbow; I may have been misled by the play of coincidence; but as I stand here in this mystic hush and silence amidst the woods and the wild hills, I am more than ever sure that I am hot on the scent. Come, it is time we went in.'

To me in all this there was something both of wonder and excitement; I knew how in his ordinary work Professor Gregg moved step by step, testing every inch of the

way, and never venturing on assertion without proof that
was impregnable. Yet I divined more from his glance and
the vehemence of his tone than from the spoken word,
that he had in his every thought the vision of the almost
incredible continually with him; and I, who was with some
share of imagination no little of a sceptic, offended at a
hint of the marvellous, could not help asking myself
whether he were cherishing a monomania, and barring out
from this one subject all the scientific method of his other
life.

Yet, with this image of mystery haunting my thoughts,
I surrendered wholly to the charm of the country. Above
the faded house on the hillside began the great forest—
a long, dark line seen from the opposing hills, stretching
above the river for many a mile from north to south, and
yielding in the north to even wilder country, barren and
savage hills, and ragged common-land, a territory all
strange and unvisited, and more unknown to Englishmen
than the very heart of Africa. The space of a couple of
steep fields alone separated the house from the wood, and
the children were delighted to follow me up the long alleys
of undergrowth, between smooth pleached walls of shining
beech, to the highest point in the wood, whence one looked
on one side across the river and the rise and fall of the
country to the great western mountain wall, and on the
other over the surge and dip of the myriad trees of the
forest, over level meadows and the shining yellow sea to
the faint coast beyond. I used to sit at this point on the
warm sunlit turf which marked the track of the Roman
Road, while the two children raced about hunting for the
whinberries that grew here and there on the banks. Here
beneath the deep blue sky and the great clouds rolling, like
olden galleons with sails full-bellied, from the sea to the
hills, as I listened to the whispered charm of the great and
ancient wood, I lived solely for delight, and only remembered strange things when we would return to the house
and find Professor Gregg either shut up in the little room
he had made his study, or else pacing the terrace with
the look, patient and enthusiastic, of the determined seeker.

One morning, some eight or nine days after our arrival,

I looked out of my window and saw the whole landscape transmuted before me. The clouds had dipped low and hidden the mountain in the west; a southern wind was driving the rain in shifting pillars up the valley, and the little brooklet that burst the hill below the house now raged, a red torrent, down the river. We were perforce obliged to keep snug within-doors; and when I had attended to my pupils, I sat down in the morning-room where the ruins of a library still encumbered an old-fashioned bookcase. I had inspected the shelves once or twice, but their contents had failed to attract me; volumes of eighteenth-century sermons, an old book on farriery, a collection of *Poems* by 'persons of quality,' Prideaux's *Connection,* and an odd volume of Pope, were the boundaries of the library, and there seemed little doubt that everything of interest or value had been removed. Now however, in desperation, I began to re-examine the musty sheepskin and calf bindings, and found, much to my delight, a fine old quarto printed by the Stephani, containing the three books of Pomponius Mela, *De Situ Orbis,* and other of the ancient geographers. I knew enough of Latin to steer my way through an ordinary sentence, and I soon became absorbed in the odd mixture of fact and fancy—light shining on a little space of the world, and beyond, mist and shadow and awful forms. Glancing over the clear-printed pages, my attention was caught by the heading of a chapter in Solinus, and I read the words:—

'Mira de intimis gentibus Libyae, de lapide
Hexecontalitho,'

—'The wonders of the people that inhabit the inner part of Libya, and of the stone called Sixtystone.'

The odd title attracted me, and I read on:—

'Gens ista avia et secreta habitat, in montibus horrendis foeda mysteria celebrat. De hominibus nihil aliud illi praeferunt quam figuram, ab humano ritu prorsus exulant, oderunt deum lucis. Stridunt potius quam loquuntur; vox absona nec sine horrore auditur. Lapide quodam gloriantur, quem Hexecontalithon vocant; dicunt enim hunc lapidem sexaginta notas ostendere. Cujus lapidis nomen secretum ineffabile colunt: quod Ixaxar.'

'This folk,' I translated to myself, 'dwells in remote and secret places, and celebrates foul mysteries on savage hills. Nothing have they in common with men save the face, and the customs of humanity are wholly strange to them; and they hate the sun. They hiss rather than speak; their voices are harsh, and not to be heard without fear. They boast of a certain stone, which they call Sixtystone; for they say that it displays sixty characters. And this stone has a secret unspeakable name; which is Ixaxar.'

I laughed at the queer inconsequence of all this, and thought it fit for 'Sinbad the Sailor,' or other of the supplementary Nights. When I saw Professor Gregg in the course of the day, I told him of my find in the bookcase, and fantastic rubbish I had been reading. To my surprise he looked up at me with an expression of great interest.

'That is really very curious,' he said. 'I have never thought it worth while to look into the old geographers, and I dare say I have missed a good deal. Ah, that is the passage, is it? It seems a shame to rob you of your entertainment, but I really think I must carry off the book.'

The next day the professor called me to come to the study. I found him sitting at a table in the full light of the window, scrutinizing something very attentively with a magnifying glass.

'Ah, Miss Lally,' he began, 'I want to use your eyes. This glass is pretty good, but not like my old one that I left in town. Would you mind examining the thing yourself, and telling me how many characters are cut on it?'

He handed me the object in his hand. I saw that it was the black seal he had shown me in London, and my heart began to beat with the thought that I was presently to know something. I took the seal, and, holding it up to the light, checked off the grotesque dagger-shaped characters one by one.

'I make sixty-two,' I said at last.

'Sixty-two? Nonsense; it's impossible. Ah, I see what you have done, you have counted that and that,' and he pointed to two marks which I had certainly taken as letters with the rest.

'Yes, yes,' Professor Gregg went on, 'but those are obvious scratches, done accidentally; I saw that at once. Yes, then that's quite right. Thank you very much, Miss Lally.'

I was going away, rather disappointed at my having been called in merely to count the number of marks on the black seal, when suddenly there flashed into my mind what I had read in the morning.

'But, Professor Gregg,' I cried, breathless, 'the seal, the seal. Why, it is the stone Hexecontalithos that Solinus writes of; it is Ixaxar.'

'Yes,' he said, 'I suppose it is. Or it may be a mere coincidence. It never does to be too sure, you know, in these matters. Coincidence killed the professor.'

I went away puzzled at what I had heard, and as much as ever at a loss to find the ruling clue in this maze of strange evidence. For three days the bad weather lasted, changing from driving rain to a dense mist, fine and dripping, and we seemed to be shut up in a white cloud that veiled all the world away from us. All the while Professor Gregg was darkling in his room, unwilling, it appeared, to dispense confidences or talk of any kind, and I heard him walking to and fro with a quick, impatient step, as if he were in some way wearied of inaction. The fourth morning was fine, and at breakfast the professor said briskly—

'We want some extra help around the house; a boy of fifteen or sixteen, you know. There are a lot of little odd jobs that take up the maids' time which a boy could do much better.'

'The girls have not complained to me in any way,' I replied. 'Indeed, Anne said there was much less work than in London, owing to there being so little dust.'

'Ah, yes, they are very good girls. But I think we shall do much better with a boy. In fact, that is what has been bothering me for the last two days.'

'Bothering you?' I said in astonishment, for as a matter

of fact the professor never took the slightest interest in the affairs of the house.

'Yes,' he said, 'the weather, you know. I really couldn't go out in that Scotch mist; I don't know the country very well, and I should have lost my way. But I am going to get the boy this morning.'

'But how do you know there is such a boy as you want anywhere about?'

"Oh, I have no doubt as to that. I may have to walk a mile or two at the most, but I am sure to find just the boy I require.'

I thought the professor was joking, but though his tone was airy enough there was something grim and set about his features that puzzled me. He got his stick, and stood at the door looking meditatively before him, and as I passed through the hall he called to me.

'By the way, Miss Lally, there was one thing I wanted to say to you. I dare say you may have heard that some of these country lads are not over bright; idiotic would be a harsh word to use, and they are usually called "naturals," or something of the kind. I hope you won't mind if the boy I am after should turn out not too keen-witted; he will be perfectly harmless, of course, and blacking boots doesn't need much mental effort.'

With that he was gone, striding up the road that led to the wood, and I remained stupified; and then for the first time my astonishment was mingled with a sudden note of terror, arising I knew not whence, and all unexplained even to myself, and yet I felt about my heart for an instant something of the chill of death, and that shapeless, formless dread of the unknown that is worse than death itself. I tried to find courage in the sweet air that blew up from the sea, and in the sunlight after rain, but the mystic woods seemed to darken around me; and the vision of the river coiling between the reeds, and the silver grey of the ancient bridge, fashioned in my mind symbols of vague dread, as the mind of a child fashions terror from things harmless and familiar.

Two hours later Professor Gregg returned. I met him

as he came down the road, and asked quietly if he had been able to find a boy.

'Oh, yes,' he answered; 'I found one easily enough. His name is Jervase Cradock, and I expect he will make himself very useful. His father has been dead for many years, and the mother, whom I saw, seemed very glad at the prospect of a few shillings extra coming in on Saturday nights. As I expected, he is not too sharp, has fits at times, the mother said; but as he will not be trusted with the china, that doesn't much matter, does it? And he is not in any way dangerous, you know, merely a little weak.'

'When is he coming?'

'To-morrow morning at eight o'clock. Anne will show him what he has to do, and how to do it. At first he will go home every night, but perhaps it may ultimately turn out more convenient for him to sleep here, and only go home for Sundays.'

I found nothing to say to all this; Professor Gregg spoke in a quiet tone of matter-of-fact, as indeed was warranted by the circumstance; and yet I could not quell my sensation of astonishment at the whole affair. I knew that in reality no assistance was wanted in the housework, and the professor's prediction that the boy he was to engage might prove a little 'simple,' followed by so exact a fulfilment, struck me as bizarre in the extreme. The next morning I heard from the house-maid that the boy Cradock had come at eight, and that she had been trying to make him useful. 'He doesn't seem quite all there, I don't think, miss' was her comment, and later in the day I saw him helping the old man who worked in the garden. He was a youth of about fourteen, with black hair and black eyes and an olive skin, and I saw at once from the curious vacancy of his expression that he was mentally weak. He touched his forehead awkwardly as I went by, and I heard him answering the gardener in a queer, harsh voice that caught my attention; it gave me the impression of some one speaking deep below under the earth, and there was a strange sibilance, like the hissing of the phonograph as the pointer travels over the cylinder. I heard that he seemed anxious to do what he could, and was quite docile and obedient, and Morgan the gardener, who knew his mother, assured me he was perfectly harmless. 'He's always been a bit queer,' he said, 'and no wonder, after what his mother went through before he was born. I did know his father, Thomas Cradock, well, and a very fine workman he was too, indeed. He got something wrong with his lungs owing to working in the wet woods, and never got over it, and went off quite sudden like. And they do say as how Mrs. Cradock was quite off her head; anyhow, she was found by Mr. Hillyer and Ty Coch, all crouched up on the Grey Hills, over there, crying and weeping like a lost soul. And Jervase, he was born about eight months afterwards, and as I was saying, he was a bit queer always; and they do say when he could scarcely walk he would frighten the other children into fits with the noises he would make.'

A word in the story had stirred up some remembrance within me, and, vaguely curious, I asked the old man where the Grey Hills were.

'Up there,' he said, with the same gesture he had used before; 'you go past the "Fox and Hounds," and through the forest, by the old ruins. It's a good five miles from here, and a strange sort of a place. The poorest soil between this and Monmouth, they do say, though it's good feed for sheep. Yes, it was a sad thing for poor Mrs. Cradock.'

The old man turned to his work, and I strolled on down the path between the espaliers, gnarled and gouty with age, thinking of the story I had heard, and groping for the point in it that had some key to my memory. In an instant it came before me; I had seen the phrase 'Grey Hills' on the slip of yellowed paper that Professor Gregg had taken from the drawer in his cabinet. Again I was seized with pangs of mingled curiosity and fear; I remembered the strange characters copied from the limestone rock, and then again their identity with the inscription on the age-old seal, and the fantastic fables of the Latin geographer. I saw beyond doubt that, unless coincidence had set all the scene and disposed all these bizarre events with curious art, I was to be a spectator of things far removed from the usual and customary traffic and jostle of life. Professor Gregg I noted day by day; he was hot on his trail, growing lean with eagerness; and in the evenings, when the sun was swimming on the verge of the mountain, he would pace the terrace to and fro with his eyes on the ground, while the mist grew white in the valley, and the stillness of the evening brought far voices near, and the blue smoke rose a straight column from the diamond-shaped chimney of the grey farmhouse, just as I had seen it on the first morning. I have told you I was of sceptical habit; but though I understood little or nothing, I began to dread, vainly proposing to myself the iterated dogmas of science that all life is material, and that in the system of things there is no undiscovered land, even beyond the remotest stars, where the supernatural can find a footing. Yet there struck in on this the thought that matter is as really awful and unknown as spirit, that science itself but dallies on the threshold, scarcely gaining more than a glimpse of the wonders of the inner place.

There is one day that stands up from amidst the others as a grim red beacon, betokening evil to come. I was sitting on a bench in the garden, watching the boy Cradock weeding, when I was suddenly alarmed by a harsh and choking sound, like the cry of a wild beast in anguish, and I was unspeakably shocked to see the unfortunate lad standing in full view before me, his whole body quivering and shaking at short intervals as though shocks of electricity were passing through him, his teeth grinding, foam gathering on his lips, and his face all swollen and blackened to a hideous mask of humanity. I shrieked with terror, and Professor Gregg came running; and as I pointed to Cradock, the boy with one convulsive shudder fell face forward, and lay on the wet earth, his body writhing like a wounded blind worm, and an inconceivable babble of sounds bursting and rattling and hissing from his lips. He seemed to pour forth an infamous jargon, with words, or what seemed words, that might have belonged to a tongue dead since untold ages, and buried deep beneath Nilotic mud, or in the inmost recesses of the Mexican forest. For a moment the thought passed through my mind, as my ears were still revolted with that infernal clamour, 'Surely this is the very speech of hell,' and then I cried out again and again, and ran away shuddering to my inmost soul. I had seen Professor Gregg's face as he stooped over the wretched boy and raised him, and I was appalled by the glow of exultation that shone on every lineament and feature. As I sat in my room with drawn blinds, and my eyes hidden in my hands, I heard heavy steps beneath, and I was told afterwards that Professor Gregg had carried Cradock to his study, and had locked the door. I heard voices murmur indistinctly, and I trembled to think of what might be passing within a few feet of where I sat; I longed to escape to the woods and sunshine, and yet I dreaded the sights that might confront me on the way; and at last, as I held the handle of the door nervously, I heard Professor Gregg's voice calling to me with a cheerful ring. 'It's all right now, Miss Lally,' he said. 'The poor fellow has got over it, and I have been arranging for him to sleep here after to-morrow. Perhaps I may be able to do something for him.'

'Yes,' he said later, 'it was a very painful sight, and I don't wonder you were alarmed. We may hope that good food will build him up a little, but I am afraid he will never be really cured,' and he affected the dismal and conventional air with which one speaks of hopeless illness; and yet beneath it I detected the delight that leapt up rampant within him, and fought and struggled to find utterance. I was as if one glanced down on the even surface of the sea, clear and immobile, and saw beneath raging depths and a storm of contending billows. It was indeed to me a torturing and offensive problem that this man, who had so bounteously rescued me from the sharpness of death, and showed himself in all the relations of life full of benevolence, and pity, and kindly forethought, should so manifestly be for once on the side of the demons, and take a ghastly pleasure in the torments of an afflicted fellow-creature. Apart, I struggled with the horned difficulty, and strove to find the solution; but without the hint of a clue, beset by mystery and contradiction. I saw nothing that might help me, and began to wonder whether, after all, I had not escaped from the white mist of the suburb at too dear a rate. I hinted something of my thought to the professor; I said enough to let him know that I was in the most acute perplexity, but the moment after regretted what I had done when I saw his face contort with a spasm of pain.

'My dear Miss Lally,' he said, 'you surely do not wish to leave us? No, no, you would not do it. You do not know how I rely on you; how confidently I go forward, assured that you are here to watch over my children. You, Miss Lally, are my rearguard; for let me tell you the business in which I am engaged is not wholly devoid of peril. You have not forgotten what I said the first morning here; my lips are shut by an old and firm resolve till they can open to utter no ingenious hypothesis or vague surmise but irrefragable fact, as certain as a demonstration in mathematics. Think over it, Miss Lally: not for a moment would I endeavour to keep you here against your own instincts, and yet I tell you frankly that I am persuaded it is here, here amidst the woods, that your duty lies.'

I was touched by the eloquence of his tone, and by the remembrance that the man, after all, had been my salvation, and I gave him my hand on a promise to serve him loyally and without question. A few days later the rector of our church—a little church, grey and severe and quaint, that hovered on the very banks of the river and watched the tides swim and return—came to see us, and Professor Gregg easily persuaded him to stay and share our dinner. Mr. Meyrick was a member of an antique family of squires, whose old manorhouse stood amongst the hills some seven miles away, and thus rooted in the soil, the rector was a living store of all the old fading customs and lore of the country. His manner, genial, with a deal of retired oddity, won on Professor Gregg; and towards the cheese, when a curious Burgundy had begun its incantations, the two men glowed like the wine, and talked of philology with the enthusiasm of a burgess over the peerage. The parson was expounding the pronunciation of the Welsh *ll*, and producing sounds like the gurgle of his native brooks, when Professor Gregg struck in.

'By the way,' he said, 'that was a very odd word I met

the other day. You know my boy, poor Jervase Cradock? Well, he has got the bad habit of talking to himself, and the day before yesterday I was walking in the garden here and heard him; he was evidently quite unconscious of my presence. A lot of what he said I couldn't make out, but one word struck me distinctly. It was such an odd sound, half sibilant, half guttural, and as quaint as those double *ls* you have been demonstrating. I do not know whether I can give you an idea of the sound: "Ishakshar" is perhaps as near as I can get. But the *k* ought to be a Greek *chi* or a Spanish *j*. Now what does it mean in Welsh?'

'In Welsh?' said the parson. 'There is no such word in Welsh, nor any word remotely resembling it. I know the book-Welsh, as they call it, and the colloquial dialects as well as any man, but there's no word like that from Anglesea to Usk. Besides, none of the Cradocks speaks a word of Welsh; it's dying out about here.'

'Really. You interest me extremely, Mr. Meyrick. I confess the word didn't strike me as having the Welsh ring. But I thought it might be some local corruption.'

'No, I never heard such a word, or anything like it. Indeed,' he added, smiling whimsically, 'if it belongs to any language, I should say it must be that of the fairies—the Tylwydd Têg, as we call them.'

The talk went on to the discovery of a Roman villa in the neighbourhood; and soon after I left the room, and sat down apart to wonder at the drawing together of such strange clues of evidence. As the professor had spoken of the curious word, I had caught the glint of his eye upon me; and though the pronunciation he gave was grotesque in the extreme, I recognized the name of the stone of sixty characters mentioned by Solinus, the black seal shut up in some secret drawer of the study, stamped for ever by a vanished race with signs that no man could read, signs that might, for all I knew, be the veils of awful things done long ago, and forgotten before the hills were moulded into form.

When the next morning I came down, I found Professor Gregg pacing the terrace in his eternal walk.

'Look at that bridge,' he said, when he saw me; 'observe the quaint and Gothic design, the angles between the arches, and the silvery grey of the stone in the awe of the morning light. I confess it seems to me symbolic; it should illustrate a mystical allegory of the passage from one world to another.'

'Professor Gregg,' I said quietly, 'it is time that I knew something of what has happened, and of what is to happen'.

For the moment he put me off, but I returned again with the same question in the evening, and then Professor Gregg flamed with excitement. 'Don't you understand yet?' he cried. 'But I have told you a good deal; yes, and shown you a good deal; you have heard pretty nearly all that I have heard, and seen what I have seen; or at least,' and his voice chilled as he spoke, 'enough to make a good deal clear as noonday. The servants told you, I have no doubt, that the wretched boy Cradock had another seizure the night before last; he awoke me with cries in that voice you heard in the garden, and I went to him, and God forbid you should see what I saw that night. But all this is useless; my time here is drawing to a close; I must be back in town in three weeks, as I have a course of lectures to prepare, and need all my books about me. In a very few days it will all be over, and I shall no longer hint, and no longer be liable to ridicule as a madman and a quack. No, I shall speak plainly, and I shall be heard with such emotions as perhaps no other man has ever drawn from the breasts of his fellows.'

He paused, and seemed to grow radiant with the joy of great and wonderful discovery.

'But all that is for the future, the near future certainly, but still the future,' he went on at length. 'There is something to be done yet; you will remember my telling you that my researches were not altogether devoid of peril? Yes, there is a certain amount of danger to be faced; I did not know how much when I spoke on the subject before, and to a certain extent I am still in the dark. But it will be a strange adventure, the last of all, the last demonstration in the chain.'

He was walking up and down the room as he spoke, and

I could hear in his voice the contending tones of exultation and despondence, or perhaps I should say awe, the
awe of a man who goes forth on unknown waters, and
I thought of his allusion to Columbus on the night he had
laid his book before me. The evening was a little chilly,
and a fire of logs had been lighted in the study where we
were; the remittent flame and the glow on the walls reminded me of the old days. I was sitting silent in an arm-
chair by the fire, wondering over all I had heard, and still
vainly speculating as to the secret springs concealed from
me under all the phantasmagoria I had witnessed, when I
became suddenly aware of a sensation that change of some
sort had been at work in the room, and that there was
something unfamiliar in its aspect. For some time I looked
about me, trying in vain to localize the alteration that I
knew had been made; the table by the window, the chairs,
the faded settee were all as I had known them. Suddenly,
as a sought-for recollection flashes into mind, I knew what
was amiss. I was facing the professor's desk, which stood
on the other side of the fire, and above the desk was a
grimy-looking bust of Pitt, that I had never seen there
before. And then I remembered the true position of this
work of art; in the furthest corner by the door was an old
cupboard, projecting into the room, and on the top of the
cupboard, fifteen feet from the floor, the bust had been,
and there, no doubt, it had delayed, accumulating dirt,
since the early years of the century.

I was utterly amazed, and sat silent still, in a confusion
of thought. There was, so far as I knew, no such thing as
a step-ladder in the house, for I had asked for one to make
some alterations in the curtains of my room, and a tall
man standing on a chair would have found it impossible
to take down the bust. It had been placed, not on the
edge of the cupboard, but far back against the wall; and
Professor Gregg was, if anything, under the average height.

'How on earth did you manage to get down Pitt?' I said
at last.

The professor looked curiously at me, and seemed to
hesitate a little.

'They must have found you a step-ladder, or perhaps the gardener brought in a short ladder from outside?'

'No, I have had no ladder of any kind. Now, Miss Lally," he went on with an awkward simulation of jest, 'there is a little puzzle for you; a problem in the manner of the inimitable Holmes; there are the facts, plain and patent; summon your acuteness to the solution of the puzzle. For Heaven's sake,' he cried with a breaking voice, 'say no more about it! I tell you, I never touched the thing,' and he went out of the room with horror manifest on his face, and his hand shook and jarred the door behind him.

I looked round the room in vague surprise, not at all realizing what had happened, making vain and idle surmises by way of explanation, and wondering at the stirring of black waters by an idle word and the trivial change of an ornament. 'This is some petty business, some whim on which I have jarred,' I reflected; 'the professor is perhaps scrupulous and superstitious over trifles, and my question may have outraged unacknowledged fears, as though one killed a spider or spilled the salt before the very eyes of a practical Scotchwoman.' I was immersed in these fond suspicions, and began to plume myself a little on my immunity for such empty fears, when the truth fell heavily as lead upon my heart, and I recognized with cold terror that some awful influence had been at work. The bust was simply inaccessible; without a ladder no one could have touched it.

I went out to the kitchen and spoke as quietly as I could to the housemaid.

'Who moved that bust from the top of the cupboard, Anne?' I said to her. 'Professor Gregg says he has not touched it. Did you find an old step-ladder in one of the outhouses?'

The girl looked at me blankly.

'I never touched it,' she said. 'I found it where it is now the other morning when I dusted the room. I remember now, it was Wednesday morning, because it was the morning after Cradock was taken bad in the night. My room is next to his, you know, miss,' the girl went on

piteously, 'and it was awful to hear how he cried and
called out names that I couldn't understand. It made me
feel all afraid; and then master came, and I heard him
speak, and he took down Cradock to the study and gave
him something.'

'And you found that bust moved the next morning?'

'Yes, miss. There was a queer sort of smell in the study
when I came down and opened the windows; a bad smell
it was, and I wondered what it could be. Do you know,
miss, I went a long time ago to the Zoo in London with
my cousin Thomas Barker, one afternoon that I had off,
when I was at Mrs. Prince's in Stanhope Gate, and we
went into the snake-house to see the snakes, and it was
just the same sort of smell; very sick it made me feel, I
remember, and I got Barker to take me out. And it was
just the same kind of a smell in the study, as I was saying, and I was wondering what it could be from, when I
see that bust with Pitt cut in it, standing on the master's
desk, and I thought to myself, Now who has done that,
and how have they done it? And when I came to dust the
things, I looked at the bust, and I saw a great mark on it
where the dust was gone, for I don't think it can have
been touched with a duster for years and years, and it
wasn't like finger-marks, but a large patch like, broad and
spread out. So I passed my hand over it, without thinking
what I was doing, and where that patch was it was all
sticky and slimy, as if a snail had crawled over it. Very
strange, isn't it, miss? and I wonder who can have done it,
and how that mess was made.'

The well-meant gabble of the servant touched me to
the quick; I lay down upon my bed, and bit my lip that I
should not cry out loud in the sharp anguish of my terror
and bewilderment. Indeed, I was almost mad with dread;
I believe that if it had been daylight I should have fled hot
foot, forgetting all courage and all the debt of gratitude
that was due to Professor Gregg, not caring whether my
fate were that I must starve slowly, so long as I might
escape from the net of blind and panic fear that every day
seemed to draw a little closer round me. If I knew, I
thought, if I knew what there were to dread, I could guard

against it; but here, in this lonely house, shut in on all sides by the olden woods and the vaulted hills, terror seems to spring inconsequent from every covert, and the flesh is aghast at the half-heard murmurs of horrible things. All in vain I strove to summon scepticism to my aid, and endeavoured by cool common sense to buttress my belief in a world of natural order, for the air that blew in at the open window was a mystic breath, and in the darkness I felt the silence go heavy and sorrowful as a mass of requiem, and I conjured images of strange shapes gathering fast amidst the reeds, beside the wash of the river.

In the morning from the moment that I set foot in the breakfast-room, I felt that the unknown plot was drawing to a crisis; the professor's face was firm and set, and he seemed hardly to hear our voices when we spoke.

'I am going out for a rather long walk,' he said when the meal was over. 'You mustn't be expecting me, now, or thinking anything has happened if I don't turn up to dinner. I have been getting stupid lately, and I dare say a miniature walking tour will do me good. Perhaps I may even spend the night in some little inn, if I find any place that looks clean and comfortable.'

I heard this and knew by my experience of Professor Gregg's manner that it was no ordinary business or pleasure that impelled him. I knew not, nor even remotely guessed, where he was bound, nor had I the vaguest notion of his errand, but all the fear of the night before returned; and as he stood, smiling, on the terrace, ready to set out, I implored him to stay, and to forget all his dreams of the undiscovered continent.

'No, no, Miss Lally,' he replied still smiling, 'it's too late now. *Vestigia nulla retrorsum*, you know, is the device of all true explorers, though I hope it won't be literally true in my case. But, indeed, you are wrong to alarm yourself so; I look upon my little expedition as quite commonplace; no more exciting than a day with the geological hammers. There is a risk, of course, but so there is on the commonest excursion. I can afford to be jaunty! I am doing nothing so hazardous as 'Arry does a hundred times over in the course of every Bank Holiday. Well, then, you must look more cheerfully; and so good-bye till to-morrow at latest.'

He walked briskly up the road, and I saw him open the gate that marks the entrance of the wood, and then he vanished in the gloom of the trees.

All the day passed heavily with a strange darkness in the air, and again I felt as if imprisoned amidst the ancient woods, shut in an olden land of mystery and dread, and as if all was long ago and forgotten by the living outside. I hoped and dreaded; and when the dinner-hour came I waited, expecting to hear the professor's step in the hall, and his voice exulting at I knew not what triumph. I composed my face to welcome him gladly, but the night descended dark, and he did not come.

In the morning, when the maid knocked at my door, I called out to her, and asked if her master had returned; and when she replied that his bedroom stood open and empty, I felt the cold clasp of despair. Still, I fancied he might have discovered genial company, and would return for luncheon, or perhaps in the afternoon, and I took the children for a walk in the forest, and tried my best to play and laugh with them, and to shut out the thoughts of mystery and veiled terror. Hour after hour I waited, and my thoughts grew darker; again the night came and found me watching, and at last, as I was making much ado to finish my dinner, I heard steps outside and the sound of a man's voice.

The maid came in and looked oddly at me. 'Please, miss,' she began, 'Mr. Morgan the gardener wants to speak to you for a minute, if you didn't mind.'

'Show him in, please,' I answered, and set my lips tight.

The old man came slowly into the room, and the servant shut the door behind him.

'Sit down, Mr. Morgan,' I said: 'what is it that you want to say to me?'

'Well, miss, Mr. Gregg he gave me something for you yesterday morning, just before he went off; and he told me particular not to hand it up before eight o'clock this evening exactly, if so be as he wasn't back home again before, and if he should come home before I was just to return it to him in his own hands. So, you see, as Mr. Gregg isn't here yet, I suppose I'd better give you the parcel directly.'

He pulled out something from his pocket, and gave it to me, half rising. I took it silently, and seeing that Morgan seemed doubtful as to what he was to do next, I thanked him and bade him good-night, and he went out. I was left alone in the room with the parcel in my hand—a paper parcel neatly sealed and directed to me, with the instructions Morgan had quoted, all written in the professor's large loose hand. I broke the seals with a choking at my heart, and found an envelope inside, addressed also, but open, and I took the letter out.

'MY DEAR MISS LALLY,' it began,—'To quote the old logic manual, the case of your reading this note is a case of my having made a blunder of some sort, and, I am afraid, a blunder that turns these lines into a farewell. It is practically certain that neither you nor any one else will ever see me again. I have made my will with provision for this eventuality, and I hope you will consent to accept the small remembrance addressed to you, and my sincere thanks for the way in which you joined your fortunes to mine. The fate which has come upon me is desperate and terrible beyond the remotest dreams of man; but this fate you have a right to know—if you please. If you look in the left-hand drawer of my dressing-table, you will find the key of the escritoire, properly labelled. In the well of the escritoire is a large envelope sealed and addressed to your name. I advise you to throw it forthwith into the fire; you will sleep better of nights if you do so. But if you must know the history of what has happened, it is all written down for you to read.'

The signature was firmly written below, and again I turned the page and read out the words one by one, aghast and white to the lips, my hands cold as ice, and sickness choking me. The dead silence of the room, and the thought of the dark woods and hills closing me in on every side, oppressed me, helpless and without capacity, and not knowing where to turn for counsel. At last I resolved that though knowledge should haunt my whole life and all the days to come, I must know the meaning of the strange terrors that had so long tormented me, rising grey, dim, and awful, like the shadows in the wood at dusk. I carefully carried out Professor Gregg's directions, and not without reluctance broke the seal of the envelope, and spread out his manuscript before me. That manuscript I always carry with me, and I see that I cannot deny your unspoken request to read it. This, then, was what I read that night, sitting at the desk, with a shaded lamp beside me.

The young lady who called herself Miss Lally then proceeded to recite

The Statement of William Gregg, F. R. S., etc.

It is many years since the first glimmer of the theory which is now almost, if not quite, reduced to fact dawned on my mind. A somewhat extensive course of miscellaneous and obsolete reading had done a good deal to prepare the way, and, later, when I became somewhat of a specialist, and immersed myself in the studies known as ethnological, I was now and then startled by facts that would not square with orthodox scientific opinion, and by discoveries that seemed to hint at something still hidden for all our research. More particularly I became convinced that much of the folk-lore of the world is but an exaggerated account of events that really happened, and I was especially drawn to consider the stories of the fairies, the good folk of the Celtic races. Here I thought I could detect the fringe of embroidery and exaggeration, the fantastic guise, the little people dressed in green and gold sporting in the flowers, and I thought I saw a distinct analogy between the name given to this race (supposed to be imaginary) and the description of their appearance and manners. Just as our remote ancestors called the dreadful beings 'fair' and 'good' precisely because they dreaded them, so they had dressed them up in charming forms, knowing the truth to be the very reverse. Literature, too, had gone early to work, and had lent a powerful hand in the transformation, so that the playful elves of Shakespeare are already far removed from the true original, and the real horror is disguised in a form of prankish mischief. But in the older tales, the stories that used to make men cross themselves as they sat round the burning logs, we tread a different stage; I saw a widely opposed spirit in certain histories of children and of men and women who vanished strangely from the earth. They would be seen by a peasant in the fields walking towards some green and rounded hillock, and seen no more on earth; and there are stories of mothers who have left a child quietly sleeping, with the cottage door rudely barred with a piece of wood, and have returned, not to find the plump and rosy little Saxon, but a thin and wizened creature, with sallow skin and black, piercing eyes, the child of another race. Then, again, there were myths darker still; the dread of witch and wizard, the lurid evil of the Sabbath, and the hint of demons who mingled with the daughters of men. And just as we have turned the terrible 'fair folk' into a company of benignant, if freakish, elves, so we have hidden from us the black foulness of the witch and her companions under a popular *diablerie* of old women and broomsticks and a comic cat with tail on end. So the Greeks called the hideous furies benevolent ladies, and thus the northern nations have followed their example. I pursued my investigations, stealing odd hours from other and more imperative labours, and I asked myself the question: Supposing these traditions to be true, who were the demons who are reported to have attended the Sabbaths? I need not say that I laid aside what I may call the supernatural hypothesis of the Middle Ages, and came to the conclusion that fairies and devils were of one and the same race and origin; invention, no doubt, and the Gothic fancy of old days, had done much in the way of exaggeration and distortion; yet I firmly believe that beneath all this imagery there was a black background of truth. As for some of the alleged wonders, I hesitated. While I should be very loath to receive any one specific instance of modern spiritualism as containing even a grain of the genuine, yet I was not wholly prepared to deny that human flesh may now and then, once perhaps in ten million cases, be the veil of powers which seem magical to us—powers which, so far from proceeding from the heights and leading men thither, are in reality survivals from the depth of being. The amœba and the snail have powers which we do not possess; and I thought it possible that the theory of reversion might explain many things which seem wholly inexplicable. Thus stood my position; I saw good reason to believe that much of the tradition, a vast deal of the earliest and uncorrupted tradition of the so-called fairies, represented solid fact, and I thought that the purely supernatural element in these traditions was to be accounted for on the hypothesis that a race which had fallen out of the grand march of evolution might have retained, as a survival, certain powers which would be to us wholly miraculous. Such was my theory as it stood conceived in my mind; and working with this in view, I seemed to gather confirmation from every side, from the spoils of a tumulus or a barrow, from a local paper reporting an antiquarian meeting in the country, and from general literature of all kinds. Amongst other instances, I remember being struck by the phrase 'articulate-speaking men' in Homer, as if the writer knew or had heard of men whose speech was so rude that it could hardly be termed articulate; and on my hypothesis of a race who had lagged far behind the rest, I could easily conceive that such a folk would speak a jargon but little removed from the inarticulate noises of brute beasts.

Thus I stood, satisfied that my conjecture was at all events not far removed from fact, when a chance paragraph in a small country print one day arrested my attention. It was a short account of what was to all appearance the usual sordid tragedy of the village—a young girl unaccountably missing, and evil rumour blatant and busy with her reputation. Yet, I could read between the lines that all this scandal was purely hypocritical, and in all probability invented to account for what was in any other manner unaccountable. A flight to London or Liverpool, or an undiscovered body lying with a weight about its neck in the foul depths of a woodland pool, or perhaps murder—such were the theories of the wretched girl's neighbours. But as I idly scanned the paragraph, a flash of thought passed through me with the violence of an electric shock: what if the obscure and horrible race of the hills still survived, still remained haunting the wild places and barren hills, and now and then repeating the evil of Gothic legend, unchanged and unchangeable as the Turanian Shelta, or the Basques of Spain? I have said that the thought came with violence; and indeed I drew in my breath sharply, and clung with both hands to my elbow-chair, in a strange confusion of horror and elation. It was as if one of my *confrères* of physical science, roaming in a quiet English wood, had been suddenly stricken aghast by the presence of the slimy and loathsome terror of the ichthyosaurus, the original of the stories of the awful worms killed by valorous knights, or had seen the sun darkened by the pterodactyl, the dragon of tradition. Yet as a resolute explorer of knowledge, the thought of such a discovery threw me into a passion of joy, and I cut out the slip from the paper and put it in a drawer in my old bureau, resolved that it should be but the first piece in a collection of the strangest significance. I sat long that evening dreaming of the conclusions I should establish, nor did cooler reflection at first dash my confidence. Yet as I began to put the case fairly, I saw that I might be building on an unstable foundation; the facts might possibly be in accordance with local opinion, and I regarded the affair with a mood of some reserve. Yet I resolved to remain perched on the look-out, and I hugged to myself the thought that I alone was watching and wakeful, while the great crowd of thinkers and searchers stood heedless and indifferent, perhaps letting the most prerogative facts pass by unnoticed.

Several years elapsed before I was enabled to add to the contents of the drawer; and the second find was in reality not a valuable one, for it was a mere repetition of the first, with only the variation of another and distant locality. Yet I gained something; for in the second case, as in the first, the tragedy took place in a desolate and lonely country, and so far my theory seemed justified. But the third piece was to me far more decisive. Again, amongst outland hills, far even from a main road of traffic, an old man was found done to death, and the instrument of execution was left beside him. Here, indeed, there were rumour and conjecture, for the deadly tool was a primitive stone axe, bound by gut to the wooden handle, and surmises the most extravagant and improbable were indulged in. Yet, as I thought with a kind of glee, the wildest conjectures went far astray; and I took the pains to enter into correspondence with the local doctor, who was called at the inquest. He, a man of some acuteness, was dumbfoundered. 'It will not do to speak of these things in country places,' he wrote to me; 'but frankly, there is some hideous mystery here. I have obtained possession of the stone axe, and have been so curious as to test its powers. I took it into the back-garden of my house one Sunday afternoon when my family and the servants were all out, and there, sheltered by the poplar hedges, I made my experiments. I found the thing utterly unmanageable; whether there is some peculiar balance, some nice adjustment of weights, which require incessant practice, or whether an effectual blow can be struck only by a certain trick of the muscles, I do not know; but I can assure you that I went into the house with but a sorry opinion of my athletic capacities. It was like an inexperienced man trying "putting the hammer"; the force exerted seemed to return on oneself, and I found myself hurled backwards with violence, while the axe fell harmless to the ground. On another occasion I tried the experiment with a clever woodman of the place; but this man, who had handled his axe for forty years, could do nothing with the stone implement, and missed every stroke most ludicrously. In short, if it were not so supremely absurd, I should say that for four thousand years no one on earth could have struck an effective blow with the tool that undoubtedly was used to murder the old man.' This, as may be imagined, was to me rare news; and afterwards, when I heard the whole story, and learned that the unfortunate old man had babbled tales of what might be seen at night on a certain wild hillside, hinting at unheard-of wonders, and that he had been found cold one morning on the very hill in question, my exultation was extreme, for I felt I was leaving conjecture far behind me. But the next step was of still greater importance. I had possessed for many years an extraordinary stone seal—a piece of dull black stone, two inches long from the handle to the stamp, and the stamping end a rough hexagon an inch and a quarter in diameter. Altogether, it presented the appearance of an enlarged tobacco stopper of an old-fashioned make. It had been sent to me by an agent in the East, who informed me that it had been found near the site of the ancient Babylon. But the characters engraved on the seal were to me an intolerable puzzle. Somewhat of the cuneiform pattern, there were yet striking differences, which I detected at the first glance, and all efforts to read the inscription on the hypothesis that the rules for deciphering the arrow-headed writing would apply proved futile. A riddle such as this stung my pride, and at odd moments I would take the Black Seal out of the cabinet, and scrutinize it with so much idle perseverence that every letter was familiar to my mind, and I could have drawn the inscription from memory without the slightest error. Judge, then, of my surprise when I one day received from a correspondent in the west of England a letter and an enclosure that positively left me thunderstruck. I saw carefully traced on a large piece of paper the very characters of the Black Seal, without alteration of any kind, and above the inscription my friend had written: *Inscription found on a limestone rock on the Grey Hills, Monmouthshire. Done in some red earth, and quite recent.* I turned to the letter. My friend wrote: 'I sent you the enclosed inscription with all due reserve. A shepherd who passed by the stone a week ago swears that there was then no mark of any kind. The characters, as I have noted, are formed by drawing some red earth over the stone, and are of an average height of one inch. They look to me like a kind of cuneiform character, a good deal altered, but this, of course, is impossible. It may be either a hoax, or more probably some scribble of the gipsies, who are plentiful enough in this wild country. They have, as you are aware, many hieroglyphics which they use in communicating with one another. I happened to visit the stone in question two days ago in connection with a rather painful incident which has occurred here.'

As may be supposed, I wrote immediately to my friend, thanking him for the copy of the inscription, and asking him in a casual manner the history of the incident he mentioned. To be brief, I heard that a woman named Cradock, who had lost her husband a day before, had set out to communicate the sad news to a cousin who lived some five miles away. She took a short cut which led by the Grey Hills. Mrs. Cradock, who was then quite a young woman, never arrived at her relative's house. Late that night a farmer who had lost a couple of sheep, supposed to have wandered from the flock, was walking over the Grey Hills, with a lantern and his dog. His attention was attracted by a noise, which he described as a kind of wailing, mournful and pitiable to hear; and, guided by the sound, he found the unfortunate Mrs. Cradock crouched on the ground by the limestone rock, swaying her body to and fro, and lamenting and crying in so heart-rending a manner that the farmer was, as he says, at first obliged to stop his ears, or he would have run away. The woman allowed herself to be taken home, and a neighbour came to see to her necessities. All the night she never ceased her crying, mixing her lament with words of some unintelligible jargon, and when the doctor arrived he pronounced her insane. She lay on her bed for a week, now wailing, as people said, like one lost and damned for eternity, and now sunk in a heavy coma; it was thought that grief at the loss of her husband had unsettled her mind, and the medical man did not at one time expect her to live. I need not say that I was deeply interested in this story, and I made my friend write to me at intervals with all the particulars of the case. I heard then that in the course of six weeks the woman gradually recovered the use of her faculties, and some months later she gave birth to a son, christened Jervase, who unhappily proved to be of weak intellect. Such were the facts known to the village; but to me, while I whitened at the sug-

gested thought of the hideous enormities that had doubt-
less been committed, all this was nothing short of conviction, and I incautiously hazarded a hint of something
like the truth to some scientific friends. The moment the
words had left my lips I bitterly regretted having spoken,
and thus given way the great secret of my life, but with a
good deal of relief mixed with indignation I found my
fears altogether misplaced, for my friends ridiculed me to
my face, and I was regarded as a madman; and beneath
a natural anger I chuckled to myself, feeling as secure
amidst these blockheads as if I had confided what I knew
to the desert sands.

But now, knowing so much, I resolved I would know
all, and I concentrated my efforts on the task of deciphering the inscription on the Black Seal. For many years I
made this puzzle the sole object of my leisure moments;
for the greater portion of my time was, of course, devoted
to other duties, and it was only now and then that I could
snatch a week of clear research. If I were to tell the full
history of this curious investigation, this statement would
be wearisome in the extreme, for it would contain simply
the account of long and tedious failure. By what I knew
already of ancient scripts I was well equipped for the
chase, as I always termed it to myself. I had correspondents amongst all the scientific men in Europe, and indeed,
in the world, and I could not believe that in these days any
character, however ancient and however perplexed, could
long resist the search-light I should bring to bear upon
it. Yet, in point of fact, it was fully fourteen years before
I succeeded. With every year my professional duties increased, and my leisure became smaller. This no doubt
retarded me a good deal; and yet, when I look back on
those years, I am astonished at the vast scope of my
investigation of the Black Seal. I made my bureau a
centre, and from all the world and from all the ages I
gathered transcripts of ancient writing. Nothing, I resolved,
should pass me unawares, and the faintest hint should be
welcomed and followed up. But as one covert after another was tried and proved empty of result, I began in
the course of years to despair, and to wonder whether

the Black Seal were the sole relic of some race that had vanished from the world and left no other trace of its existence—had perished, in fine, as Atlantis is said to have done, in some great cataclysm, its secrets perhaps drowned beneath the ocean or moulded into the heart of the hills. The thought chilled my warmth a little, and though I still persevered, it was no longer with the same certainty of faith. A chance came to the rescue. I was staying in a considerable town in the north of England, and took the opportunity of going over the very creditable museum that had for some time been established in the place. The curator was one of my correspondents; and, as we were looking through one of the mineral cases, my attention was struck by a specimen, a piece of black stone some four inches square, the appearance of which reminded me in a measure of the Black Seal. I took it up carelessly, and was turning it over in my hand, when I saw, to my astonishment, that the under side was inscribed. I said, quietly enough, to my friend the curator that the specimen interested me, and that I should be much obliged if he would allow me to take it with me to my hotel for a couple of days. He, of course, made no objection, and I hurried to my rooms and found that my first glance had not deceived me. There were two inscriptions; one in the regular cuneiform character, another in the character of the Black Seal, and I realized that my task was accomplished. I made an exact copy of the two inscriptions; and when I got to my London study, and had the Seal before me, I was able seriously to grapple with the great problem. The interpreting inscription of the museum specimen, though in itself curious enough, did not bear on my quest, but the transliteration made me master of the secret of the Black Seal. Conjecture, of course, had to enter into my calculations; there was here and there uncertainty about a particular ideograph, and one sign recurring again and again on the seal baffled me for many successive nights. But at last the secret stood open before me in plain English, and I read the key of the awful transmutation of the hills. The last word was hardly written, when with fingers all trembling and unsteady I tore the scrap of paper into the minutest fragments, and saw them flame and blacken in the red hollow of the fire, and then I crushed the grey films that remained into finest powder. Never since then have I written those words; never will I write the phrases which tell how man can be reduced to the slime from which he came, and be forced to put on the flesh of the reptile and the snake. There was now but one thing remaining. I knew, but I desired to see, and I was after some time able to take a house in the neighbourhood of the Grey Hills, and not far from the cottage where Mrs. Cradock and her son Jervase resided. I need not go into a full and detailed account of the apparently inexplicable events which have occurred here, where I am writing this. I knew that I should find in Jervase Cradock something of the blood of the 'Little People,' and I found later that he had more than once encountered his kinsmen in lonely places in that lonely land. When I was summoned one day to the garden, and found him in a seizure speaking or hissing the ghastly jargon of the Black Seal, I am afraid that exultation prevailed over pity. I heard bursting from his lips the secrets of the underworld, and the word of dread, 'Ishakshar,' signification of which I must be excused from giving.

But there is one incident I cannot pass over unnoticed. In the waste hollow of the night I awoke at the sound of those hissing syllables I knew so well; and on going to the wretched boy's room, I found him convulsed and foaming at the mouth, struggling on the bed as if he strove to escape the grasp of writhing demons. I took him down to my room and lit the lamp, while he lay twisting on the floor, calling on the power within his flesh to leave him. I saw his body swell and become distended as a bladder, while the face blackened before my eyes; and then at the crisis I did what was necessary according to the directions on the Seal, and putting all scruple on one side, I became a man of science, observant of what was passing. Yet the sight I had to witness was horrible, almost beyond the power of human conception and the most fearful fantasy. Something pushed out from the body there on the floor, and stretched forth, a slimy, wavering tentacle, across the room, grasped the bust upon the cupboard, and laid it down on my desk.

When it was over, and I was left to walk up and down all the rest of the night, white and shuddering, with sweat pouring from my flesh, I vainly tried to reason with myself: I said, truly enough, that I had seen nothing really supernatural, that a snail pushing out his horns and drawing them in was but an instance on a smaller scale of what I had witnessed; and yet horror broke through all such reasonings and left me shattered and loathing myself for the share I had taken in the night's work.

There is little more to be said. I am going now to the final trial and encounter; for I have determined that there shall be nothing wanting, and I shall meet the 'Little People' face to face. I shall have the Black Seal and the knowledge of its secrets to help me, and if I unhappily do not return from my journey, there is no need to conjure up here a picture of the awfulness of my fate.

Pausing a little at the end of Professor Gregg's statement, Miss Lally continued her tale in the following words:—

Such was the almost incredible story that the professor had left behind him. When I had finished reading it, it was late at night, but the next morning I took Morgan with me, and we proceeded to search the Grey Hills for some trace of the lost professor. I will not weary you with a description of the savage desolation of that tract of country, a tract of utterest loneliness, of bare green hills dotted over with grey limestone boulders, worn by the ravages of time into fantastic semblances of men and beasts. Finally, after many hours of weary searching, we found what I told you—the watch and chain, the purse, and the ring—wrapped in a piece of coarse parchment. When Morgan cut the gut that bound the parcel together, and I saw the professor's property, I burst into tears, but the sight of the dreaded characters of the Black Seal repeated on the parchment froze me to silent horror, and I think I understood for the first time the awful fate that had come upon my late employer.

I have only to add that Professor Gregg's lawyer treated my account of what had happened as a fairy tale, and refused even to glance at the documents I laid before him. It was he who was responsible for the statement that appeared in the public press, to the effect that Professor Gregg had been drowned, and that his body must have been swept into the open sea.

Miss Lally stopped speaking, and looked at Mr. Phillipps, with a glance of some inquiry. He, for his part, was sunken in a deep reverie of thought; and when he looked up and saw the bustle of the evening gathering in the square, men and women hurrying to partake of dinner, and crowds already besetting the music-halls, all the hum and press of actual life seemed unreal and visionary, a dream in the morning after an awakening.

'I thank you,' he said at last, 'for your most interesting story; interesting to me, because I feel fully convinced of its exact truth.'

'Sir,' said the lady, with some energy of indignation, 'you grieve and offend me. Do you think I should waste my time and yours by concocting fictions on a bench in Leicester Square?'

'Pardon me, Miss Lally, you have a little misunderstood me. Before you began I knew that whatever you told would be told in good faith, but your experiences have a far higher value than that of *bona fides*. The most extraordinary circumstances in your account are in perfect harmony with the very latest scientific theories. Professor Lodge would, I am sure, value a communication from you extremely; I was charmed from the first by his daring hypothesis in explanation of the wonders of spiritualism (so called), but your narrative puts the whole matter out of the range of mere hypothesis.'

'Alas! sir, all this will not help me. You forget, I have lost my brother under the most startling and dreadful circumstances. Again, I ask you, did you not see him as you came here? His black whiskers, his spectacles, his timid glance to right and left; think, do not these particulars recall his face to your memory?'

'I am sorry to say I have never seen any one of the kind,' said Phillipps, who had forgotten all about the missing brother. 'But let me ask you a few questions. Did you notice whether Professor Gregg——'

'Pardon me, sir, I have stayed too long. My employers will be expecting me. I thank you for your sympathy. Good-bye.'

Before Mr. Phillipps had recovered from his amazement at this abrupt departure Miss Lally had disappeared from his gaze, passing into the crowd that now thronged the approaches to the Empire. He walked home in a pensive frame of mind, and drank too much tea. At ten o'clock he had made his third brew, and had sketched out the outlines of a little work to be called 'Protoplasmic Reversion.'

you. I am sure we should have a little talk together. We turn up here?'

The theatres were filling as they crossed the Strand; the street seemed alive, and Dyson looked fondly about him. The glittering lines of gas-lamps, with here and there the blinding radiance of an electric light, the hansoms that flashed to and fro with ringing bells, the laden 'buses, and the eager hurrying east and west of the foot passengers, made his most enchanting picture; and the graceful spire of St. Mary le Strand on the one hand, and the last flush of sunset on the other, were to him a cause of thanksgiving, as the gorse blossom to Linnæus. Mr. Burton caught his look of fondness as they crossed the street.

'I see you can find the picturesque in London,' he said. 'To me this great town is as I see it is to you—the study and the love of life. Yet how few there are that can pierce the veils of apparent monotony and meanness! I have read in a paper, which is said to have the largest circulation in the world, a comparison between the aspects of London and Paris, a comparison which should be positively laureate as the great masterpiece of fatuous stupidity. Conceive if you can a human being of ordinary intelligence preferring the Boulevards to our London streets; imagine a man calling for the wholesale destruction of our most charming city, in order that the dull uniformity of that whited sepulchre called Paris should be reproduced here in London. Is it not positively incredible?'

'My dear sir,' said Dyson, regarding Burton with a good deal of interest, 'I agree most heartily with your opinions, but I really can't share your wonder. Have you heard how much George Eliot received for "Romola"? Do you know what the circulation of "Robert Elsmere" was? Do you read "Tit-Bits" regularly? To me, on the contrary, it is constant matter for wonder and thanksgiving that London was not boulevardized twenty years ago. I praise that exquisite jagged skyline that stands up against the pale greens and fading blues and flushing clouds of sunset, but I wonder even more than I praise. As for St. Mary le Strand, its preservation is a miracle, nothing more or less. A thing of exquisite beauty versus four 'buses abreast! Really, the conclusion is too obvious. Didn't you read the letter of the man who proposed that the whole mysterious system, the immemorial plan of computing Easter, should be abolished off-hand, because he doesn't like his son having his holidays as early as March 25th? But shall we be going on?'

They had lingered at the corner of a street on the north side of the Strand, enjoying the contrasts and the glamour of the scene. Dyson pointed the way with a gesture, and they strolled up the comparatively deserted streets, slanting a little to the right, and thus arriving at Dyson's lodging on the verge of Bloomsbury. Mr. Burton took a comfortable arm-chair by the open window, while Dyson lit the candles and produced the whiskey and soda and cigarettes.

'They tell me these cigarettes are very good,' he said; 'but I know nothing about it myself. I hold at last that there is only one tobacco, and that is shag. I suppose I could not tempt you to try a pipeful?'

Mr. Burton smilingly refused the offer, and picked out a cigarette from the box. When he had smoked it half through, he said with some hesitation—

'It is really kind of you to have me here, Mr. Dyson; the fact is that the interests at issue are far too serious to be discussed in a bar, where, as you found for yourself, there may be listeners, voluntary or involuntary, on each side. I think the remark I heard you make was something about the oddity of an individual going about London in deadly fear of a young man with spectacles?'

'Yes; that was it.'

'Well, would you mind confiding to me the circumstances that gave rise to the reflection?'

'Not in the least. It was like this.' And he ran over in brief outline the adventure in Oxford Street, dwelling on the violence of Mr. Wilkins's gestures, but wholly suppressing the tale told in the café. 'He told me he lived in constant terror of meeting this man; and I left him when I thought he was cool enough to look after himself,' said Dyson, ending his narrative.

'Really,' said Mr. Burton. 'And you actually saw this mysterious person?'

'Yes.'

'And could you describe him?'

'Well, he looked to me a youngish man, pale and nervous. He had small black side-whiskers, and wore rather large spectacles.'

'But this is simply marvellous! You astonish me. For I must tell you that my interest in the matter is this. I'm not in the least in terror of meeting a dark young man with spectacles, but I shrewdly suspect a person of that description would much rather not meet me. And yet the account you give of the man tallies exactly. A nervous glance to right and left—is it not so? And, as you observed, he wears prominent spectacles, and has small black whiskers. There cannot be, surely, two people exactly identical— one a cause of terror, and the other, I should imagine, extremely anxious to get out of the way. But have you seen this man since?'

'No, I have not; and I have been looking out for him pretty keenly. But of course he may have left London, and England too, for the matter of that.'

'Hardly, I think. Well, Mr. Dyson, it is only fair that I should explain my story, now that I have listened to yours. I must tell you, then, that I am an agent for curiosities and precious things of all kinds. An odd employment, isn't it? Of course, I wasn't brought up to the business; I gradually fell into it. I have always been fond of things queer and rare, and by the time I was twenty I had made half a dozen collections. It is not generally known how often farm-labourers come upon rarities; you would be astonished if I told you what I have seen turned up by the plough. I lived in the country in those days, and I used to buy anything the men on the farms brought me; and I had the queerest set of rubbish, as my friends called my collection. But that's how I got the scent of the business, which means everything; and, later on, it struck me that I might very well turn my knowledge to account and add to my income. Since those early days I have been in most quarters of the world, and some very valuable things have passed through my hands, and I have had to engage in difficult and delicate negotiations. You have possibly heard of the Khan opal—called in the East "The Stone of a Thousand and One Colours"? Well, perhaps the conquest of that stone was my greatest achievement. I call it myself the stone of the thousand and one lies, for I assure you that I had to invent a cycle of folk-lore before the Rajah who owned it would consent to sell the thing. I subsidized wandering story-tellers, who told tales in which the opal played a frightful part; I hired a holy man —a great ascetic—to prophesy against the thing in the language of Eastern symbolism; in short, I frightened the Rajah out of his wits. So, you see, there is room for diplomacy in the traffic I am engaged in. I have to be ever on my guard, and I have often been sensible that unless I watched every step and weighed every word, my life would not last me much longer. Last April I became aware of the existence of a highly valuable antique gem; it was in southern Italy, and in the possession of persons who were ignorant of its real value. It has always been my experience that it is precisely the ignorant who are most difficult to deal with. I have met farmers who were under the impression that a shilling of George the First was a find of almost incalculable value; and all the defects I have sustained have been at the hands of people of this description. Reflecting on these facts, I saw that the acquisition of the gem would be an affair demanding the nicest diplomacy; I might possibly have got it by offering a sum approaching its real value, but I need not point out to you that such a proceeding would be most unbusinesslike. Indeed, I doubt whether it would have been successful; for the cupidity of such persons is aroused by a sum which seems enormous, and the low cunning which serves them in place of intelligence immediately suggests that the object for which such an amount is offered must be worth at least double. Of course, when it is a matter of an ordinary curiosity—an old jug, a carved chest, or a queer brass lantern—one does not much care; the cupidity of the owner defeats its object; the collector laughs and goes away, for he is aware that such things are by no means unique. But this gem I fervently desired to possess; and as I did not see my way to giving more than a hundredth part of its value, I was conscious that all my, let us say, imaginative and diplomatic powers would have to be exerted. I am sorry to say that I came to the conclusion that I could not undertake to carry the matter through single-handed, and I determined to confide in my assistant, a young man named William Robbins, whom I judged to be by no means devoid of capacity. My idea was that Robbins should get himself up as a low-class dealer in precious stones; he could patter a little Italian, and would go to the town in question and manage to see the gem we were after, possibly by offering some trifling articles of jewellery for sale, but that I left to be decided. Then my work was to begin, but I will not trouble you with a tale told twice over. In due course, then, Robbins went off to Italy with an assortment of uncut stones and a few rings, and some jewellery I bought in Birmingham on purpose for his expedition. A week later I followed him, travelling leisurely, so that I was a fortnight later in arriving at our common destination. There was a decent hotel in the town, and on my inquiring of the landlord whether there were many strangers in the place, he told me very few; he had heard there was an Englishman staying in a small tavern, a pedlar, he said, who sold beautiful trinkets very cheaply, and wanted to buy old rubbish. For five or six days I took life leisurely, and I must say I enjoyed myself. It was part of my plan to make the people think I was an enormously rich man; and I knew that such items as the extravagance of my meals, and the price of every bottle of wine I drank, would not be suffered, as Sancho Panza puts it, to rot in the landlord's breast. At the end of the week I was fortunate enough to make the acquaintance of Signor Melini, the owner of the gem I coveted, at the café, and with his ready hospitality, and my geniality, I was soon established as a friend of the house. On my third or fourth visit I managed to make the Italians talk about the English pedlar, who, they said, spoke a most detestable Italian. "But that does not matter," said the Signora Melini, "for he has beautiful things, which he sells very,

very cheap." "I hope you may not find he has cheated you," I said, "for I must tell you that English people give these fellows a very wide berth. They usually make a great parade of the cheapness of their goods, which often turn out to be double the price of better articles in the shops." They would not hear of this, and Signora Melini insisted on showing me the three rings and the bracelet she had bought of the pedlar. She told me the price she had paid; and after scrutinizing the articles carefully, I had to confess that she had made a bargain, and indeed Robbins had sold her the things at about fifty per cent below market value. I admired the trinkets as I gave them back to the lady, and I hinted that the pedlar must be a somewhat foolish specimen of his class. Two days later, as I was taking my vermouth at the café with Signor Melini, he led the conversation back to the pedlar, and mentioned casually that he had shown the man a little curiosity, for which he had made rather a handsome offer. "My dear sir," I said, "I hope you will be careful. I told you that the travelling tradesman does not bear a very high reputation in England; and notwithstanding his apparent simplicity, this fellow may turn out to be an arrant cheat. May I ask you what is the nature of the curiosity you have shown him?" He told me it was a little thing, a pretty little stone with some figures cut on it: people said it was old. "I should like to examine it;" I replied, "as it happens I have seen a good deal of these gems. We have a fine collection of them in our Museum at London." In due course I was shown the article, and I held the gem I so coveted between my fingers. I looked at it coolly, and put it down carelessly on the table. "Would you mind telling me, Signor," I said, "how much my fellow-countryman offered you for this?" "Well," he said, "my wife says the man must be mad; he said he would give me twenty lire for it."

'I looked at him quietly, and took up the gem and pretended to examine it in the light more carefully; I turned it over and over, and finally pulled out a magnifying glass from my pocket, and seemed to search every line in the cutting with minutest scrutiny. "My dear sir," I said at last, "I am inclined to agree with Signora Melini. If this gem were genuine, it would be worth some money; but as it happens to be a rather bad forgery, it is not worth twenty centesimi. It was sophisticated, I should imagine, some time in the last century, and by a very unskilful hand." "Then we had better get rid of it," said Melini. "I never thought it was worth anything myself. Of course, I am sorry for the pedlar, but one must let a man know his own trade. I shall tell him we will take the twenty lire." "Excuse me," I said, "the man wants a lesson. It would be a charity to give him one. Tell him that you will not take anything under eighty lire, and I shall be much surprised if he does not close with you at once."

'A day or two later I heard that the English pedlar had gone away, after debasing the minds of the country people with Birmingham art jewellery; for I admit that the gold sleeve-links like kidney beans, the silver chains made apparently after the pattern of a dog-chain, and the initial brooches, have always been heavy on my conscience. I cannot acquit myself of having indirectly contributed to debauch the taste of a simple folk; but I hope that the end I had in view may finally outbalance this heavy charge. Soon afterwards I paid a farewell visit at the Melinis', and the signor informed me with an oily chuckle that the plan I had suggested had been completely successful. I congratulated him on his bargain, and went away after expressing a wish that Heaven might send many such pedlars in his path.

'Nothing of interest occurred on my return journey. I had arranged that Robbins was to meet me at a certain place on a certain day, and I went to the appointment full of the coolest confidence; the gem had been conquered, and I had only to reap the fruits of victory. I am sorry to shake that trust in our common human nature which I am sure you possess, but I am compelled to tell you that up to the present date I have never set eyes on my man Robbins, or on the antique gem in his custody. I have found out that he actually arrived in London, for he was seen three days before my arrival in England by a pawnbroker of my acquaintance, consuming his favourite beverage—four ale—in the tavern where we met tonight. Since then he has not been heard of. I hope you will now pardon my curiosity as to the history and adventures of dark young men with spectacles. You will, I am sure, feel for me in my position; the savour of life has disappeared for me; it is a bitter thought that I have rescued one of the most perfect and exquisite specimens of antique art from the hands of ignorant, and indeed unscrupulous persons, only to deliver it into the keeping of a man who is evidently utterly devoid of the very elements of commercial morality.'

'My dear sir,' said Dyson, 'you will allow me to compliment you on your style; your adventures have interested me exceedingly. But, forgive me, you just now used the word morality; would not some persons take exception to your own methods of business? I can conceive, myself, flaws of a moral kind being found in the very original conception you have just described to me; I can imagine the Puritan shrinking in dismay from your scheme, pronouncing it unscrupulous—nay, dishonest.'

Mr. Burton helped himself very frankly to some more whisky.

'Your scruples entertain me,' he said. 'Perhaps you have not gone very deeply into these questions of ethics. I have been compelled to do so myself, just as I was forced to master a system of book-keeping. Without book-keeping, and still more without a system of ethics, it is impossible to conduct a business such as mine. But I assure you that I am often profoundly saddened, as I pass through the crowded streets and watch the world at work, by the thought of how few amongst all these hurrying individuals, black-hatted, well-dressed, educated we may presume sufficiently,—how few amongst them have any reasoned system of morality. Even you have not weighed the question; although you study life and affairs, and to a certain extent penetrate the veils and masks of the comedy of man, even you judge by empty conventions, and the false money which is allowed to pass current as sterling coin. Allow me to play the part of Socrates; I shall teach you nothing that you do not know. I shall merely lay aside the wrappings of prejudice and bad logic, and show you the real image which you possess in your soul. Come, then. Do you allow that happiness is anything?'

'Certainly,' said Dyson.

'And happiness is desirable or undesirable?'

'Desirable, of course.'

'And what shall we call the man who gives happiness? Is he not a philanthropist?'

'I think so.'

'And such a person is praiseworthy, and the more praiseworthy in the proportion of the persons whom he makes happy?'

'By all means.'

'So that he who makes a whole nation happy is praiseworthy in the extreme, and the action by which he gives happiness is the highest virtue?'

'It appears so, O Burton,' said Dyson, who found something very exquisite in the character of his visitor.

'Quite so; you find the several conclusions inevitable. Well, apply them to the story I have told you. I conferred happiness on myself by obtaining (as I thought) possession of the gem; I conferred happiness on the Melinis by getting them eighty lire instead of an object for which they had not the slightest value, and I intended to confer happiness on the whole British nation by selling the thing to the British Museum, to say nothing of the happiness a profit of about nine thousand per cent would have conferred on me. I assure you, I regard Robbins as an interferer with the cosmos and fair order of things. But that is nothing; you perceive that I am an apostle of the very highest morality; you have been forced to yield to argument.'

'There certainly seems a great deal in what you advance,' said Dyson. 'I admit that I am a mere amateur of ethics, while you, as you say, have brought the most acute scrutiny to bear on these perplexed and doubtful questions. I can well understand your anxiety to meet the fallacious Robbins, and I congratulate myself on the chance which has made us acquainted. But you will pardon my seeming inhospitality; I see it is half-past eleven, and I think you mentioned a train.'

'A thousand thanks, Mr. Dyson. I have just time, I see. I will look you up some evening, if I may. Goodnight.'

The Decorative Imagination

In the course of a few weeks Dyson became accustomed to the constant incursions of the ingenious Mr. Burton, who showed himself ready to drop in at all hours, not averse to refreshment, and a profound guide in the complicated questions of life. His visits at once terrified and delighted Dyson, who could no longer seat himself at his bureau secure from interruption, while he embarked on literary undertakings, each one of which was to be a masterpiece. On the other hand, it was a vivid pleasure to be confronted with views so highly original; and if here and there Mr. Burton's reasonings seemed tinged with fallacy, yet Dyson freely yielded to the joy of strangeness, and never failed to give his visitor a frank and hearty welcome. Mr. Burton's first inquiry was always after the unprincipled Robbins, and he seemed to feel the stings of disappointment when Dyson told him that he had failed to meet this outrage on all morality, as Burton styled him, vowing that sooner or later he would take vengeance on such a shameless betrayal of trust.

One evening they had sat together for some time discussing the possibility of laying down for this present generation and our modern and intensely complicated order of society, some rules of social diplomacy, such as Lord Bacon gave to the courtiers of King James I. 'It is a book to make,' said Mr. Burton, 'but who is there capable of making it? I tell you people are longing for such a book; it would bring fortune to its publisher. Bacon's Essays are exquisite, but they have now no practical application; the modern strategist can find but little use in a treatise "De Re Military," written by a Florentine

in the fifteenth century. Scarcely more dissimilar are the
social conditions of Bacon's time and our own; the rules
that he lays down so exquisitely for the courtier and
diplomatist of James the First's age will avail us little in
the rough-and-tumble struggle of to-day. Life, I am afraid,
has deteriorated; it gives little play for fine strokes such
as formerly advanced men in the state. Except in such
businesses as mine, where a chance does occur now and
then, it has all become, as I said, an affair of rough and
tumble; men still desire to attain, it is true, but what is
their *moyen de parvenir?* A mere imitation, and not a
gracious one, of the arts of the soap-vender and the
proprietor of baking powder. When I think of these things,
my dear Dyson, I confess that I am tempted to despair of
my century.'

'You are too pessimistic, my dear fellow; you set up
too high a standard. Certainly, I agree with you that the
times are decadent in many ways. I admit a general appearance of squalor; it needs much philosophy to extract
the wonderful and the beautiful from the Cromwell Road
or the Nonconformist conscience. Australian wines of
fine Burgundy character, the novels alike of the old
women and the new women, popular journalism,—these
things indeed make for depression. Yet we have our advantages. Before us is unfolded the greatest spectacle the
world has ever seen,—the mystery of the innumerable
unending streets, the strange adventures that must in-
fallibly arise from so complicated a press of interests. Nay,
I will say that he who has stood in the ways of a suburb
and has seen them stretch before him all shining, void,
and desolate at noonday, has not lived in vain. Such a
sight is in reality more wonderful than any perspective of
Bagdad or Grand Cairo. And, to set on one side the
entertaining history of the gem which you told me, surely
you must have had many singular adventures in your own
career?'

'Perhaps not so many as you would think; a good deal
—the larger part—of my business has been as commonplace as linen-drapery. But of course things happen now
and then. It is ten years since I have established my

agency, and I suppose that a house and estate agent who had been in trade for an equal time could tell you some queer stories. But I must give you a sample of my experiences some night.'

'Why not to-night?' said Dyson. 'This evening seems to me admirably adapted for an odd chapter. Look out into the street; you can catch a view of it, if you crane your neck from that chair of yours. Is it not charming? The double row of lamps growing closer in the distance, the hazy outline of the plane-tree in the square, and the lights of the hansoms swimming to and fro, gliding and vanishing; and above, the sky all clear and blue and shining. Come, let us have one of your *cent nouvelles nouvelles.*'

'My dear Dyson, I am delighted to amuse you.'

With these words Mr. Burton prefaced the

NOVEL OF THE IRON MAID

I think the most extraordinary event which I can recall took place about five years ago. I was then still feeling my way; I had declared for business, and attended regularly at my office, but I had not succeeded in establishing a really profitable connection, and consequently I had a good deal of leisure time on my hands. I have never thought fit to trouble you with the details of my private life; they would be entirely devoid of interest. I must briefly say, however, that I had a numerous circle of acquaintance, and was never at a loss as to how to spend my evenings. I was so fortunate as to have friends in most of the ranks of the social order; there is nothing so unfortunate, to my mind, as a specialized circle, wherein a certain round of ideas is continually traversed and retraversed. I have always tried to find out new types and persons whose brains contained something fresh to me; one may chance to gain information even from the conversation of city men on an omnibus. Amongst my acquaintance I knew a young doctor who lived in a far outlying suburb, and I used often to brave the intolerably slow railway journey, to have the pleasure of listening to his talk. One night we conversed so eagerly together over our pipes and whiskey that the clock passed unnoticed, and when I glanced up I realized with a shock that I had just five minutes in which to catch the last train. I made a dash for my hat and stick, and jumped out of the house and down the steps, and tore at full speed up the street. It was no good, however; there was a shriek of the engine whistle, and I stood there at the station door and saw far on the long dark line of the embankment a red light shine and vanish, and a porter came down and shut the door with a bang.

'How far to London?' I asked him.

'A good nine miles to Waterloo Bridge;' and with that he went off.

Before me was the long suburban street, its dreary distance marked by rows of twinkling lamps, and the air was poisoned by the faint sickly smell of burning bricks; it was not a cheerful prospect by any means, and I had to walk through nine miles of such streets, deserted as those of Pompeii. I knew pretty well what direction to take; so I set out wearily, looking at the stretch of lamps vanishing in perspective; and as I walked, street after street branched off to right and left,—some far reaching to distances that seemed endless, communicating with other systems of thoroughfare; and same mere protoplasmic streets, beginning in orderly fashion with serried two-storied houses, and ending suddenly in waste, and pits, and rubbish heaps, and fields whence the magic had departed. I have spoken of systems of thoroughfare, and I assure you that, walking alone through these silent places, I felt phantasy growing on me, and some glamour of the infinite. There was here, I felt, an immensity as in the outer void of the universe. I passed from unknown to unknown, my way marked by lamps like stars, and on either hand was an unknown world where myriads of men dwelt and slept, street leading into street, as it seemed to world's end. At first the road by which I was travelling was lined with houses of unutterable monotony,—a wall of grey brick pierced by two stories of windows, drawn close to the very pavement. But by degrees I noticed an improvement: there were gardens, and these grew larger. The suburban builder began to allow himself a wider scope; and for a certain distance each flight of steps was guarded by twin lions of plaster, and scents of flowers prevailed over the fume of heated bricks. The road began to climb a hill, and, looking up a side street, I saw the half moon rise over plane-trees, and there on the other side was as if a white cloud had fallen, and the air around it was sweetened as with incense; it was a may-tree in full bloom. I pressed on stubbornly, listening for the wheels and the clatter of some belated hansom; but into that land of men who go to the city in the morning and return in the evening, the hansom rarely enters, and I had resigned myself once more to the walk, when I suddenly became aware that some one was advancing to meet me along the sidewalk. The man was strolling rather aimlessly; and though the time and the place would have allowed an unconventional style of dress, he was vested in the ordinary frock coat, black tie, and silk hat of civilization. We met each other under the lamp, and, as often happens in this great town, two casual passengers brought face to face found each in the other an acquaintance.

'My. Mathias, I think?' I said.

'Quite so. And you are Frank Burton. You know you are a man with a Christian name, so I won't apologize for my familiarity. But may I ask where you are going?'

I explained the situation to him, saying I had traversed a region as unknown to me as the darkest recesses of Africa. 'I think I have only about five miles farther,' I concluded.

'Nonsense; you must come home with me. My house is close by; in fact, I was just taking my evening walk when we met. Come along; I dare say you will find a makeshift bed easier than a five-mile walk.'

I let him take my arm and lead me along, though I was a good deal surprised at so much geniality from a man who was, after all, a mere casual club acquaintance. I suppose I had not spoken to Mr. Mathias half-a-dozen times; he was a man who would sit silent in an arm-chair for hours, neither reading nor smoking, but now and again moistening his lips with his tongue and smiling queerly to himself. I confess he had never attracted me, and on the whole I should have preferred to continue my walk. But he took my arm and led me up a side street, and stopped at a door in a high wall. We passed through the still, moonlit garden, beneath the black shadow of an old cedar, and into an old red brick house with many gables. I was tired enough, and I sighed with relief as I let myself fall into a great leather arm-chair. You know the infernal grit with which they strew the sidewalk in those suburban districts; it makes walking a penance, and I felt my four-mile tramp had made me more weary than ten miles on an honest country road. I looked about the room with some curiosity. There was a shaded lamp which threw a circle of brilliant light on a heap of papers lying on an old brass-bound secretaire of the last century; but the room was all vague and shadowy, and I could only see that it was long and low, and that it was filled with indistinct objects which might be furniture. Mr. Mathias sat down in a second arm-chair, and looked about him with that odd smile of his. He was a queer-looking man, clean-shaven, and white to the lips. I should think his age was something between fifty and sixty.

'Now I have got you here,' he began, 'I must inflict my hobby on you. You knew I was a collector? Oh, yes, I have devoted many years to collecting curiosities, which I think are really curious. But we must have a better light.'

He advanced into the middle of the room, and lit a lamp which hung from the ceiling; and as the bright light flashed round the wick, from every corner and space there seemed to start a horror. Great wooden frames with complicated apparatus of ropes and pulleys stood against the wall; a wheel of strange shape had a place beside a thing that looked like a gigantic gridiron. Little tables glittered with bright steel instruments carelessly put down as if ready for use; a screw and vice loomed out, casting ugly shadows; and in another nook was a saw with cruel jagged teeth.

'Yes,' said Mr. Mathias; 'they are, as you suggest, instruments of torture—of torture and death. Some—many, I may say—have been used; a few are reproductions after ancient examples. Those knives were used for flaying; that frame is a rack, and a very fine specimen. Look at this; it comes from Venice. You see that sort of collar, something like a big horse-shoe? Well, the patient, let us call him, sat down quite comfortably, and the horse-shoe was neatly fitted round his neck. Then the two ends were joined with a silken band, and the executioner began to turn a handle connected with the band. The horse-shoe contracted very gradually as the band tightened, and the turning continued till the man was strangled. It all took place quietly, in one of those queer garrets under the Leads. But these things are all European; the Orientals are, of course, much more ingenious. These are the Chinese contrivances. You have heard of the "heavy death"? It is my hobby, this sort of thing. Do you know, I often sit here, hour after hour, and meditate over the collection. I fancy I see the faces of the men who have suffered—faces lean with agony and wet with sweats of death—growing distinct out of the gloom, and I hear the echoes of their cries for mercy. But I must show you my latest acquisition. Come into the next room.'

I followed Mr. Mathias out. The weariness of the walk, the late hour, and the strangeness of it all, made me feel like a man in a dream; nothing would have surprised me very much. The second room was, as the first, crowded with ghastly instruments; but beneath the lamp was a wooden platform, and a figure stood on it. It was a large statue of a naked woman, fashioned in green bronze; the arms were stretched out, and there was a smile on the lips; it might well have been intended for a Venus, and yet there was about the thing an evil and a deadly look.

Mr. Mathias looked at it complacently. 'Quite a work of art, isn't it?' he said. 'It's made of bronze, as you see, but it has long had the name of the Iron Maid. I got it from Germany, and it was only unpacked this afternoon; indeed, I have not yet had time to open the letter of advice. You see that very small knob between the breasts? Well, the victim was bound to the Maid, the knob was pressed, and the arms slowly tightened round the neck. You can imagine the result.'

As Mr. Mathias talked, he patted the figure affectionately. I had turned away, for I sickened at the sight of the man and his loathsome treasure. There was a slight click, of which I took no notice,—it was not much louder than the tick of a clock; and then I heard a sudden whir, the noise of machinery in motion, and I faced round. I have never forgotten the hideous agony on Mathias's face as those relentless arms tightened about his neck; there was a wild struggle as of a beast in the toils, and then a shriek that ended in a choking groan. The whirring noise had suddenly changed into a heavy droning. I tore with all my might at the bronze arms, and strove to wrench them apart, but I could do nothing. The head had slowly bent down, and the green lips were on the lips of Mathias.

Of course I had to attend at the inquest. The letter which had accompanied the figure was found unopened on the study table. The German firm of dealers cautioned their client to be most careful in touching the Iron Maid, as the machinery had been put in thorough working order.

For many revolving weeks Mr. Burton delighted Dyson by his agreeable conversation, diversified by anecdote, and interspersed with the narration of singular adventures. Finally, however, he vanished as suddenly as he had appeared, and on the occasion of his last visit he contrived to loot a copy of his namesake's Anatomy. Dyson, considering this violent attack on the rights of property, and certain glaring inconsistencies in the talk of his late friend, arrived at the conclusion that his stories were fabulous, and that the Iron Maid only existed in the sphere of a decorative imagination.

The Recluse of Bayswater

Amongst the many friends who were favoured with the occasional pleasure of Mr. Dyson's society was Mr. Edgar Russell, realist and obscure struggler, who occupied a small back room on the second floor of a house in Abingdon Grove, Notting Hill. Turning off from the main street, and walking a few paces onward, one was conscious of a certain calm, a drowsy peace, which made the feet inclined to loiter, and this was ever the atmosphere of Abingdon Grove. The houses stood a little back, with gardens where the lilac, and laburnum, and blood-red may blossomed gaily in their seasons, and there was a corner where an older house in another street had managed to keep a back garden of real extent, a walled-in garden, whence there came a pleasant scent of greenness after the rains of early summer, where old elms held memories of the open fields, where there was yet sweet grass to walk on. The houses in Abingdon Grove belonged chiefly to the nondescript stucco period of thirty-five years ago, tolerably built, with passable accommodation for moderate incomes; they had largely passed into the state of lodgings, and cards bearing the inscription 'Furnished Apartments' were not infrequent over the doors. Here, then, in a house of sufficiently good appearance, Mr. Russell had established himself; for he looked upon the traditional dirt and squalor of Grub Street as a false and obsolete convention, and preferred, as he said, to live within sight of green leaves. Indeed, from his room one had a magnificent view of a long line of gardens, and a screen of poplars shut out the melancholy back premises of Wilton Street during the summer months. Mr. Russell lived chiefly on bread and tea, for his means were of the smallest; but when Dyson came to see him, he would send out the slavey for six ale, and Dyson was always at liberty to smoke as much of his tobacco as he pleased. The landlady had been so unfortunate as to have her drawing-room floor vacant for many months; a card had long proclaimed the void within; and Dyson, when he walked up the steps one evening in early autumn, had a sense that something was missing, and, looking at the fanlight, saw the appealing card had disappeared.

'You have let your first floor, have you?' he said, as he greeted Mr. Russell.

'Yes; it was taken about a fortnight ago by a lady.'

'Indeed,' said Dyson, always curious; 'a young lady?'

'Yes; I believe so. She is a widow, and wears a thick crape veil. I have met her once or twice on the stairs and in the street; but I should not know her face.'

'Well,' said Dyson, when the beer had arrived, and the pipes were in full blast, 'and what have you been doing? Do you find the work getting any easier?'

'Alas!' said the young man, with an expression of great gloom, 'the life is a purgatory, and all but a hell. I write, picking out my words, weighing and balancing the force of every syllable, calculating the minutest effects that language can produce, erasing and rewriting, and spending a whole evening over a page of manuscript. And then, in the morning, when I read what I have written—— Well, there is nothing to be done but to throw it in the wastepaper basket, if the verso has been already written on, or to put it in the drawer if the other side happens to be clean. When I have written a phrase which undoubtedly embodies a happy turn of thought, I find it dressed up in feeble commonplace; and when the style is good, it serves only to conceal the baldness of superannuated fancies. I sweat over my work, Dyson—every finished line means so much agony. I envy the lot of the carpenter in the side street who has a craft which he understands. When he gets an order for a table he does not writhe with anguish; but if I were so unlucky as to get an order for a book, I think I should go mad.'

'My dear fellow, you take it all too seriously. You should let the ink flow more readily. Above all, firmly believe, when you sit down to write, that you are an artist, and that whatever you are about is a masterpiece. Suppose ideas fail you, say, as I heard one of our most exquisite artists say, "It's of no consequence; the ideas are all there, at the bottom of that box of cigarettes!" You, indeed, smoke a pipe, but the application is the same. Besides, you must have some happy moments; and these should be ample consolation.'

'Perhaps you are right. But such moments are so few; and then there is the torture of a glorious conception matched with execution beneath the standard of the "Family Story Paper." For instance, I was happy for two hours a night or two ago; I lay awake and saw visions. But then the morning!'

'What was your idea?'

'It seemed to me a splendid one: I thought of Balzac and the "Comédie Humaine," of Zola and the Rougon-Macquart family. It dawned on me that I would write the history of a street. Every house should form a volume. I fixed upon the street, I saw each house, and read as clearly as in letters the physiology and psychology of each; the little byway stretched before me in its actual shape—a street that I know and have passed down a hundred times, with some twenty houses, prosperous and mean, and lilac bushes in purple blossom. And yet it was, at the same time, a symbol, a *via dolorosa* of hopes cherished and disappointed, of years of monotonous existence without content or discontent, of tragedies and obscure sorrows; and on the door of one of those houses I saw the red stain of blood, and behind a window two shadows, blackened and faded on the blind, as they swayed on tightened cords—the shadows of a man and a woman hanging in a vulgar gaslit parlour. These were my fancies; but when pen touched paper they shrivelled and vanished away.'

'Yes,' said Dyson, 'there is a lot in that. I envy you the pains of transmuting vision into reality, and, still more, I envy you the day when you will look at your bookshelf and see twenty goodly books upon the shelves—the series complete and done for ever. Let me entreat you to have them bound in solid parchment, with gold lettering. It is the only real cover for a valiant book. When I look in at the windows of some choice shop, and see the bindings of levant morocco, with pretty tools and panellings, and your sweet contrasts of red and green, I say to myself, "These are not books, but *bibelots*." A book bound so—a true book, mind you—is like a Gothic statue draped in brocade of Lyons.'

'Alas!' said Russell, 'we need not discuss the binding —the books are not begun.'

The talk went on as usual till eleven o'clock, when Dyson bade his friend good-night. He knew the way downstairs, and walked down by himself; but, greatly to his surprise, as he crossed the first-floor landing the door opened slightly, and a hand was stretched out, beckoning.

Dyson was not the man to hesitate under such circumstances. In a moment he saw himself involved in adventure; and, as he told himself, the Dysons had never disobeyed a lady's summons. Softly, then, with due regard for the lady's honour, he would have entered the room, when a low but clear voice spoke to him—

'Go downstairs and open the door and shut it again rather loudly. Then come up to me; and for Heaven's sake, walk softly.'

Dyson obeyed her commands, not without some hesitation, for he was afraid of meeting the landlady or the maid on his return journey. But, walking like a cat, and making each step he trod on crack loudly, he flattered himself that he had escaped observation; and as he gained the top of the stairs the door opened wide before him, and he found himself in the lady's drawing-room, bowing awkwardly.

'Pray be seated, sir. Perhaps this chair will be the best; it was the favoured chair of my landlady's deceased husband. I would ask you to smoke, but the odour would betray me. I know my proceedings must seem to you unconventional; but I saw you arrive this evening, and I do not think you would refuse to help a woman who is so unfortunate as I am.'

Mr. Dyson looked shyly at the young lady before him. She was dressed in deep mourning, but the piquant smiling face and charming hazel eyes ill accorded with the heavy garments and the mouldering surface of the crape.

'Madam,' he said gallantly, 'your instinct has served you well. We will not trouble, if you please, about the question of social conventions; the chivalrous gentleman knows nothing of such matters. I hope I may be privileged to serve you.'

'You are very kind to me, but I knew it would be so. Alas! sir, I have had experience of life, and I am rarely mistaken. Yet man is too often so vile and so misjudging that I trembled even as I resolved to take this step, which, for all I knew, might prove to be both desperate and ruinous.'

'With me you have nothing to fear,' said Dyson. 'I was nurtured in the faith of chivalry, and I have always endeavoured to remember the proud traditions of my race. Confide in me, then, and count upon my secrecy, and if it prove possible, you may rely on my help.'

'Sir, I will not waste your time, which I am sure is valuable, by idle parleyings. Learn, then, that I am a fugitive, and in hiding here; I place myself in your power; you have but to describe my features, and I fall into the hands of my relentless enemy.'

Mr. Dyson wondered for a passing instant how this could be, but he only renewed his promise of silence, repeating that he would be the embodied spirit of dark concealment.

'Good,' said the lady, 'the Oriental fervour of your style is delightful. In the first place, I must disabuse your mind of the conviction that I am a widow. These gloomy vestments have been forced on me by strange circumstance; in plain language, I have deemed it expedient to go disguised. You have a friend, I think, in the house, Mr. Russell? He seems of a coy and retiring nature.'

'Excuse me, madam,' said Dyson, 'he is not coy, but he is a realist; and perhaps you are aware that no Carthusian monk can emulate the cloistral seclusion in which a realistic novelist loves to shroud himself. It is his way of observing human nature.'

'Well, well,' said the lady; 'all this, though deeply interesting, is not germane to our affair. I must tell you my history.'

With these words the young lady proceeded to relate the

NOVEL OF THE WHITE POWDER

My name is Leicester; my father, Major-General Wyn Leicester, a distinguished officer of artillery, succumbed five years ago to a complicated liver complaint acquired in the deadly climate of India. A year later my only brother, Francis, came home after a exceptionally brilliant career at the University, and settled down with the resolution of a hermit to master what has been well called the great legend of the law. He was a man who seemed to live in utter indifference to everything that is called pleasure; and though he was handsomer than most men, and could talk as merrily and wittily as if he were a mere vagabond, he avoided society, and shut himself up in a large room at the top of the house to make himself a lawyer. Ten hours a day of hard reading was at first his allotted portion; from the first light in the east to the late afternoon he remained shut up with his books, taking a hasty half-hour's lunch with me as if he grudged the wasting of the moments, and going out for a short walk when it began to grow dusk. I thought that such relentless application must be injurious, and tried to cajole him from the crabbed textbooks, but his ardour seemed to grow rather than diminish, and his daily tale of hours increased. I spoke to him seriously, suggesting some occasional relaxation, if it were but an idle afternoon with a harmless novel; but he laughed, and said that he read about feudal tenures when he felt in need of amusement, and scoffed at the notions of theatres, or a month's fresh air. I confessed that he looked well, and seemed not to suffer from his labours, but I knew that such unnatural toil would take revenge at last, and I was not mistaken. A look of anxiety began to lurk about his eyes, and he seemed languid, and at last he avowed that he was no longer in perfect health; he was troubled, he said, with a sensation of dizziness, and awoke now and then of nights from fearful dreams, terrified and cold with icy sweats. 'I am taking care of myself,' he said, 'so you must not trouble; I passed the whole of yesterday afternoon in idleness, leaning back in that comfortable chair you gave me, and scribbling nonsense on a sheet of paper. No, no; I will not overdo my work; I shall be well enough in a week or two depend upon it.'

Yet in spite of his assurances I could see that he grew no better, but rather worse; he would enter the drawing-room with a face all miserably wrinkled and despondent, and endeavour to look gaily when my eyes fell on him, and I thought such symptoms of evil omen, and was frightened sometimes at the nervous irritation of his movements, and at glances which I could not decipher. Much against his will, I prevailed on him to have medical advice, and with an ill grace he called in our old doctor.

Dr. Haberden cheered me after examination of his patient.

'There is nothing really much amiss,' he said to me. 'No doubt he reads too hard and eats hastily, and then goes back again to his books in too great a hurry, and the natural sequence is some digestive trouble and a little mischief in the nervous system. But I think—I do indeed, Miss Leicester—that we shall be able to set this all right. I have written him a prescription which ought to do great things. So you have no cause for anxiety.'

My brother insisted on having the prescription made up by a chemist in the neighbourhood. It was an odd, old-fashioned shop, devoid of the studied coquetry and calculated glitter that make so gay a show on the counters and shelves of the modern apothecary; but Francis liked the old chemist, and believed in the scrupulous purity of his drugs. The medicine was sent in due course, and I saw that my brother took it regularly after lunch and dinner. It was an innocent-looking white powder, of which a little was dissolved in a glass of cold water; I stirred it in, and it seemed to disappear, leaving the water clear and colorless. At first Francis seemed to benefit greatly; the weariness vanished from his face, and he became more cheerful than he had ever been since the time when he left school; he talked gaily of reforming himself, and avowed to me that he had wasted his time.

'I have given too many hours to law,' he said, laughing; 'I think you have saved me in the nick of time. Come, I shall be Lord Chancellor yet, but I must not forget life. You and I will have a holiday together before long; we will go to Paris and enjoy ourselves, and keep away from the Bibliothèque Nationale.'

I confessed myself delighted with the prospect.

'When shall we go?' I said. 'I can start the day after to-morrow if you like.'

'Ah! that is perhaps a litle too soon; after all, I do not know London yet, and I suppose a man ought to give the pleasures of his own country the first choice. But we will go off together in a week or two, so try and furbish up your French. I only know law French myself, and I am afraid that wouldn't do.'

We were just finishing dinner, and he quaffed off his medicine with a parade of carousal as if it had been wine from some choicest bin.

'Has it any particular taste?' I said.

'No; I should not know I was not drinking water,' and he got up from his chair and began to pace up and down the room as if he were undecided as to what he should do next.

'Shall we have coffee in the drawing-room?' I said; 'or would you like to smoke?'

'No, I think I will take a turn; it seems a pleasant evening. Look at the afterglow; why, it is as if a great city were burning in flames, and down there between the dark houses it is raining blood fast. Yes, I will go out; I may be in soon, but I shall take my key; so good-night, dear, if I don't see you again.'

The door slammed behind him, and I saw him walk lightly down the street, swinging his malacca cane, and I felt grateful to Dr. Haberden for such an improvement.

I believe my brother came home very late that night, but he was in a merry mood the next morning.

'I walked on without thinking where I was going,' he said, 'enjoying the freshness of the air, and livened by the crowds as I reached more frequented quarters. And then I met an old college friend, Orford, in the press of the pavement, and then—well, we enjoyed ourselves. I have felt what it is to be young and a man; I find I have blood in my veins, as other men have. I made an appointment with Orford for to-night; there will be a little party of us at the restaurant. Yes; I shall enjoy myself for a week or two, and hear the chimes at midnight, and then we will go for our little trip together.'

Such was the transmutation of my brother's character that in a few days he became a lover of pleasure, a careless and merry idler of western pavements, a hunter out of snug restaurants, and a fine critic of fantastic dancing; he grew fat before my eyes, and said no more of Paris, for he had clearly found his paradise in London. I rejoiced, and yet wondered a little; for there was, I thought, something in his gaiety that indefinitely displeased me, though I could not have defined my feeling. But by degrees there came a change; he returned still in the cold hours of the morning, but I heard no more about his pleasures, and one morning as we sat at breakfast together I looked suddenly into his eyes and saw a stranger before me.

'Oh, Francis!' I cried. 'Oh, Francis, Francis, what have you done?' and rending sobs cut the words short. I went weeping out of the room; for though I knew nothing, yet I knew all, and by some odd play of thought I remembered the evening when he first went abroad, and the picture of the sunset sky glowed before me; the clouds like a city in burning flames, and the rain of blood. Yet I did battle with such thoughts, resolving that perhaps, after all, no great harm had been done, and in the evening at dinner I resolved to press him to fix a day for our holiday in Paris. We had talked easily enough, and my brother had just taken his medicine, which he continued all the while. I was about to begin my topic when the words forming in my mind vanished, and I wondered for a second what icy and intolerable weight oppressed my heart and suffocated me as with the unutterable horror of the coffin-lid nailed down on the living.

We had dined without candles; the room had slowly grown from twilight to gloom, and the walls and corners were indistinct in the shadow. But from where I sat I looked out into the street; and as I thought of what I would say to Francis, the sky began to flush and shine, as it had done on a well-remembered evening, and in the gap between two dark masses that were houses an awful pageantry of flame appeared—lurid whorls of writhed cloud, and utter depths burning, grey masses like the fume blown from a smoking city, and an evil glory blazing far above shot with tongues of more ardent fire, and below as if there were a deep pool of blood. I looked down to where my brother sat facing me, and the words were shaped on my lips, when I saw his hand resting on the table. Between the thumb and forefinger of the closed hand there was a mark, a small patch about the size of a six-pence, and somewhat of the colour of a bad bruise. Yet, by some sense I cannot define, I knew that what I saw was no bruise at all; oh! if human flesh could burn with flame, and if flame could be black as pitch, such was that before me. Without thought or fashioning of words grey horror shaped within me at the sight, and in an inner cell it was known to be a brand. For the moment the stained sky became dark as midnight, and when the light returned to me I was alone in the silent room, and soon after I heard my brother go out.

Late as it was, I put on my hat and went to Dr. Haberden, and in his great consulting room, ill lighted by a candle which the doctor brought in with him, with stammering lips, and a voice that would break in spite of my resolve, I told him all, from the day on which my brother began to take the medicine down to the dreadful thing I had seen scarcely half an hour before.

When I had done, the doctor looked at me for a minute with an expression of great pity on his face.

'My dear Miss Leicester,' he said, 'you have evidently

been anxious about your brother; you have been worrying over him, I am sure. Come, now, is it not so?'

'I have certainly been anxious,' I said. 'For the last week or two I have not felt at ease.'

'Quite so; you know, of course, what a queer thing the brain is?'

'I understand what you mean; but I was not deceived. I saw what I have told you with my own eyes.'

'Yes, yes of course. But your eyes had been staring at that very curious sunset we had tonight. That is the only explanation. You will see it in the proper light to-morrow, I am sure. But, remember, I am always ready to give any help that is in my power; do not scruple to come to me, or to send for me if you are in any distress.'

I went away but little comforted, all confusion and terror and sorrow, not knowing where to turn. When my brother and I met the next day, I looked quickly at him, and noticed, with a sickening at heart, that the right hand, the hand on which I had clearly seen the patch as of a black fire, was wrapped up with a handkerchief.

'What is the matter with your hand, Francis?' I said in a steady voice.

'Nothing of consequence. I cut a finger last night, and it bled rather awkwardly. So I did it up roughly to the best of my ability.'

'I will do it neatly for you, if you like.'

'No, thank you, dear; this will answer very well. Suppose we have breakfast; I am quite hungry.'

We sat down and I watched him. He scarcely ate or drank at all, but tossed his meat to the dog when he thought my eyes were turned away; there was a look in his eyes that I had never yet seen, and the thought flashed across my mind that it was a look that was scarcely human. I was firmly convinced that awful and incredible as was the thing I had seen the night before, yet it was no illusion, no glamour of bewildered sense, and in the course of the evening I went again to the doctor's house.

He shook his head with an air puzzled and incredulous, and seemed to reflect for a few minutes.

'And you say he still keeps up the medicine? But why?

As I understand, all the symptoms he complained of have disappeared long ago; why should he go on taking the stuff when he is quite well? And by the by, where did he get it made up? At Sayce's? I never send any one there; the old man is getting careless. Suppose you come with me to the chemist's; I should like to have some talk with him.'

We walked together to the shop; old Sayce knew Dr. Haberden, and was quite ready to give any information.

'You have been sending that in to Mr. Leicester for some weeks, I think, on my prescription,' said the doctor, giving the old man a pencilled scrap of paper.

The chemist put on his great spectacles with trembling uncertainty, and held up the paper with a shaking hand.

'Oh, yes,' he said, 'I have very little of it left; it is rather an uncommon drug, and I have had it in stock some time. I must get in some more, if Mr. Leicester goes on with it.'

'Kindly let me have a look at the stuff,' said Haberden, and the chemist gave him a glass bottle. He took out the stopper and smelt the contents, and looked strangely at the old man.

'Where did you get this?' he said, 'and what is it? For one thing, Mr. Sayce, it is not what I prescribed. Yes, yes, I see the label is right enough, but I tell you this is not the drug.'

'I have had it a long time,' said the old man in feeble terror; 'I got it from Burbage's in the usual way. It is not prescribed often, and I have had it on the shelf for some years. You see there is very little left.'

'You had better give it to me,' said Haberden. 'I am afraid something wrong has happened.'

We went out of the shop in silence, the doctor carrying the bottle neatly wrapped in paper under his arm.

'Dr. Haberden,' I said, when we had walked a little way—'Dr. Haberden.'

'Yes,' he said, looking at me gloomily enough.

'I should like you to tell me what my brother has been taking twice a day for the last month or so.'

'Frankly, Miss Leicester, I don't know. We will speak of this when we get to my house.'

We walked on quickly without another word till we

reached Dr. Haberden's. He asked me to sit down, and began pacing up and down the room, his face clouded over, as I could see, with no common fears.

'Well,' he said at length, 'this is all very strange; it is only natural that you should feel alarmed, and I must confess that my mind is far from easy. We will put aside, if you please, what you told me last night and this morning, but the fact remains that for the last few weeks Mr. Leicester has been impregnating his system with a drug which is completely unknown to me. I tell you, it is not what I ordered; and what the stuff in the bottle really is remains to be seen.'

He undid the wrapper, and cautiously tilted a few grains of the white powder on to a piece of paper, and peered curiously at it.

'Yes,' he said, 'it is like the sulphate of quinine, as you say; it is flaky. But smell it.'

He held the bottle to me, and I bent over it. It was a strange, sickly smell, vaporous and overpowering, like some strong anæsthetic.

'I shall have it analysed,' said Haberden; 'I have a friend who has devoted his whole life to chemistry as a science. Then we shall have something to go upon. No, no; say no more about that other matter; I cannot listen to that; and take my advice and think no more about it yourself.

That evening my brother did not go out as usual after dinner.

'I have had my fling,' he said with a queer laugh, 'and I must go back to my old ways. A little law will be quite a relaxation after so sharp a dose of pleasure,' and he grinned to himself, and soon after went up to his room. His hand was still all bandaged.

Dr. Haberden called a few days later.

'I have no special news to give you,' he said. 'Chambers is out of town, so I know no more about that stuff than you do. But I should like to see Mr. Leicester, if he is in.'

'He is in his room,' I said; 'I will tell him you are here.'

'No, no, I will go up to him; we will have a little quiet talk together. I dare say that we have made a good deal of fuss about a very little; for, after all, whatever the powder may be, it seems to have done him good.'

The doctor went upstairs, and standing in the hall I heard his knock, and the opening and shutting of the door; and then I waited in the silent house for an hour, and the stillness grew more and more intense as the hands of the clock crept round. Then there sounded from above the noise of a door shut sharply, and the doctor was coming down the stairs. His footsteps crossed the hall, and there was a pause at the door; I drew a long, sick breath with difficulty, and saw my face white in a little mirror, and he came in and stood at the door. There was an unutterable horror shining in his eyes; he steadied himself by holding the back of a chair with one hand, his lower lip trembled like a horse's, and he gulped and stammered unintelligible sounds before he spoke.

'I have seen that man,' he began in a dry whisper. 'I have been sitting in his presence for the last hour. My God! And I am alive and in my senses! I, who have dealt with death all my life, and have dabbled with the melting ruins of the earthly tabernacle. But not this, oh! not this,' and he covered his face with his hands as if to shut out the sight of something before him.

'Do not send for me again, Miss Leicester,' he said with more composure. 'I can do nothing in this house. Good-bye.'

As I watched him totter down the steps, and along the pavement towards his house, it seemed to me that he had aged by ten years since the morning.

My brother remained in his room. He called out to me in a voice I hardly recognized that he was very busy, and would like his meals brought to his door and left there, and I gave the order to the servants. From that day it seemed as if the arbitrary conception we call time had been annihilated for me; I lived in an ever-present sense of horror, going through the routine of the house mechanically, and only speaking a few necessary words to the servants. Now and then I went out and paced the streets for an hour or two and came home again; but whether I were without or within, my spirit delayed before the closed door of the upper room, and, shuddering, waited for it to open. I have said that I scarcely reckoned time; but I suppose it must have been a fortnight after Dr. Haberden's visit that I came home from my stroll a little refreshed and lightened. The air was sweet and pleasant, and the hazy form of green leaves, floating cloud-like in the square, and the smell of blossoms, had charmed my senses, and I felt happier and walked more briskly. As I delayed a moment at the verge of the pavement, waiting for a van to pass by before crossing over to the house, I happened to look up at the windows, and instantly there was the rush and swirl of deep cold waters in my ears, my heart leapt up and fell down, down as into a deep hollow, and I was amazed with a dread and terror without form or shape. I stretched out a hand blindly through the folds of thick darkness, from the black and shadowy valley, and held myself from falling, while the stones beneath my feet rocked and swayed and tilted, and the sense of solid things seemed to sink away from under me. I had glanced up at the window of my brother's study, and at that moment the blind was drawn aside, and something that had life stared out into the world. Nay, I cannot say I saw a face or any human likeness; a living thing, two eyes of burning flame glared at me, and they were in the midst of something as formless, as my fear, the symbol and presence of all evil and all hideous corruption. I stood shuddering and quaking as with the grip of ague, sick with unspeakable agonies of fear and loathing, and for five minutes I could not summon force or motion to my limbs. When I was within the door, I ran up the stairs to my brother's room and knocked.

'Francis, Francis,' I cried, 'for Heaven's sake, answer me. What is the horrible thing in your room? Cast it out, Francis; cast it from you.'

I heard a noise as of feet shuffling slowly and awkwardly, and a choking, gurgling sound, as if some one was struggling to find utterance, and then the noise of a voice, broken and stifled, and words that I could scarcely understand.

'There is nothing here,' the voice said. 'Pray do not disturb me. I am not very well to-day.'

I turned away, horrified, and yet helpless. I could do nothing, and I wondered why Francis had lied to me, for I had seen the appearance beyond the glass too plainly to be deceived, though it was but the sight of a moment. And I sat still, conscious that there had been something else, something I had seen in the first flash of terror, before those burning eyes had looked at me. Suddenly I remembered; as I lifted my face the blind was being drawn back, and I had had an instant's glance of the thing that was moving it, and in my recollection I knew that a hideous image was engraved forever on my brain. It was not a hand; there were no fingers that held the blind, but a black stump pushed it aside, the mouldering outline and the clumsy movement as of a beast's paw had glowed into my senses before the darkling waves of terror had overwhelmed me as I went down quick into the pit. My mind was aghast at the thought of this, and of the awful presence that dwelt with my brother in his room; I went to his door and cried to him again, but no answer came. That night one of the servants came up to me and told me in a whisper that for three days food had been regularly placed at the door and left untouched; the maid had knocked but had received no answer; she had heard the noise of shuffling feet that I had noticed. Day after day went by, and still my brother's meals were brought to his door and left untouched; and though I knocked and called again and again, I could get no answer. The servants began to talk to me; it appeared they were as alarmed as I; the cook said that when my brother first shut himself up in his room she used to hear him come out at night and go about the house; and once, she said, the hall door had opened and closed again, but for several nights she had heard no sound. The climax came at last; it was in the dusk of the evening, and I was sitting in the darkening dreary room when a terrible shriek jarred and rang harshly out of the silence, and I heard a frightened scurry of feet dashing down the stairs. I waited, and the servant-maid staggered into the room and faced me, white and trembling.

'Oh, Miss Helen!' she whispered; 'oh! for the Lord's sake, Miss Helen, what has happened? Look at my hand, miss; look at that hand!'

I drew her to the window, and saw there was a black wet stain upon her hand.

'I do not understand you,' I said. 'Will you explain to me?'

'I was doing your room just now,' she began. 'I was turning down the bed-clothes, and all of a sudden there was something fell upon my hand, wet, and I looked up, and the ceiling was black and dripping on me.'

I looked hard at her and bit my lip.

'Come with me,' I said. 'Bring your candle with you.'

The room I slept in was beneath my brother's, and as I went in I felt I was trembling. I looked up at the ceiling, and saw a patch, all black and wet, and a dew of black drops upon it, and a pool of horrible liquor soaking into the white bed-clothes.

I ran upstairs and knocked loudly.

'Oh, Francis, Francis, my dear brother,' I cried, 'what has happened to you.'

And I listened. There was a sound of choking, and a noise like water bubbling and regurgitating, but nothing else, and I called louder, but no answer came.

In spite of what Dr. Haberden had said, I went to him; with tears streaming down my cheeks I told him all that had happened, and he listened to me with a face set hard and grim.

'For your father's sake,' he said at last, 'I will go with you, though I can do nothing.'

We went out together; the streets were dark and silent, and heavy with heat and a drought of many weeks. I saw the doctor's face white under the gas-lamps, and when we reached the house his hand was shaking.

We did not hesitate, but went upstairs directly. I held the lamp, and he called out in a loud, determined voice—

'Mr. Leicester, do you hear me? I insist on seeing you. Answer me at once. '

There was no answer, but we both heard that choking noise I have mentioned.

'Mr. Leicester, I am waiting for you. Open the door this instant, or I shall break it down.' And he called a third time in a voice that rang and echoed from the walls—

'Mr. Leicester! For the last time I order you to open the door.'

'Ah!' he said, after a pause of heavy silence, 'we are wasting time here. Will you be so kind as to get me a poker, or something of the kind?'

I ran into a little room at the back where odd articles were kept, and found a heavy adze-like tool that I thought might serve the doctor's purpose.

'Very good,' he said, 'that will do, I dare say. I give you notice, Mr. Leicester,' he cried loudly at the keyhole, 'that I am now about to break into your room.'

Then I heard the wrench of the adze, and the wood-work split and cracked under it; with a loud crash the door suddenly burst open, and for a moment we started back aghast at a fearful screaming cry, no human voice, but as the roar of a monster, that burst forth inarticulate and struck at us out of the darkness.

'Hold the lamp,' said the doctor, and we went in and glanced quickly round the room.

'There it is,' said Dr. Haberden, drawing a quick breath; 'look, in that corner.'

I looked, and a pang of horror seized my heart as with a white-hot iron. There upon the floor was a dark and putrid mass, seething with corruption and hideous rotten-ness, neither liquid nor solid, but melting and changing before our eyes, and bubbling with unctuous oily bubbles like boiling pitch. And out of the midst of it shone two burning points like eyes, and I saw a writhing and stirring as of limbs, and something moved and lifted up what might have been an arm. The doctor took a step forward, raised the iron bar and struck at the burning points; he drove in the weapon, and struck again and again in the fury of loathing.

* * * * * *

A week or two later, when I had recovered to some extent from the terrible shock, Dr. Haberden came to see me.

'I have sold my practice,' he began, 'and tomorrow I am sailing on a long voyage. I do not know whether I shall ever return to England; in all probability I shall buy a little land in California, and settle there for the remainder of my life. I have brought you this packet, which you may open and read when you feel able to do so. It contains the report of Dr. Chambers on what I submitted to him. Good-bye, Miss Leicester, good-bye.'

When he was gone I opened the envelope; I could not wait, and proceeded to read the papers within. Here is the manuscript, and if you will allow me, I will read you the astounding story it contains.

'My dear Haberden,' the letter began, 'I have delayed inexcusably in answering your questions as to the white substance you sent me. To tell you the truth, I have hesitated for some time as to what course I should adopt, for there is a bigotry and orthodox standard in physical science as in theology, and I knew that if I told you the truth I should offend rooted prejudices which I once held dear myself. However, I have determined to be plain with you, and first I must enter into a short personal explanation.

'You have known me, Haberden, for many years as a scientific man; you and I have often talked of our profession together, and discussed the hopeless gulf that opens before the feet of those who think to attain to truth by any means whatsoever except the beaten way of experiment and observation in the sphere of material things. I remember the scorn with which you have spoken to me of men of science who have dabbled a little in the unseen, and have timidly hinted that perhaps the senses are not, after all, the eternal, impenetrable bounds of all knowledge, the everlasting walls beyond which no human being has ever passed. We have laughed together heartily, and I think justly, at the "occult" follies of the day, disguised under various names—the mesmerisms, spiritualisms, materializations, theosophies, all the rabble rout of imposture, with their machinery of poor tricks and feeble conjuring, the true back-parlour of shabby London streets. Yet, in spite of what I have said, I must confess to you that I am no materialist, taking the word of course in its usual signification. It is now many years since I have convinced myself—convinced myself, a sceptic, remember—that the old ironbound theory is utterly and entirely false. Perhaps this confession will not wound you so sharply as it would have done twenty years ago; for I think you cannot have failed to notice that for some time hypotheses have been advanced by men of pure science which are nothing less than transcendental, and I suspect that most modern chemists and biologists of repute would not hesitate to subscribe the *dictum* of the old Schoolman, *Omnia exeunt in mysterium,* which means, I take it, that every branch of human knowledge if traced up to its source and final principles vanished into mystery. I need not trouble you now with a detailed account of the painful steps which led me to my conclusions; a few simple experiments suggested a doubt as to my then standpoint, and a train of thought that rose from circumstances comparatively trifling brought me far; my old conception of the universe has been swept away, and I stand in a world that seems as strange and awful to me as the endless waves of the ocean seen for the first time, shining, from a peak in Darien. Now I know that the walls of sense that seemed so impenetrable, that seemed to loom up above the heavens and to be founded below the depths, and to shut us in for evermore, are no such everlasting impassable barriers as we fancied, but thinnest and most airy veils that melt away before the seeker, and dissolve as the early mist of the morning about the brooks. I know that you never adopted the extreme materialistic position; you did not go about trying to prove a universal negative, for your logical sense withheld you from that crowning absurdity; but I am sure that you will find all that I am saying strange and repellent to your habits of thought. Yet, Haberden, what I tell you is the truth, nay, to adopt our common language, the sole and scientific truth, verified by experience; and the universe is verily more splendid and more awful than we used to dream. The whole universe, my friend, is a tremendous sacrament; a mystic, ineffable force and energy, veiled by a outward form of matter; and man, and the sun and the other stars, and the flower of the grass, and the crystal in the test-tube, are each and every one as spiritual, as material, and subject to an inner working.

'You will perhaps wonder, Haberden, whence all this tends; but I think a little thought will make it clear. You will understand that from such a standpoint the whole view of things is changed, and what we thought incredible and absurd may be possible enough. In short, we must look at legend and belief with other eyes, and be prepared to accept tales that had become mere fables. Indeed this is no such great demand. After all, modern science will concede as much, in a hypocritical manner; you must not, it is true, believe in witchcraft, but you may credit hypnotism; ghosts are out of date, but there is a good deal to be said for the theory of telepathy. Give superstition a Greek name, and believe in it, should almost be a proverb.

'So much for my personal explanation. You sent me, Haberden, a phial, stoppered and sealed, containing a small quantity of flaky white powder, obtained from a chemist who has been dispensing it to one of your patients. I am not surprised to hear that this powder refused to yield any results to your analysis. It is a substance which was known to a few many hundred years ago, but which I never expected to have submitted to me from the shop of a modern apothecary. There seems no reason to doubt the truth of the man's tale; he no doubt got, as he says, the rather uncommon salt you prescribed from the wholesale chemist's; and it has probably remained on his shelf for twenty years, or perhaps longer. Here what we call chance and coincidence begin to work; during all these years the salt in the bottle was exposed to certain recurring variations of temperature, variations probably ranging from 40° to 80°. And, as it happens, such changes, recurring year after year at irregular intervals, and with varying degrees of intensity and duration, have constituted a process, and a process, so complicated and so delicate, that I question whether modern scientific apparatus directed with the utmost precision could produce the same result. The white powder you sent me is something very different from the drug you prescribed; it is the powder from which the wine of the Sabbath, the *Vinum Sabbati,* was prepared. No doubt you have read of the Witches' Sabbath, and have laughed at the tales which terrified our ancestors; the black cats, and the broomsticks, and dooms pronounced against some old woman's cow. Since I have known the truth I have often reflected that it is on the whole a happy thing that such burlesque as this is believed, for it serves to conceal much that it is better should not be known generally. However, if you care to read the appendix to Payne Knight's monograph, you will find that the true Sabbath was something very different, though the writer has very nicely refrained from printing all he knew. The secrets of the true Sabbath were the secrets of remote times surviving into the Middle Ages, secrets of an evil science which existed long before Aryan man entered Europe. Men and women, seduced from their homes on specious pretences, were met by beings well qualified to assume, as they did assume, the part of devils, and taken by their guides to some desolate and lonely place, known to the initiate by long tradition, and unknown to all else. Perhaps it was a cave in some bare and wind-swept hill, perhaps some inmost recess of a great forest, and there the Sabbath was held. There, in the blackest hour of night, the *Vinum Sabbati* was prepared, and this evil graal was poured forth and offered to the neophytes, and they partook of an infernal sacrament; *sumentes calicem principis inferorum,* as an old author well expresses it. And suddenly, each one that had drunk found himself attended by a companion, a share of glamour and unearthly allurement, beckoning him apart, to share in joys more exquisite, more piercing than the thrill of any dream, to the consummation of the marriage of the Sabbath. It is hard to write of such things as these, and chiefly because that shape that allured with loveliness was no hallucination, but, awful as it is to express the man himself. By the power of that Sabbath wine, a few grains of white powder thrown into a glass of water, the house of life was riven asunder and the human trinity dissolved, and the worm which never dies, that which lies sleeping within us all, was made tangible and an external thing, and clothed with a garment of flesh. And then, in the hour of midnight, the primal fall was repeated and re-presented, and the awful thing veiled in the mythos of the Tree in the Garden was done anew. Such was the *nuptiæ Sabbati*.

'I prefer to say no more; you, Haberden, know as well as I do that the most trivial laws of life are not to be broken with impunity; and for so terrible an act as this, in which the very inmost place of the temple was broken open and defiled, a terrible vengeance followed. What began with corruption ended also with corruption.'

Underneath is the following in Dr. Haberden's writing:—

'The whole of the above is unfortunately strictly and entirely true. Your brother confessed all to me on that morning when I saw him in his room. My attention was first attracted to the bandaged hand, and I forced him to show it to me. What I saw made me, a medical man of many years' standing, grow sick with loathing, and the story I was forced to listen to was infinitely more frightful than I could have believed possible. It has tempted me to doubt the Eternal Goodness which can permit nature to offer such hideous possibilities; and if you had not with your own eyes seen the end, I should have said to you— disbelieve it all. I have not, I think, many more weeks to live, but you are young, and may forget all this.

'JOSEPH HABERDEN, M. D.'

In the course of two or three months I heard that Dr. Haberden had died at sea shortly after the ship left England.

Miss Leicester ceased speaking, and looked pathetically at Dyson, who could not refrain from exhibiting some symptoms of uneasiness.

He stuttered out some broken phrases expressive of his

deep interest in her extraordinary history, and then said with a better grace—

'But pardon me, Miss Leicester, I understood you were in some difficulty. You were kind enough to ask me to assist you in some way.'

'Ah,' she said, 'I had forgotten that; my own present trouble seems of such little consequence in comparison with what I have told you. But as you are so good to me, I will go on. You will scarcely believe it, but I found that certain persons suspected, or rather pretended to suspect, that I had murdered my brother. These persons were relatives of mine, and their motives were extremely sordid ones; but I actually found myself subject to the shameful indignity of being watched. Yes, sir, my steps were dogged when I went abroad, and at home I found myself exposed to constant if artful observation. With my high spirit this was more than I could brook, and I resolved to set my wits to work and elude the persons who were shadowing me. I was so fortunate as to succeed; I assumed this disguise, and for some time have lain snug and unsuspected. But of late I have reason to believe that the pursuer is on my track; unless I am greatly deceived, I saw yesterday the detective who is charged with the odious duty of observing my movements. You, sir, are watchful and keen-sighted; tell me, did you see any one lurking about this evening?'

'I hardly think so,' said Dyson, 'but perhaps you would give me some description of the detective in question.'

'Certainly; he is a youngish man, dark, with dark whiskers. He has adopted spectacles of large size in the hope of disguising himself effectually, but he cannot disguise his uneasy manner, and the quick, nervous glances he casts to right and left.'

This piece of description was the last straw for the unhappy Dyson, who was foaming with impatience to get out of the house, and would gladly have sworn eighteenth-century oaths, if propriety had not frowned on such a course.

'Excuse me, Miss Leicester,' he said with cool politeness, 'I cannot assist you.'

'Ah,' she said sadly, 'I have offended you in some way. Tell me what I have done, and I will ask you to forgive me.'

'You are mistaken,' said Dyson, grabbing his hat, but speaking with somes difficulty; 'you have done nothing. But, as I say, I cannot help you. Perhaps,' he added, with some tinge of sarcasm, 'my friend Russell might be of service.'

'Thank you,' she replied; 'I will try him,' and the lady went off into a shriek of laughter, which filled up Mr. Dyson's cup of scandal and confusion.

He left the house shortly afterwards, and had the peculiar delight of a five-mile walk, through streets which slowly changed from black to grey, and from grey to shining passages of glory for the sun to brighten. Here and there he met or overtook strayed revellers, but he reflected that no one could have spent the night in a more futile fashion than himself; and when he reached his home he had made resolves for reformation. He decided that he would abjure all Milesian and Arabian methods of entertainment, and subscribe to Mudie's for a regular supply of mild and innocuous romance.

Strange Occurrence in Clerkenwell

Mr. Dyson had inhabited for some years a couple of rooms in a moderately quiet street in Bloomsbury, where, as he somewhat pompously expressed it, he held his finger on the pulse, of life without being deafened with the thousand rumours of the main arteries of London. It was to him a source of peculiar, if esoteric, gratification that from the adjacent corner of Tottenham Court Road a hundred lines of omnibuses went to the four quarters of the town; he would dilate on the facilities for visiting Dalston, and dwell on the admirable line that knew extremest Ealing and the streets beyond Whitechapel. His rooms, which had been originally 'furnished apartments,' he had gradually purged of their more peccant parts; and though one would not find here the glowing splendour of his old chambers in the street off the Strand, there was something of severe grace about the appointments which did credit to his taste. The rugs were old, and of the true faded beauty; the etchings, nearly all of them proofs printed by the artist, made a good show with broad white margins and black frames, and there was no spurious black oak. Indeed, there was but little furniture of any kind: a plain and honest table, square and sturdy, stood in one corner; a seventeenth-century settle fronted the hearth; and two wooden elbow-chairs and a bookshelf of the Empire made up the equipment, with an exception worthy of note. For Dyson cared for none of these things; his place was at his own bureau, a quaint old piece of lacquered-work, at which he would sit for hour after hour, with his back to the room, engaged in the desperate pursuit of literature, or, as he termed his profession, the chase of the phrase. The neat array of pigeon-holes and drawers teemed and overflowed with manuscripts and notebooks, the experiments and efforts of many years; and the inner well, a vast and cavernous receptacle, was stuffed with accumulated ideas. Dyson was a craftman who loved all the detail and the technique of his work intensely; and if, as has been hinted, he deluded himself a little with the name of artist, yet his amusements were eminently harmless, and, so far as can be ascertained, he (or the publishers) had chosen the good part of not tiring the world with printed matter.

Here, then, Dyson would shut himself up with his fancies, experimenting with words, and striving, as his friend the recluse of Bayswater strove, with the almost invincible problem of style, but always with a fine confidence, extremely different from the chronic depression of the realist. He had been almost continuously at work on some scheme that struck him as well-nigh magical in its possibilities since the night of his adventure with the ingenious tenant of the first floor in Abingdon Grove; and as he laid down the pen with a glow of triumph, he reflected that he had not viewed the streets for five days in succession. With all the enthusiasm of his accomplished labour still working in his brain, he put away his papers and went out, pacing the pavement at first in that rare mood of exultation which finds in every stone upon the way the possibilities of a masterpiece. It was growing late, and the autumn evening was drawing to a close amidst veils of haze and mist, and in the stilled air the voices, and the roaring traffic, and incessant feet seemed to Dyson like the noise upon the stage when all the house is silent. In the square the leaves rippled down as quick as summer rain, and the street beyond was beginning to flare with the lights in the butcher's shops and the vivid illumination of the greengrocer. It was a Saturday night, and the swarming populations of the slums were turning out in force; the battered women in rusty black had begun to paw the lumps of cagmag, and others gloated over unwholesome cabbages, and there was a brisk demand for four ale. Dyson passed through these night-fires with some relief; he loved to meditate, but his thoughts were not as De

Quincey's after his dose; he cared not two straws whether onions were dear or cheap, and would not have exulted if meat had fallen to twopence a pound. Absorbed in the wilderness of the tale he had been writing, weighing nicely the points of plot and construction, relishing the recollection of this and that happy phrase, and dreading failure here and there, he left the rush and whistle of the gas-flares behind him, and began to touch upon pavements more deserted.

He had turned, without taking note, to the northward, and was passing through an ancient fallen street, where now notices of floors and offices to let hung out, but still about it lingered the grace and the stiffness of the Age of Wigs—a broad roadway, a broad pavement, and on each side a grave line of houses with long and narrow windows flush with the walls, all of mellowed brick-work. Dyson walked with quick steps, as he resolved that short work must be made of a certain episode; but he was in that happy humour of invention, and another chapter rose in the inner chamber of his brain, and he dwelt on the circumstances he was to write down with curious pleasure. It was charming to have the quiet streets to walk in, and and in his thought he made a whole district the cabinet of his studies, and vowed he would come again. Heedless of his course, he struck off to the east again, and soon found himself involved in a squalid network of grey two-storied houses, and then in the waste void and elements of brick-work, the passages and unmade roads behind great factory walls, encumbered with the refuse of the neighbourhood, forlorn, ill-lighted, and desperate. A brief turn, and there rose before him the unexpected, a hill suddenly lifted from the level ground, its steep ascent marked by the lighted lamps, and eager as an explorer, Dyson found his way to the place, wondering where his crooked paths had brought him. Here all was again decorous, but hideous in the extreme. The builder, some one lost in the deep gloom of the early 'twenties, had conceived the idea of twin villas in grey brick, shaped in a manner to recall the outlines of the Parthenon, each with its classic form broadly marked with raised bands of stucco. The name of the street was all strange, and for a further surprise the top on the hill was crowned with an irregular plot of grass and fading trees, called a square, and here again the Parthenon-motive had persisted. Beyond, the streets were curious, wild in their irregularities, here a row of sordid, dingy dwellings, dirty and disreputable in appearance, and there, without warning, stood a house, genteel and prim, with wire blinds and brazen knocker, as clean and trim as if it had been the doctor's house in some benighted little country town. These surprises and discoveries began to exhaust Dyson, and he hailed with delight the blazing windows of a public-house, and went in with the intention of testing the beverage provided for the dwellers in this region, as remote as Libya and Pamphylia and the parts about Mesopotamia. The babble of voices from within warned him that he was about to assist at the true parliament of the London workman, and he looked about him for that more retired entrance called private. When he had settled himself on an exiguous bench, and had ordered some beer, he began to listen to the jangling talk in the public bar beyond; it was a senseless argument, alternately furious and maudlin, with appeals to Bill and Tom, and mediæval survivals of speech, words that Chaucer wrote belched out with zeal and relish, and the din of pots jerked down and coppers rapped smartly on the zinc counter made a thorough bass for it all. Dyson was calmly smoking his pipe between the sips of beer, when an indefinite-looking figure slid rather than walked into the compartment. The man started violently when he saw Dyson placidly sitting in the corner, and glanced keenly about him. He seemed to be on wires, controlled by some electric machine, for he almost bolted out of the door when the barman asked with what he could serve him, and his hand shivered as he took the glass. Dyson inspected him with a little curiosity. He was muffled up almost to the lips, and a soft felt hat was drawn down over his eyes; he looked as if he shrank from every glance, and a more raucous voice suddenly uplifted in the public bar seemed to find in him a sympathy that made him shake and quiver like a jelly. It was pitiable to see any one so thrilled with nervousness, and Dyson was about to address some trivial remark of casual inquiry to the man, when another person came into the compartment, and, laying his hand on his arm, muttered something in an undertone, and vanished as he came. But Dyson had recognized him as the smooth-tongued and smooth-shaven Burton; and yet he thought little of it, for his whole faculty of observation was absorbed in the lamentable and yet grotesque spectacle before him. At the first touch of the hand on his arm the unfortunate man had wheeled round as if spun on a pivot, and shrank back with a low, piteous cry, as if some dumb beast were caught in the toils. The blood fled away from the wretch's face, and the skin became grey as if a shadow of death had passed in the air and fallen on it, and Dyson caught a choking whisper—

'Mr. Davies! For God's sake, have pity on me, Mr. Davies! On my oath, I say——' and his voice sank to silence as he heard the message, and strove in vain to bite his lips, and summon up to his aid some tinge of manhood. He stood there a moment, wavering as the leaves of an aspen, and then he was gone out into the street, as Dyson thought silently, with his doom upon his head. He had not been gone a minute when it suddenly flashed into Dyson's mind that he knew the man; it was undoubtedly the young man with spectacles for whom so many ingenious persons were searching; the spectacles indeed were missing, but the pale face, the dark whiskers, and the timid glances were enough to identify him. Dyson saw at once that by a succession of hazards he had unawares hit upon the scent of some desperate conspiracy, wavering as the track of a loathsome snake in and out of the highways and byways of the London cosmos; the truth was instantly pictured before him, and he divined that all unconscious and unheeding he had been privileged to see the shadows of hidden forms, chasing and hurrying, and grasping and vanishing across the bright curtain of common life, soundless and silent, or only babbling fables and pretences. For him in an instant the jargoning of voices, the garish splendour, and all the vulgar tumult of the public-house became part of magic; for here before his eyes a scene in this grim mystery play had been enacted, and he had seen human flesh grow cold with a palsy of fear; the very hell of cowardice and terror had gaped wide within an arm's-breadth. In the midst of these reflections the barman came up and stared at him as if to hint that he had exhausted his right to take his ease, and Dyson bought another lease of the seat by an order for more beer. As he pondered the brief glimpse of tragedy, he recollected that with his first start of haunted fear the young man with whiskers had drawn his hand swiftly from his greatcoat pocket, and that he had heard something fall to the ground; and pretending to have dropped his pipe, Dyson began to grope in the corner, searching with his fingers. He touched something and drew it gently to him, and with one brief glance, as he put it quietly in his pocket, he saw it was a little old-fashioned notebook, bound in faded green morocco.

He drank down his beer at a gulp, and left the place, overjoyed at his fortunate discovery, and busy with conjecture as to the possible importance of the find. By turns he dreaded to find perhaps mere blank leaves, or the laboured follies of a betting-book, but the faded morocco cover seemed to promise better things, and to hint at mysteries. He piloted himself with no little difficulty out of the sour and squalid quarter he had entered with a light heart, and emerging at Gray's Inn Road, struck off down Guilford Street and hastened home, only anxious for a lighted candle and solitude.

Dyson sat down at his bureau, and placed the little book before him; it was an effort to open the leaves and dare disappointment. But in desperation at last he laid his fingers between the pages at haphazard, and rejoiced to see a compact range of writing with a margin, and as it chanced, three words caught his glance and stood out apart from the mass. Dyson read—

'*the Gold Tiberius,*'

and his face flushed with fortune and the lust of the hunter.

He turned at once to the first leaf of the pocket-book, and proceeded to read with rapt interest the

HISTORY OF THE YOUNG MAN WITH SPECTACLES

From the filthy and obscure lodging, situated, I verily
believe, in one of the foulest slums of Clerkenwell, I indite
this history of a life which, daily threatened, cannot last
very much longer. Every day—nay, every hour, I know
too well my enemies are drawing their nets closer about
me; even now I am condemned to be a close prisoner in
my squalid room, and I know that when I go out I shall
go to my destruction. This history, if it chance to fall into
good hands, may, perhaps, be of service in warning
young men of the dangers and pitfalls that most surely
must accompany any deviation from the ways of rectitude.

My name is Joseph Walters. When I came of age I
found myself in possession of a small but sufficient income,
and I determined that I would devote my life to scholarship. I do not mean the scholarship of these days; I had
no intention of associating myself with men whose lives
are spent in the unspeakably degrading occupation of 'edit-
ing' classics, befouling the fair margins of the fairest
books with idle and superfluous annotation, and doing
their utmost to give a lasting disgust of all that is beautiful.
An abbey church turned to the base use of a stable or
bakehouse is a sorry sight; but more pitiable still is a
masterpiece spluttered over with the commentator's pen,
and his hideous mark 'cf.'

For my part, I chose the glorious career of scholar in
its ancient sense; I longed to possess encyclopædic learning, to grow old amongst books, to distil day by day, and
year after year, the inmost sweetness of all worthy writings.
I was not rich enough to collect a library, and I was there-
fore forced to betake myself to the reading-room of the
British Museum.

O dim, far-lifted, and mighty dome, Mecca of many
minds, mausoleum of many hopes, sad house where all
desires fail! For there men enter in with hearts uplifted, and
dreaming minds, seeing in those exalted stairs a ladder

to fame, in that pompous portico the gate of knowledge, and going in, find but vain vanity, and all but in vain. There, when the long streets are ringing, is silence, there eternal twilight, and the odour of heaviness. But there the blood flows thin and cold, and the brain burns adust; there is the hunt of shadows, and the chase of embattled phantoms; a striving against ghosts, and a war that has no victory. O dome, tomb of the quick! surely in thy galleries, where no reverberant voice can call, sighs whisper ever, and mutterings of dead hopes; and there men's souls mount like moths towards the flame, and fall scorched and blackened beneath thee, O dim, far-lifted, and mighty dome!

Bitterly do I now regret the day when I took my place at a desk for the first time, and began my studies. I had not been an habitué of the place for many months, when I became acquainted with a serene and benevolent gentleman, a man somewhat past middle age, who nearly always occupied a desk next to mine. In the reading-room it takes little to make an acquaintance—a casual offer of assistance, a hint as to the search in the catalogue, and the ordinary politeness of men who constantly sit near each other; it was thus I came to know the man calling himself Dr. Lipsius. By degrees I grew to look for his presence, and to miss him when he was away, as was sometimes the case, and so a friendship sprang up between us. His immense range of learning was placed freely at my service; he would often astonish me by the way in which he would sketch out in a few minutes the bibliography of a given subject, and before long I had confided to him my ambitions.

'Ah,' he said, 'you should have been a German. I was like that myself when I was a boy. It is a wonderful resolve, an infinite career. I will know all things; yes, it is a device indeed. But it means this—a life of labour without end, and a desire unsatisfied at last. The scholar has to die, and die saying, "I know very little!"'

Gradually, by speeches such as these, Lipsius seduced me: he would praise the career, and at the same time hint that it was as hopeless as the search for the philoso-

pher's stone, and so by artful suggestions, insinuated with
infinite address, he by degrees succeeded in undermining
all my principles. 'After all,' he used to say, 'the greatest of all sciences, the key to all knowledge, is the science
and art of pleasure. Rabelais was perhaps the greatest of
all the encyclopædic scholars; and he, as you know, wrote
the most remarkable book that has ever been written. And
what does he teach men in this book? Surely the joy of
living. I need not remind you of the words, suppressed in
most of the editions, the key of all the Rabelaisian mythology, of all the enigmas of his grand philosophy, *Vivez
joyeux*. There you have all his learning; his work is the
institutes of pleasure as the fine art; the finest art there
is; the art of all arts. Rabelais had all science, but he had
all life too. And we have gone a long way since his time.
You are enlightened, I think; you do not consider all the
petty rules and bylaws that a corrupt society has made for
its own selfish convenience as the immutable decrees of
the Eternal.'

Such were the doctrines that he preached; and it was by
such insidious arguments, line upon line, here a little and
there a little, that he at last succeeded in making me a man
at war with the whole social system. I used to long for some
opportunity to break the chains and to live a free life, to be
my own rule and measure. I viewed existence with the eyes
of a pagan, and Lipsius understood to perfection the art
of stimulating the natural inclinations of a young man
hitherto a hermit. As I gazed up at the great dome I
saw it flushed with the flames and colours of a world of
enticement unknown to me, my imagination played me a
thousand wanton tricks, and the forbidden drew me as
surely as a loadstone draws on iron. At last my resolution
was taken, and I boldly asked Lipsius to be my guide.

He told me to leave the Museum at my usual hour,
haft-past four, to walk slowly along the northern pavement
of Great Russell Street, and to wait at the corner of the
street till I was addressed, and then to obey in all things
the instructions of the person who came up to me. I
carried out these directions, and stood at the corner looking about me anxiously, my heart beating fast, and my

breath coming in gasps. I waited there for some time, and had begun to fear I had been made the object of a joke, when I suddenly became conscious of a gentleman who was looking at me with evident amusement from the opposite pavement of Tottenham Court Road. He came over, and raising his hat, politely begged me to follow him, and I did so without a word, wondering where we were going, and what was to happen. I was taken to a house of quiet and respectable aspect in a street lying to the north of Oxford Street, and my guide rang the bell. A servant showed us into a large room, quietly furnished, on the ground floor. We sat there in silence for some time, and I noticed that the furniture, though unpretending, was extremely valuable. There were large oak presses, two bookcases of extreme elegance, and in one corner a carved chest which must have been mediæval. Presently Dr. Lipsius came in and welcomed me with his usual manner, and after some desultory conversation my guide left the room. Then an elderly man dropped in and began talking to Lipsius, and from their conversation I understood that my friend was a dealer in antiques; they spoke of the Hittite seal, and of the prospects of further discoveries, and later, when two or three more persons joined us, there was an argument as to the possibility of a systematic exploration of the pre-Celtic monuments in England. I was, in fact, present at an archæological reception of an informal kind; and at nine o'clock, when the antiquaries were gone, I stared at Lipsius in a manner that showed I was puzzled, and sought an explanation.

'Now,' he said, 'we will go upstairs.'

As we passed up the stairs, Lipsius lighting the way with a hand-lamp, I heard the sound of a jarring lock and bolts and bars shot on at the front door. My guide drew back a baize door and we went down a passage, and I began to hear odd sounds, a noise of curious mirth; then he pushed me through a second door, and my initiation began. I cannot write down what I witnessed that night; I cannot bear to recall what went on in those secret rooms fast shuttered and curtained so that no light should escape into the quiet street; they gave me red wine to drink, and a woman told me as I sipped it that it was wine of the Red Jar that Avallaunius had made. Another asked me how I liked the wine of the Fauns, and I heard a dozen fantastic names, while the stuff boiled in my veins, and stirred, I think, something that had slept within me from the moment I was born. It seemed as if my self-consciousness deserted me; I was no longer a thinking agent, but at once subject and object; I mingled in the horrible sport, and watched the mystery of the Greek groves and fountains enacted before me, saw the reeling dance and heard the music calling as I sat beside my mate, and yet I was outside it all, and viewed my own part an idle spectator. Thus with strange rites they made me drink the cup, and when I woke up in the morning I was one of them, and had sworn to be faithful. At first I was shown the enticing side of things; I was bidden enjoy myself and care for nothing but pleasure, and Lipsius himself indicated to me as the acutest enjoyment the spectacle of the terrors of the unfortunate persons who were from time to time decoyed into the evil house. But after a time it was pointed out to me that I must take my share in the work, and so I found myself compelled to be in my turn a seducer; and thus it is on my conscience that I have held many to the depths of the pit.

One day Lipsius summoned me to his private room, and told me that he had a difficult task to give me. He unlocked a drawer and gave me a sheet of type-written paper, and bade me read it.

It was without place, or date, or signature, and ran as follows:—

Mr. James Headley, F. S. A. will receive from his agent in Armenia, on the 12th inst., a unique coin, the gold Tiberius. It bears on the reverse a faun with the legend VICTORIA. It is believed that this coin is of immense value. Mr. Headley will come up to town to show the coin to his friend, Professor Memys, of Chenies Street, Oxford Street, on some date between the 13th and the 18th.

Dr. Lipsius chuckled at my face of blank surprise when I laid down this singular communication.

'You will have a good chance of showing your discretion,' he said. 'This is not a common case; it requires great management and infinite tact. I am sure I wish I had a Panurge in my service, but we will see what you can do.'

'But is it not a joke?' I asked him. 'How can you know—or rather, how can this correspondent of yours know—that a coin has been despatched from Armenia to Mr. Headley? And how is it possible to fix the period in which Mr. Headley will take it into his head to come up to town? It seems to me a lot guesswork.'

'My dear Mr. Walters,' he replied, 'we do not deal in guesswork here. It would bore you if I went into all these little details, the cogs and wheels, if I may say so, which move the machine. Don't you think it is much more amusing to sit in front of the house and be astonished than to be behind the scenes and see the mechanism? Better tremble at the thunder, believe me, than see the man rolling the cannon-ball. But, after all, you needn't bother about the how and why; you have your share to do. Of course I shall give you full instructions, but a great deal depends on the way the thing is carried out. I have often heard very young men maintain that style is everything in literature, and I can assure you that the same maxim holds good in our far more delicate profession. With us style is absolutely everything, and that is why we have friends like yourself.'

I went away in some perturbation: he had no doubt designedly left everything in mystery, and I did not know what part I should have to play. Though I had assisted at scenes of hideous revelry, I was not yet dead to all echo of human feeling, and I trembled lest I should receive the order to be Mr. Headley's executioner.

A week later, it was on the sixteenth of the month, Dr. Lipsius made me a sign to come into his room.

'It is for to-night,' he began. 'Please to attend carefully to what I am going to say, Mr. Walters, and on peril of your life, for it is a dangerous mater,—on peril of your life, I say, follow these instructions to the letter. You understand? Well, to-night at about half-past seven, you will stroll quietly up the Hampstead Road till you come to

Vincent Street. Turn down here and walk along, taking the third turning to your right, which is Lambert Terrace. Then follow the terrace, cross the road, and go along Hertford Street, and so into Lillington Square. The second turning you will come to in the square is called Sheen Street; but in reality it is more a passage between blank walls than a street. Whatever you do, take care to be at the corner of this street at eight o'clock precisely. You will walk along it, and just at the bend where you lose sight of the square you will find an old gentleman with white beard and whiskers. He will in all probability be abusing a cabman for having brought him to Sheen Street instead of Chenies Street. You will go up to him quietly and offer your services; he will tell you where he wants to go, and you will be so courteous as to offer to show him the way. I may say that Professor Memys moved into Chenies Street a month ago; thus Mr. Headley has never been to see him there, and, moreover, he is very shortsighted, and knows little of the topography of London. Indeed, he has quite lived the life of a learned hermit at Audley Hall.

'Well, need I say more to a man of your intelligence? You will bring him to this house, he will ring the bell, and a servant in quiet livery will let him in. Then your work will be done, and I am sure done well. You will leave Mr. Headley at the door, and simply continue your walk, and I shall hope to see you the next day. I really don't think there is anything more I can tell you.'

These minute instructions I took care to carry out to the letter. I confess that I walked up the Tottenham Court Road by no means blindly, but with an uneasy sense that I was coming to a decisive point in my life. The noise and rumour of the crowded pavements were to me but dumb show; I revolved again and again in ceaseless iteration the task that had been laid on me, and I questioned myself as to the possible results. As I got near the point of turning, I asked myself whether danger were not about my steps; the cold thought struck me that I was suspected and observed, and every chance foot-passenger who gave me a second glance seemed to me an officer of police. My time was running out, the sky had darkened, and I hesitated, half resolved to go no farther, but to abandon Lipsius and his friends for ever. I had almost determined to take this course, when the conviction suddenly came to me that the whole thing was a gigantic joke, a fabrication of rank improbability. Who could have procured the information about the Armenian agent? I asked myself. By what means could Lipsius have known the particular day and the very train that Mr. Headley was to take? how engage him to enter one special cab amongst the dozens waiting at Paddington? I vowed it a mere Milesian tale, and went forward merrily, turned down Vincent Street, and threaded out the route that Lipsius had so carefully impressed upon me. The various streets he had named were all places of silence and an oppressive cheap gentility; it was dark, and I felt alone in the musty squares and crescents, where people pattered by at intervals, and the shadows were growing blacker. I entered Sheen street, and found it as Lipsius had said, more a passage than a street; it was a byway, on one side a low wall and neglected gardens, and grim backs of a line of houses, and on the other a timber-yard. I turned the corner, and lost sight of the square, and then, to my astonishment, I saw the scene of which I had been told. A hansom cab had come to a stop beside the pavement, and an old man, carrying a handbag, was fiercely abusing the cabman, who sat on his perch the image of bewilderment.

'Yes, but I'm sure you said Sheen Street, and that's where I brought you,' I heard him saying as I came up, and the old gentleman boiled in a fury, and threatened police and suits at law.

The sight gave me a shock, and in an instant I resolved to go through with it. I strolled on, and without noticing the cabman, lifted my hat politely to old Mr. Headley.

'Pardon me, sir,' I said, 'but is there any difficulty? I see you are a traveller; perhaps the cabman has made a mistake. Can I direct you?'

The old fellow turned to me, and I noticed that he snarled and showed his teeth like an ill-tempered cur as he spoke.

'This drunken fool has brought me here,' he said. 'I told

him to drive to Chenies Street, and he brings me to this infernal place. I won't pay him a farthing, and I meant to have given him a handsome sum. I am going to call for the police and give him in charge.'

At this threat the cabman seemed to take alarm; he glanced round, as if to make sure that no policeman was in sight, and drove off grumbling loudly, and Mr. Headley grinned savagely with satisfaction at having saved his fare, and put back one and sixpence into his pocket, the 'handsome sum' the cabman had lost.

'My dear sir,' I said, 'I am afraid this piece of stupidity has annoyed you a great deal. It is a long way to Chenies Street, and you will have some difficulty in finding the place unless you know London pretty well.'

'I know it very little,' he replied. 'I never come up except on important business, and I've never been to Chenies Street in my life.'

'Really? I should be happy to show you the way. I have been for a stroll, and it will not at all inconvenience me to take you to your destination.'

'I want to go to Professor Memys, at Number 15. It's most annoying to me; I'm short-sighted, and I can never make out the numbers on the doors.'

'This way if you please,' I said, and we set out.

I did not find Mr. Headley an agreeable man; indeed, he grumbled the whole way. He informed me of his name, and I took care to say, 'The well-known antiquary?' and thenceforth I was compelled to listen to the history of his complicated squabbles with publishers, who treated him, as he said, disgracefully; the man was a chapter in the Irritability of Authors. He told me that he had been on the point of making the fortune of several firms, but had been compelled to abandon the design owing to their rank ingratitude. Besides these ancient histories of wrong, and the more recent misadventure of the cabman, he had another grievous complaint to make. As he came along in the train, he had been sharpening a pencil, and the sudden jolt of the engine as it drew up at a station had driven the penknife against his face, inflicting a small triangular wound just on the cheek-bone, which he showed me. He denounced the railway company, heaped imprecations on the head of the driver, and talked of claiming damages. Thus he grumbled all the way, not noticing in the least where he was going; and so unamiable did his conduct appear to me, that I began to enjoy the trick I was playing on him.

Nevertheless, my heart beat a little faster as we turned into the street where Lipsius was waiting. A thousand accidents, I thought, might happen; some chance might bring one of Headley's friends to meet us; perhaps, though he knew not Chenies Street, he might know the street where I was taking him; in spite of his short sight, he might possibly make out the number, or, in a sudden fit of suspicion, he might make an inquiry of the policeman at the corner. Thus every step upon the pavement, as we drew nearer to the goal, was to me a pang and a terror, and every approaching passenger carried a certain threat of danger. I gulped down my excitement with an effort, and made shift to say pretty quietly—

'Number 15, I think you said? That is the third house from this. If you will allow me, I will leave you now; I have been delayed a little, and my way lies on the other side of Tottenham Court Road.'

He snarled out some kind of thanks, and I turned my back and walked swiftly in the opposite direction. A minute or two later I looked round and saw Mr. Headley standing on the doorstep, and then the door opened and he went in. For my part, I gave a sigh of relief; I hastened to get away from the neighbourhood, and endeavoured to enjoy myself in merry company.

The whole of the next day I kept away from Lipsius. I felt anxious, but I did not know what had happened, or what was happening, and a reasonable regard for my own safety told me that I should do well to remain quietly at home. My curiosity, however, to learn the end of the odd drama in which I had played a part stung me to the quick, and late in the evening I made up my mind to see how events had turned out. Lipsius nodded when I came in, and asked if I could give him five minutes' talk. We went to his room, and he began to walk up and down, while I sat waiting for him to speak.

'My dear Mr. Walters,' he said at length, 'I congratulate you warmly; your work was done in the most thorough and artistic manner. You will go far. Look.'

He went to his escritoire and pressed a secret spring; a drawer flew out, and he laid something on the table. It was a gold coin; I took it up and examined it eagerly, and read the legend about the figure of the faun.

'Victoria,' I said, smiling.

'Yes; it was a great capture, which we owe to you. I had great difficulty in persuading Mr. Headley that a little mistake had been made; that was how I put it. He was very disagreeable, and indeed ungentlemanly, about it; didn't he strike you as a very cross old man?'

I held the coin, admiring the choice and rare design, clear cut as if from the mint; and I thought the fine gold glowed and burnt like a lamp.

'And what finally became of Mr. Headley?' I said at last.

Lipsius smiled, and shrugged his shoulders.

'What on earth does it matter?' he said. 'He might be here, or there, or anywhere; but what possible consequence could it be? Besides, your question rather surprises me; you are an intelligent man, Mr. Walters. Just think it over, and I'm sure you won't repeat the question.'

'My dear sir,' I said, 'I hardly think you are treating me fairly. You have paid me some handsome compliments on my share in the capture, and I naturally wish to know how the matter ended. From what I saw of Mr. Headley I should think you must have had some difficulty with him.'

He gave me no answer for the moment, but began again to walk up and down the room, apparently absorbed in thought.

'Well,' he said at last, 'I suppose there is something in what you say. We are certainly indebted to you. I have said that I have a high opinion of your intelligence, Mr. Walters. Just look here, will you?'

He opened a door communicating with another room, and pointed.

There was a great box lying on the floor, a queer, coffin-shaped thing. I looked at it, and saw it was a mummy case, like those in the British Museum, vividly painted in the brilliant Egyptian colours, with I knew not what proclamation of dignity or hopes of life immortal. The mummy swathed about in the robes of death was lying within, and the face had been uncovered.

'You are going to send this away?' I said, forgetting the question I had put.

'Yes; I have an order from a local museum. Look a little more closely, Mr. Walters.'

Puzzled by his manner, I peered into the face, while he held the lamp. The flesh was black with the passing of the centuries; but as I looked I saw upon the right cheek bone a small triangular scar, and the secret of the mummy flashed upon me: I was looking at the dead body of the man whom I had decoyed into that house.

There was no thought or design of action in my mind. I held the accursed coin in my hand, burning me with a foretaste of hell, and I fled as I would have fled from pestilence and death, and dashed into the street in blind horror, not knowing where I went. I felt the gold coin grasped in my clenched first, and throwing it away, I knew not where, I ran on and on through by-streets and dark ways, till at last I issued out into a crowded thoroughfare and checked myself. Then as consciousness returned I realized my instant peril, and understood what would happen if I fell into the hands of Lipsius. I knew that I had put forth my finger to thwart a relentless mechanism rather than a man. My recent adventure with the unfortunate Mr. Headley had taught me that Lipsius had agents in all quarters; and I foresaw that if I fell into his hands, he would remain true to his doctrine of style, and cause me to die a death of some horrible and ingenious torture. I bent my whole mind to the task of outwitting him and his emissaries, three of whom I knew to have proved their ability for tracking down persons who for various reasons preferred to remain obscure. These servants of Lipsius were two men and a woman, and the woman was incomparably the most subtle and the most deadly. Yet I considered that I too had some portion of craft, and I took my resolve. Since then I have matched myself day by day and hour by hour against the ingenuity of Lipsius and his myrmidons. For a time I was successful; though they beat furiously after me in the covert of London, I remained *perdu,* and watched with some amusement their frantic efforts to recover the scent lost in two or three minutes. Every lure and wile was put forth to entice me from my hiding-place; I was informed by the medium of the public prints that what I had taken had been recovered, and meetings were proposed in which I might hope to gain a great deal without the slightest risk. I laughed at their endeavours, and began a little to despise the organization I had so dreaded, and ventured more abroad. Not once or twice, but several times, I recognized the two men who were charged with my capture, and I succeeded in eluding them at close quarters; and a little too hastily I decided that I had nothing to dread, and that my craft was greater than theirs. But in the meanwhile, while I congratulated myself on my cunning, the third of Lipsius's emissaries was weaving her nets; and in an evil hour I paid a visit to an old friend, a literary man named Russell, who lived in a quiet street in Bayswater. The woman, as I found out too late, a day or two ago occupied rooms in the same house, and I was followed and tracked down. Too late, as I have said I recognized that I had made a fatal mistake, and that I was besieged. Sooner or later I shall find myself in the power of an enemy without pity; and so surely as I leave this house I shall go to receive doom. I hardly dare to guess how it will at last fall upon me; my imagination, always a vivid one, paints to me appalling pictures of the unspeakable torture which I shall probably endure; and I know that I shall die with Lipsius standing near and gloating over the refinements of my suffering and my shame.

Hours, nay minutes, have become precious to me. I sometimes pause in the midst of anticipating my tortures, to wonder whether even now I cannot hit upon some supreme stroke, some design of infinite subtlety, to free myself from the toils. But I find that the faculty of combination has left me; I am as the scholar in the old myth, deserted by the power which has helped me hitherto. I do not know when the supreme moment will come, but sooner or later it is inevitable; before long I shall receive sentence, and from the sentence to execution will not be long.

     .   .   .   .

I cannot remain here a prisoner any longer. I shall go out to-night when the streets are full of crowds and clamours, and make a last effort to escape.

     .   .   .   .   .   .

It was with profound astonishment that Dyson closed the little book, and thought of the strange series of incidents which had brought him into touch with the plots and counterplots connected with the Gold Tiberius. He had bestowed the coin carefully away, and he shuddered at the bare possibility of its place of deposit becoming known to the evil band who seemed to possess such extraordinary sources of information.

It had grown late while he read, and he put the pocket-book away, hoping with all his heart that the unhappy Walters might even at the eleventh hour escape the doom he dreaded.

Adventure of the
Deserted Residence

'A wonderful story, as you say, an extraordinary sequence and play of coincidence. I confess that your expressions when you first showed me the Gold Tiberius were not exaggerated. But do you think that Walters has really some fearful fate to dread?'

'I cannot say. Who can presume to predict events when life itself puts on the robe of coincidence and plays at drama? Perhaps we have not yet reached the last chapter in the queer story. But, look, we are drawing near to the verge of London; there are gaps, you see, in the serried ranks of brick, and a vision of green fields beyond.'

Dyson had persuaded the ingenious Mr. Phillipps to accompany him on one of those aimless walks to which he was himself so addicted. Starting from the very heart of London, they had made their way westward through the stony avenues, and were now just emerging from the red lines of an extreme surburb, and presently the half-finished road ended, a quiet lane began, and they were beneath the shade of elm trees. The yellow autumn sunlight that had lit up the bare distance of the suburban street now filtered down through the boughs of the trees and shone on the glowing carpet of fallen leaves, and the pools of rain glittered and shot back the gleam of light. Over all the broad pastures there was peace and the happy rest of autumn before the great winds begin, and afar off London lay all vague and immense amidst the

veiling mist; here and there a distant window catching the
sun and kindling with fire, and a spire gleaming high, and
below the streets in shadow, and the turmoil of life. Dyson
and Phillipps walked on in silence beneath the high hedges,
till at a turn of the lane they saw a mouldering and
ancient gate standing open, and the prospect of a house
at the end of a moss-grown carriage drive.

'There is a survival for you,' said Dyson; 'it has come
to its last days, I imagine. Look how the laurels have
grown gaunt and weedy, and black and bare beneath; look
at the house, covered with yellow wash, and patched with
green damp. Why, the very notice-board, which informs all
and singular that the place is to be let, has cracked and
half fallen.'

'Suppose we go in and see it,' said Phillipps; 'I don't
think there is anybody about.'

They turned up the drive, and walked slowly towards
this remnant of old days. It was a large, straggling house,
with curved wings at either end, and behind a series of
irregular roofs and projections, showing that the place
had been added to at divers dates; the two wings were
roofed in cupola fashion, and at one side, as they came
nearer, they could see a stableyard, and a clock turret
with a bell, and the dark masses of gloomy cedars. Amidst
all the lineaments of dissolution there was but one note
of contrast: the sun was setting beyond the elm trees;
and all the west and south were in flames; on the upper
windows of the house the glow shone reflected, and it
seemed as if blood and fire were mingled. Before the
yellow front of the mansion, stained, as Dyson had remarked, with gangrenous patches, green and blackening,
stretched what had once been, no doubt, a well-kept lawn,
but it was now rough and ragged, and nettles and great
docks, and all manner of coarse weeds, struggled in the
places of the flower-beds. The urns had fallen from their
pillars beside the walk, and lay broken in shards upon the
ground, and everywhere from grass-plot and path a
fungoid growth had sprung up and multiplied, and lay
dank and slimy like a festering sore upon the earth. In
the middle of the rank grass of the lawn was a desolate

fountain; the rim of the basin was crumbling and pulverized with decay, and within the water stood stagnant, with green scum for the lilies that had once bloomed there; rust had eaten into the bronze flesh of the Triton that stood in the middle, and the conch-shell he held was broken.

'Here,' said Dyson, 'one might moralize over decay and death. Here all the stage is decked out with the symbols of dissolution; the cedarn gloom and twilight hang heavy around us, and everywhere within the pale dankness has found a harbour, and the very air is changed and brought to accord with the scene. To me, I confess, this deserted house is as moral as a graveyard, and I find something sublime in that lonely Triton, deserted in the midst of his water-pool. He is the last of the gods; they have left him, and he remembers the sound of water falling on water, and the days that were sweet.'

'I like your reflections extremely,' said Phillipps; 'but I may mention that the door of the house is open.'

'Let us go in, then.'

The door was just ajar, and they passed into the mouldy hall and looked in at a room on one side. It was a large room, going far back, and the rich, old, red flock paper was peeling from the walls in long strips, and blackened with vague patches of rising damp; the ancient clay, the dank reeking earth rising up again, and subduing all the work of men's hands after the conquest of many years. The floor was thick with the dust of decay, and the painted ceiling fading from all gay colours and light fancies of cupids in a career, and disfigured with sores of dampness, seemed transmuted into other work. No longer the amorini chased one another pleasantly, with limbs that sought not to advance, and hands that merely simulated the act of grasping at the wreathed flowers; but it appeared some savage burlesque of the old careless world and of its cherished conventions, and the dance of the Loves had become a Dance of Death; black pustules and festering sores swelled and clustered on fair limbs and smiling faces showed corruption, and the fairy blood had boiled with the germs of foul disease; it was a parable of the leaven working, and worms devouring for a banquet the heart of the rose.

Strangely, under the painted ceiling, against the decaying walls, two old chairs still stood alone, the sole furniture of the empty place. High-backed, with curving arms and twisted legs, covered with faded gold leaf, and upholstered in tattered damask, they too were a part of the symbolism, and struck Dyson with surprise. 'What have we here?' he said. 'Who has sat in these chairs? Who, clad in peach-bloom satin, with lace ruffles and diamond buckles, all golden, a *conté fleurettes* to his companion? Phillipps, we are in another age. I wish I had some snuff to offer you, but failing that I beg to offer you a seat, and we will sit and smoke tobacco. A horrid practice, but I am no pedant.'

They sat down on the queer old chairs, and looked out of the dim and grimy panes to the ruined lawn, and the fallen urns, and the deserted Triton.

Presently Dyson ceased his imitation of eighteenth-century airs; he no longer pulled forward imaginary ruffles, or tapped a ghostly snuff-box.

'It's a foolish fancy,' he said at last; 'but I keep thinking I hear a noise like some one groaning. Listen; no, I can't hear it now. There it is again! Did you notice it, Phillipps?'

'No, I can't say I heard anything. But I believe that old places like this are like shells from the shore, ever echoing with noises. The old beams, mouldering piece-meal, yield a little and groan; and such a house as this I can fancy all resonant at night with voices, the voices of matter so slowly and so surely transformed into other shapes, the voice of the worm that gnaws at last the very heart of the oak, the voice of stone grinding on stone, and the voice of the conquest of Time.'

They sat still in the old arm-chairs, and grew graver in the musty ancient air, the air of a hundred years ago.

'I don't like the place,' said Phillipps, after a long pause. 'To me it seems as if there were a sickly, unwholesome smell about it, a smell of something burning.'

'You are right; there is an evil odour here. I wonder what it is. Hark! Did you hear that?'

A hollow sound, a noise of infinite sadness and infinite pain, broke in upon the silence, and the two men looked fearfully at one another, horror, and the sense of unknown things, glimmering in their eyes.

'Come,' said Dyson, 'we must see into this,' and they went into the hall and listened in the silence.

'Do you know,' said Phillipps, 'it seems absurd, but I could almost fancy that the smell is that of burning flesh.'

They went up the hollow-sounding stairs, and the odour became thick and noisome, stifling the breath, and a vapour, sickening as the smell of the chamber of death, choked them. A door was open, and they entered the large upper room, and clung hard to one another, shuddering at the sight they saw.

A naked man was lying on the floor, his arms and legs stretched wide apart, and bound to pegs that had been hammered into the boards. The body was torn and mutilated in the most hideous fashion, scarred with the marks of red-hot irons, a shameful ruin of the human shape. But upon the middle of the body a fire of coals was smouldering; the flesh had been burnt through. The man was dead, but the smoke of his torment mounted still, a black vapour.

'The young man with spectacles,' said Mr. Dyson.

The Red Hand

A Note on *The Red Hand*

Those of my readers who have managed to find their way this far in the book will by now be familiar with Dyson, that armchair supersleuth who somehow fails, throughout the length of *The Three Impostors,* to actually capture a single culprit.

During those same years, the 1890s, in which Arthur Machen composed *The Three Impostors,* he wrote another tale of Dyson's less-than-effective sleuthings, *The Red Hand,* which follows next.

Machen seems to have developed a certain fondness for his drawing-room Sherlock, and in *The Red Hand* (which was originally written as an entry in a short story contest) he permits him, at long last, to capture a real criminal.

Although *The Red Hand* is not really a sequel to *The Three Impostors,* it seems fitting to include the remainder of Dyson's detectings in the same volume with his initial exploits.

—LIN CARTER

The Problem
of the Fish-Hooks

'There can be no doubt whatever,' said Mr. Phillipps, 'that my theory is the true one; these flints are prehistoric fish-hooks.'

'I dare say; but you know that in all probability the things were forged the other day with a door-key.'

'Stuff!' said Phillipps; 'I have some respect, Dyson, for your literary abilities, but your knowledge of ethnology is insignificant, or rather nonexistent. These fish-hooks satisfy every test; they are perfectly genuine.'

'Possibly, but as I said just now, you go to work at the wrong end. You neglect the opportunities that confront you and await you, obvious, at every corner; you positively shrink from the chance of encountering primitive man in this whirling and mysterious city, and you pass the weary hours in your agreeable retirement of Red Lion Square fumbling with bits of flint, which are, as I said, in all probability, rank forgeries.'

Phillipps took one of the little objects, and held it up in exasperation.

'Look at that ridge,' he said. 'Did you ever see such a ridge as that on a forgery?'

Dyson merely grunted and lit his pipe, and the two sat smoking in rich silence, watching through the open window the children in the square as they flitted to and fro in the twilight of the lamps, as elusive as bats flying on the verge of a dark wood.

'Well,' said Phillipps at last, 'it is really a long time since you have been round. I suppose you have been working at your told task.'

'Yes,' said Dyson, 'always the chase of the phrase. I shall grow old in the hunt. But it is a great consolation to meditate on the fact that there are not a dozen people in England who know what style means.'

'I suppose not; for the matter of that, the study of ethnology is far from popular. And the difficulties! Primitive man stands dim and very far off across the great bridge of years.'

'By the way,' he went on after a pause, 'what was that stuff you were talking just now about shrinking from the chance of encountering primitive man at the corner, or something of the kind? There are certainly people about here whose ideas are very primitive.'

'I wish, Phillipps, you would not rationalize my remarks. If I recollect the phrase correctly, I hinted that you shrank from the chance of encountering primitive man in this whirling and mysterious city, and I meant exactly what I said. Who can limit the age of survival? The troglodyte and the lake-dweller, perhaps representatives of yet darker races, may very probably be lurking in our midst, rubbing shoulders with frock-coated and finely-draped humanity, ravening like wolves at heart and boiling with the foul passions of the swamp and the black cave. Now and then as I walk in Holborn or Fleet Street I see a face which I pronounce abhorred, and yet I could not give a reason for the thrill of loathing that stirs within me.'

'My dear Dyson, I refuse to enter myself in your literary "trying-on" department. I know that survivals do exist, but all things have a limit, and your speculations are absurd. You must catch me your troglodyte before I will believe in him.'

'I agree to that with all my heart,' said Dyson, chuckling at the ease with which he had succeeded in 'drawing' Phillipps. 'Nothing could be better. It's a fine night for a walk,' he added, taking up his hat.

'What nonsense you are talking, Dyson!' said Phillipps.

'However, I have no objection to taking a walk with you: as you say, it is a pleasant night.'

'Come along then,' said Dyson, grinning, 'but remember our bargain.'

The two men went out into the square, and threading one of the narrow passages that serve as exits, struck towards the north-east. As they passed along a flaring causeway they could hear at intervals between the clamour of the children and the triumphant *Gloria* played on a piano-organ the long deep hum and roll of the traffic in Holborn, a sound so persistent that it echoed like the turning of everlasting wheels. Dyson looked to right and left and conned the way, and presently they were passing through a more peaceful quarter, touching on deserted squares and silent streets black as midnight. Phillipps had lost all count of direction, and as by degrees the region of faded respectability gave place to the squalid, and dirty stucco offended the eye of the artistic observer, he merely ventured the remark that he had never seen a neighbourhood more unpleasant or more commonplace.

'More mysterious, you mean,' said Dyson. 'I warn you, Phillipps, we are now not upon the scent.'

They dived yet deeper into the maze of brickwork; some time before they had crossed a noisy thoroughfare running east and west, and now the quarter seemed all amorphous, without character; here a decent house with sufficient garden, here a faded square, and here factories surrounded by high, blank walls, with blind passages and dark corners; but all ill-lighted and unfrequented and heavy with silence.

Presently, as they paced down a forlorn street of two-story houses, Dyson caught sight of a dark and obscure turning.

'I like the look of that,' he said; 'it seems to me promising.' There was a street lamp at the entrance, and another, a mere glimmer, at the further end. Beneath the lamp, on the pavement, an artist had evidently established his academy in the daytime, for the stones were all a blur of crude colours rubbed into each other, and a few broken fragments of chalk lay in a little heap beneath the wall.

'You see people do occasionally pass this way,' said Dyson, pointing to the ruins of the screever's work. 'I confess I should not have thought it possible. Come, let us explore.'

On one side of this by-way of communication was a great timber-yard, with vague piles of wood looming shapeless above the enclosing wall; and on the other side of the road a wall still higher seemed to enclose a garden, for there were shadows like trees, and a faint murmur of rustling leaves broke the silence. It was a moonless night, and clouds that had gathered after sunset had blackened, and midway between the feeble lamps the passage lay all dark and formless, and when one stopped and listened, and the sharp echo of reverberant footsteps ceased, there came from far away, as from beyond the hills, a faint roll of the noise of London. Phillipps was bolstering up his courage to declare that he had had enough of the excursion, when a loud cry from Dyson broke in upon his thoughts.

'Stop, stop for Heaven's sake, or you will tread on it! There! almost under your feet!' Phillipps looked down, and saw a vague shape, dark, and framed in surrounding darkness, dropped strangely on the pavement, and then a white cuff glimmered for a moment as Dyson lit a match, which went out directly.

'It's a drunken man,' said Phillipps very coolly.

'It's a murdered man,' said Dyson, and he began to call for police with all his might, and soon from the distance running footsteps echoed and grew louder, and cries sounded.

A policeman was the first to come up.

'What's the matter?' he said, as he drew to a stand, panting. 'Anything amiss here?' for he had not seen what was on the pavement.

'Look!' said Dyson, speaking out of the gloom. 'Look there! My friend and I came down this place three minutes ago, and that is what we found.'

The man flashed his light on the dark shape and cried out.

'Why, it's murder,' he said; 'there's blood all about him,

and a puddle of it in the gutter there. He's not dead long, either. Ah! there's the wound! It's in the neck.'

Dyson bent over what was lying there. He saw a prosperous gentleman, dressed in smooth, well-cut clothes. The neat whiskers were beginning to grizzle a little; he might have been forty-five an hour before; and a handsome gold watch had half slipped out of his waistcoat pocket. And there in the flesh of the neck, between chin and ear, gaped a great wound, clean cut, but all clotted with dry blood, and the white of the cheeks shone like a lighted lamp above the red.

Dyson turned, and looked curiously about him; the dead man lay across the path with his head inclined towards the wall, and the blood from the wound streamed away across the pavement, and lay a dark puddle, as the policeman had said, in the gutter. Two more policemen had come up, the crowd gathered, humming from all quarters, and the officers had as much as they could do to keep the curious at a distance. The three lanterns were flashing here and there, searching for more evidence, and in the gleam of one of them Dyson caught sight of an object in the road, to which he called the attention of the policeman nearest to him.

'Look, Phillipps,' he said, when the man had secured it and held it up. 'Look, that should be something in your way!'

It was a dark flinty stone, gleaming like obsidian, and shaped to a broad edge something after the manner of an adze. One end was rough, and easily grasped in the hand, and the whole thing was hardly five inches long. The edge was thick with blood.

'What is that, Phillipps?' said Dyson; and Phillipps looked hard at it.

'It's a primitive flint knife,' he said. 'It was made about ten thousand years ago. One exactly like this was found near Aubury, in Wiltshire, and all the authorities gave it that age.'

The policeman stared astonished at such a development of the case; and Phillipps himself was all aghast at his own words. But Mr. Dyson did not notice him. An inspector who had just come up and was listening to the outlines of the case, was holding a lantern to the dead man's head. Dyson, for his part, was staring with a white heat of curiosity at something he saw on the wall, just above where the man was lying; there were a few rude marks done in red chalk.

'This is a black business,' said the inspector at length; 'does anybody know who it is?'

A man stepped forward from the crowd. 'I do, governor,' he said, 'he's a big doctor, his name's Sir Thomas Vivian; I was in the 'orspital abart six months ago, and he used to come round; he was a very kind man.'

'Lord,' cried the inspector, 'this is a bad job indeed. Why, Sir Thomas Vivian goes to the Royal Family. And there's a watch worth a hundred guineas in his pocket, so it isn't robbery.'

Dyson and Phillipps gave their cards to the authorities, and moved off, pushing with difficulty through the crowd that was still gathering, gathering fast; and the alley that had been lonely and desolate now swarmed with white staring faces and hummed with the buzz of rumour and horror, and rang with the commands of the officers of police. The two men, once free from this swarming curiosity, stepped out briskly, but for twenty minutes neither spoke a word.

'Phillipps,' said Dyson, as they came into a small but cheerful street, clean and brightly lit, 'Phillipps, I owe you an apology. I was wrong to have spoken as I did to-night. Such infernal jesting,' he went on, with heat, 'as if there were no wholesome subjects for a joke. I feel as if I had raised an evil spirit.'

'For Heaven's sake say nothing more,' said Phillipps, choking down horror with visible effort. 'You told the truth to me in my room; the troglodyte, as you said, is still lurking about the earth, and in these very streets around us, slaying for mere lust of blood.'

'I will come up for a moment,' said Dyson when they reached Red Lion Square, 'I have something to ask you. I think there should be nothing hidden between us at all events.'

Phillipps nodded gloomily, and they went up to the room, where everything hovered indistinct in the uncertain glimmer of the light from without. When the candle was lighted and the two men sat facing each other, Dyson spoke.

'Perhaps,' he began, 'you did not notice me peering at the wall just above the place where the head lay. The light from the inspector's lantern was shining full on it, and I saw something that looked queer to me, and I examined it closely. I found that some one had drawn in red chalk a rough outline of a hand—a human hand—upon the wall. But it was the curious position of the fingers that struck me; it was like this'; and he took a pencil and a piece of paper and drew rapidly, and then handed what he had done to Phillipps. It was a rough sketch of a hand seen from the back, with the fingers clenched, and the top of the thumb protruded between the first and second fingers, and pointed downwards, as if to something below.

'It was just like that,' said Dyson, as he saw Phillipps's face grow still whiter. 'The thumb pointed down as if to the body; it seemed almost a live hand in ghastly gesture. And just beneath there was a small mark with the powder of the chalk lying on it—as if some one had commenced a stroke and had broken the chalk in his hand. I saw the bit of chalk lying on the ground. But what do you make of it?'

'It's a horrible old sign,' said Phillipps—'one of the most horrible signs connected with the theory of the evil eye. It is used still in Italy, but there can be no doubt that it has been known for ages. It is one of the survivals; you must look for the origin of it in the black swamp whence man first came.'

Dyson took up his hat to go.

'I think, jesting apart,' said he, 'that I kept my promise, and that we were and are hot on the scent, as I said. It seems as if I had really shown you primitive man, or his handiwork at all events.'

Incident of the Letter

About a month after the extraordinary and mysterious murder of Sir Thomas Vivian, the well-known and universally respected specialist in heart disease, Mr. Dyson called again on his friend Mr. Phillipps, whom he found, not, as usual, sunk deep in painful study, but reclining in his easy-chair in an attitude of relaxation. He welcomed Dyson with cordiality.

'I am very glad you have come,' he began; 'I was thinking of looking you up. There is no longer the shadow of doubt about the matter.'

'You mean the case of Sir Thomas Vivian?'

'Oh, no, not at all. I was referring to the problem of the fish-hooks. Between ourselves, I was a little too confident when you were here last, but since then other facts have turned up; and only yesterday I had a letter from a distinguished F. R. S. which quite settles the affair. I have been thinking what I should tackle next; and I am inclined to believe that there is a good deal to be done in the way of so-called undecipherable inscriptions.'

'Your line of study pleases me,' said Dyson. 'I think it may prove useful. But in the meantime, there was surely something extremely mysterious about the case of Sir Thomas Vivian.'

'Hardly, I think. I allowed myself to be frightened that night; but there can be no doubt that the facts are patient of a comparatively commonplace explanation.'

'Really! What is your theory then?'

'Well, I imagine that Vivian must have been mixed up at some period of his life in an adventure of a not very creditable description, and that he was murdered out of revenge by some Italian whom he had wronged.'

'Why Italian?'

'Because of the hand, the sign of the *mano in fica*. That gesture is now only used by Italians. So you see that what appeared the most obscure feature in the case turns out to be illuminant.'

'Yes, quite so. And the flint knife?'

'That is very simple. The man found the thing in Italy, or possibly stole it from some museum. Follow the line of least resistance, my dear fellow, and you will see there is no need to bring up primitive man from his secular grave beneath the hills.'

'There is some justice in what you say,' said Dyson. 'As I understand you, then, you think that your Italian, having murdered Vivian, kindly chalked up that hand as a guide to Scotland Yard?'

'Why not? Remember a murderer is always a madman. He may plot and contrive nine-tenths of his scheme with the acuteness and the grasp of a chess-player or a pure mathematician; but somewhere or other his wits leave him and he behaves like a fool. Then you must take into account the insane pride or vanity of the criminal; he likes to leave his mark, as it were, upon his handiwork.'

'Yes, it is all very ingenious; but have you read the reports of the inquest?'

'No, not a word. I simply gave my evidence, left the court, and dismissed the subject from my mind.'

'Quite so. Then if you don't object I should like to give you an account of the case. I have studied it rather deeply, and I confess it interests me extremely.'

'Very good. But I warn you I have done with mystery. We are to deal with facts now.'

'Yes, it is fact that I wish to put before you. And this is fact the first. When the police moved Sir Thomas Vivian's body they found an open knife beneath him. It was an ugly-looking thing such as sailors carry, with a blade that the mere opening rendered rigid, and there the blade was all ready, bare and gleaming, but without a trace of blood on it, and the knife was found to be quite new; it had never been used. Now, at the first glance it looks as if your imaginary Italian were just the man to have such a tool. But consider a moment. Would he be likely to buy a new knife expressly to commit murder? And, secondly, if he had such a knife, why didn't he use it, instead of that very odd flint instrument?

'And I want to put this to you. You think the murderer chalked up the hand after the murder as a sort of "melo-dramatic Italian assassin his mark" touch. Passing over the question as to whether the real criminal ever does such a thing, I would point out that, on the medical evidence, Sir Thomas Vivian hadn't been dead for more than an hour. That would place the stroke at about a quarter to ten, and you know it was perfectly dark when we went out at 9.30. And that passage was singularly gloomy and ill-lighted, and the hand was drawn roughly, it is true, but correctly and without the bungling of strokes and the bad shots that are inevitable when one tries to draw in the dark or with shut eyes. Just try to draw such a simple figure as a square without looking at the paper, and then ask me to conceive that your Italian, with the rope waiting for his neck, could draw the hand on the wall so firmly and truly, in the black shadow of that alley. It is absurd. By consequence, then, the hand was drawn early in the evening, long before any murder was committed; or else —mark this, Phillipps—it was drawn by some one to whom darkness and gloom were familiar and habitual; by some one to whom the common dread of the rope was unknown!

'Again: a curious note was found in Sir Thomas Vivian's pocket. Envelope and paper were of a common make, and the stamp bore the West Central postmark. I will come to the nature of the contents later on, but it is the question of the handwriting that is so remarkable. The address on the outside was neatly written in a small clear hand, but the letter itself might have been written by a Persian who had learnt the English script. It was upright, and the letters were curiously contorted, with an affectation of dashes and backward curves which really reminded me of an Oriental manuscript, though it was all perfectly legible. But—and here comes the poser—on searching the dead man's waistcoat pockets a small memorandum book was found; it was almost filled with pencil jottings. These memoranda related chiefly to matters of a private as distinct from a professional nature; there were appointments to meet friends, notes of theatrical first-nights, the address of a good hotel in Tours, and the title of a new novel—nothing in any way intimate. And the whole of these jottings were written in a hand nearly identical with the writing of the note found in the dead man's coat pocket! There was just enough difference between them to enable the expert to swear that the two were not written by the same person. I will just read you so much of Lady Vivian's evidence as bears on this point of the writing; I have the printed slip with me. Here you see she says: "I was married to my late husband seven years ago; I never saw any letter addressed him in a hand at all resembling that on the envelope produced, nor have I ever seen writing like that in the letter before me. I never saw my late husband using the memorandum book, but I am sure he did write everything in it; I am certain of that because we stayed last May at the Hotel du Faisan, Rue Royale, Tours, the address of which is given in the book; I remember his getting the novel 'A Sentinel' about six weeks ago. Sir Thomas Vivian never liked to miss the first-nights at the theatres. His usual hand was perfectly different from that used in the notebook."

'And now, last of all, we come back to the note itself. Here it is in facsimile. My possession of it is due to the kindness of Inspector Cleeve, who is pleased to be amused at my amateur inquisitiveness. Read it, Phillipps; you tell me you are interested in obscure inscriptions; here is something for you to decipher.'

Mr. Phillipps, absorbed in spite of himself in the strange circumstances Dyson had related, took the piece of paper, and scrutinized it closely. The handwriting was indeed bizarre in the extreme, and, as Dyson had noted, not unlike the Persian character in its general effect, but it was perfectly legible.

'Read it aloud,' said Dyson, and Phillipps obeyed.

' "Hand did not point in vain. The meaning of the stars is no longer obscure. Strangely enough, the black heaven vanished, or was stolen yesterday, but that does not matter in the least, as I have a celestial globe. Our old orbit remains unchanged; you have not forgotten the number of my sign, or will you appoint some other house? I have been on the other side of the moon, and can bring something to show you." '

'And what do you make of that?' said Dyson.

'It seems to me mere gibberish,' said Phillipps; 'you suppose it has a meaning?'

'Oh, surely; it was posted three days before the murder; it was found in the murdered man's pocket; it is written in a fantastic hand which the murdered man himself used for his private memoranda. There must be purpose under all this, and to my mind there is something ugly enough hidden under the circumstances of this case of Sir Thomas Vivian.'

'But what theory have you formed?'

'Oh, as to theories, I am still in a very early stage; it is too soon to state conclusions. But I think I have demolished your Italian. I tell you, Phillipps, again, the whole thing has an ugly look to my eyes. I cannot do as you do, and fortify myself with cast-iron propositions to the effect that this or that doesn't happen, and never has happened. You note that the first word in the letter is "hand." That seems to me, taken with what we know about the hand on the wall, significant enough, and what you yourself told me of the history and meaning of the symbol, its connection with a world-old belief and faiths of dim far-off years, all this speaks of mischief, for me at all events. No; I stand pretty well to what I said to you half in joke that night before we went out. There are sacraments of evil as well as of good about us, and we live and move to my belief in an unknown world, a place where there are caves and shadows and dwellers in twilight. It is possible that man may sometimes return on the track of evolution, and it is my belief that an awful lore is not yet dead.'

'I cannot follow you in all this,' said Phillipps; 'it seems to interest you strangely. What do you propose to do?'

'My dear Phillipps," replied Dyson, speaking in a lighter tone, 'I am afraid I shall have to go down a little in the world. I have a prospect of visits to the pawnbrokers before me, and the publicans must not be neglected. I must cultivate a taste for four ale; shag tobacco I already love and esteem with all my heart.'

Search for the
Vanished Heaven

For many days after the discussion with Phillipps, Mr. Dyson was resolute in the line of research he had marked out for himself. A fervent curiosity and an innate liking for the obscure were great incentives, but especially in this case of Sir Thomas Vivian's death (for Dyson began to boggle a little at the word 'murder') there seemed to him an element that was more than curious. The sign of the red hand upon the wall, the tool of flint that had given death, the almost identity between the handwriting of the note and the fantastic script reserved religiously, as it appeared, by the doctor for trifling jottings, all these diverse and variegated threads joined to weave in his mind a strange and shadowy picture, with ghastly shapes dominant and deadly, and yet ill-defined, like the giant figures wavering in an ancient tapestry. He thought he had a clue to the meaning of the note, and in his resolute search for the 'black heaven,' which had vanished, he beat furiously about the alleys and obscure streets of central London, making himself a familiar figure to the pawnbroker, and a frequent guest at the more squalid pot-houses.

For a long time he was unsuccessful, and he trembled at the thought that the 'black heaven' might be hid in the coy retirements of Peckham, or lurk perchance in distant Willesden, but finally, improbability, in which he put his trust, came to the rescue. It was a dark and rainy night, with something in the unquiet and stirring gusts that savoured of approaching winter, and Dyson, beating up a narrow street not far from the Gray's Inn Road, took shelter in an extremely dirty 'public,' and called for beer, forgetting for the moment his preoccupations, and only thinking of the sweep of the wind about the tiles and the hissing of the rain through the black and troubled air. At the bar there gathered the usual company: the frowsy women and the men in shiny black, those who appeared to mumble secretly together, others who wrangled in interminable argument, and a few shy drinkers who stood apart, each relishing his dose, and the rank and biting flavour of cheap spirit. Dyson was wondering at the enjoyment of it all, when suddenly there came a sharper accent. The folding-doors swayed open, and a middleaged woman staggered towards the bar, and clutched the pewter rim as if she stepped a deck in a roaring gale. Dyson glanced at her attentively as a pleasing specimen of her class; she was decently dressed in black, and carried a black bag of somewhat rusty leather, and her intoxication was apparent and far advanced. As she swayed at the bar, it was evidently all she could do to stand upright, and the barman, who had looked at her with disfavour, shook his head in reply to her thick-voiced demand for a drink. The woman glared at him, transformed in a moment to a fury, with bloodshot eyes, and poured forth a torrent of execration, a stream of blasphemies and early English phraseology.

'Get out of this,' said the man; 'shut up and be off, or I'll send for the police.'

'Police, you ——,' bawled the woman, 'I'll —— well give you something to fetch the police for!' and with a rapid dive into her bag she pulled out some object which she hurled furiously at the bar-man's head.

The man ducked down, and the missile flew over his head and smashed a bottle to fragments, while the woman with a peal of horrible laughter rushed to the door, and they could hear her steps pattering fast over the wet stones.

The barman looked ruefully about him.

'Not much good going after her,' he said, 'and I'm afraid what she's left won't pay for that bottle of whisky.'

He fumbled amongst the fragments of broken glass, and drew out something dark, a kind of square stone it seemed, which he held up.

'Valuable cur'osity,' he said, 'any gent like to bid?'

The habitués had scarcely turned from their pots and glasses during these exciting incidents; they gazed a moment, fishily, when the bottle smashed, and that was all, and the mumble of the confidential was resumed and the jangle of the quarrelsome, and the shy and solitary sucked in their lips and relished again the rank flavour of the spirit.

Dyson looked quickly at what the barman held before him.

'Would you mind letting me see it?' he said; 'it's a queer-looking thing, isn't it?'

It was a small black tablet, apparently of stone, about four inches long by two and a half broad, and as Dyson took it he felt rather than saw that he touched the secular with his flesh. There was some kind of carving on the surface, and, most conspicuous, a sign that made Dyson's heart leap.

'I don't mind taking it,' he said quietly. 'Would two shillings be enough?'

'Say half a dollar,' said the man, and the bargain was concluded. Dyson drained his pot of beer, finding it delicious, and lit his pipe, and went out deliberately soon after. When he reached his apartment he locked the door, and placed the tablet on his desk, and then fixed himself in his chair, as resolute as an army in its trenches before a beleaguered city. The tablet was full under the light of the shaded candle, and scrutinizing it closely, Dyson saw first the sign of the hand with the thumb protruding between the fingers; it was cut finely and firmly on the dull black surface of the stone, and the thumb pointed downward to what was beneath.

'It is a mere ornament,' said Dyson to himself, 'perhaps symbolical ornament, but surely not an inscription, or the signs of any words ever spoken.'

The hand pointed to a series of fantastic figures, spirals

and whorls of the finest, most delicate lines, spaced at intervals over the remaining surface of the tablet. The marks were as intricate and seemed almost as much as without design as the pattern of a thumb impressed on a pane of glass.

'Is it some natural marking?' though Dyson; 'there have been queer designs, likenesses of beasts and flowers, in stones with which man's hand had nothing to do;' and he bent over the stone with a magnifier, only to be convinced that no hazard of nature could have delineated those varied labyrinths of line. The whorls were different sizes; some were less than the twelfth of an inch in diameter, and the largest was a little smaller than a sixpence, and under the glass the regularity and accuracy of the cutting were evident, and in the smaller spirals the lines were graduated at intervals of a hundredth of an inch. The whole thing had a marvellous and fantastic look, and gazing at the mystic whorls beneath the hand, Dyson became subdued with an impression of vast and far-off ages, and of a living being that had touched the stone with enigmas before the hills were formed, when the hard rocks still boiled with fervent heat.

'The "black heaven" is found again,' he said, 'but the meaning of the stars is likely to be obscure for everlasting so far as I am concerned.'

London stilled without, and a chill breath came into the room as Dyson sat gazing at the tablet shining duskily under the candle-light; and at last, as he closed the desk over the ancient stone, all his wonder at the case of Sir Thomas Vivian increased tenfold, and he thought of the well-dressed prosperous gentleman lying dead mystically beneath the sign of the hand, and the insupportable conviction seized him that between the death of this fashionable West-end doctor and the weird spirals of the tablet there were most secret and unimaginable links.

For days he sat before his desk gazing at the tablet, unable to resist its loadstone fascination, and yet quite helpless, without ever the hope of solving the symbols so secretly inscribed. At last, desperate, he called in Mr.

Phillipps in consultation, and told in brief the story of the finding the stone.

'Dear me!' said Phillipps, 'this is extremely curious; you have had a find indeed. Why it looks to me even more ancient than the Hittite seal. I confess the character, if it is a character, is entirely strange to me. These whorls are really very quaint.'

'Yes, but I want to know what they mean. You must remember this tablet is the "black heaven" of the letter found in Sir Thomas Vivian's pocket; it bears directly on his death.'

'Oh, no, that is nonsense! This is, no doubt, an extremely ancient tablet, which has been stolen from some collection. Yes, the hand makes an odd coincidence, but only a coincidence after all.'

'My dear Phillipps, you are a living example of the truth of the axiom that extreme scepticism is mere credulity. But can you decipher the inscription?'

'I undertake to decipher anything,' said Phillipps. 'I do not believe in the insoluble. These characters are curious, but I cannot fancy them to be inscrutable.'

'Then take the thing away with you and make what you can of it. It has begun to haunt me; I feel as if I had gazed too long into the eyes of the Sphinx.'

Phillipps departed with the tablet in an inner pocket. He had not much doubt of success, for he had evolved thirty-seven rules for the solution of inscriptions. Yet when a week had passed and he called to see Dyson there was no vestige of triumph on his features. He found his friend in a state of extreme irritation, pacing up and down in the room like a man in a passion. He turned with a start as the door opened.

'Well,' said Dyson, 'you have got it? What is it all about?'

'My dear fellow, I am sorry to say I have completely failed. I have tried every known device in vain. I have even been so officious as to submit it to a friend at the Museum, but he, though a man of prime authority on the subject, tells me that he is quite at fault. It must be some wreckage of a vanished race, almost, I think—a fragment of another world than ours. I am not a superstitious man, Dyson, and you know that I have no truck with even the noble delusions, but I confess I yearn to be rid of this small square of blackish stone. Frankly, it has given me an ill week; it seems to me troglodytic and abhorred.'

Phillipps drew out the tablet and laid it on the desk before Dyson.

'By the way,' he went on, 'I was right at all events in one particular; it has formed part of some collection. There is a piece of grimy paper on the back that must have been a label.'

'Yes, I noticed that,' said Dyson, who had fallen into deepest disappointment; 'no doubt the paper is a label. But as I don't much care where the tablet originally came from, and only wish to know what the inscription means, I paid no attention to the paper. The thing is a hopeless riddle, I suppose, and yet it must surely be of the greatest importance.'

Phillipps left soon after, and Dyson, still despondent, took the tablet in his hand and carelessly turned it over. The label had so grimed that it seemed merely a dull stain, but as Dyson looked at it idly, and yet attentively, he could see pencil-marks, and he bent over it eagerly, with his glass to his eye. To his annoyance, he found that part of the paper had been torn away, and he could only with difficulty make out odd words and pieces of words. First he read something that looked like 'inroad,' and then beneath, 'stony-hearted step——' and a tear cut off the rest. But in an instant a solution suggested itself, and he chuckled with huge delight.

'Certainly,' he said aloud, 'this is not only the most charming but the most convenient quarter in all London; here I am, allowing for the accidents of side streets, perched on a tower of observation.'

He glanced triumphantly out of the window across the street to the gate of the British Museum. Sheltered by the boundary wall of that agreeable institution, a 'screever,' or artist in chalks, displayed his brilliant impressions on the pavement, soliciting the approval and the coppers of the gay and serious.

'This,' said Dyson, 'is more than delightful! An artist is provided to my hand.'

The Artist of the Pavement

Mr. Phillipps, in spite of all disavowals—in spite of the wall of sense of whose enclosure and limit he was wont to make his boast—yet felt in his heart profoundly curious as to the case of Sir Thomas Vivian. Though he kept a brave face for his friend, his reason could not decently resist the conclusion that Dyson had enunciated, namely, that the whole affair had a look both ugly and mysterious. There was the weapon of a vanished race that had pierced the great arteries; the red hand, the symbol of a hideous faith, that pointed to the slain man; and then the tablet which Dyson declared he had expected to find, and had certainly found, bearing the ancient impress of the hand of malediction, and a legend written beneath in a character compared with which the most antique cuneiform was a thing of yesterday. Besides all this, there were other points that tortured and perplexed. How to account for the bare knife found unstained beneath the body? And the hint that the red hand upon the wall must have been drawn by some one whose life was passed in darkness thrilled him with a suggestion of dim and infinite horror. Hence he was in truth not a little curious as to what was to come, and some ten days after he had returned the tablet he again visited the 'mystery-man,' as he privately named his friend.

Arrived in the grave and airy chambers in Great Russell Street, he found the moral atmosphere of the place had been transformed. All Dyson's irritation had disappeared, his brow was smoothed with complacency, and he sat at a table by the window gazing out into the street with an

181

expression of grim enjoyment, a pile of books and papers lying unheeded before him.

'My dear Phillipps, I am delighted to see you! Pray excuse my moving. Draw your chair up here to the table, and try this admirable shag tobacco.'

'Thank you,' said Phillipps, 'judging by the flavour of the smoke, I should think it is a little strong. But what on earth is all this? What are you looking at?'

'I am on my watch-tower. I assure you that the time seems short while I contemplate this agreeable street and the classic grace of the Museum portico.'

'Your capacity for nonsense is amazing,' replied Phillipps, 'but have you succeeded in deciphering the tablet? It interests me.'

'I have not paid much attention to the tablet recently,' said Dyson. 'I believe the spiral character may wait.'

'Really! And how about the Vivian murder?'

'Ah, you do take an interest in that case? Well, after all, we cannot deny that it was a queer business. But is not "murder" rather a coarse word? It smacks a little, surely, of the police poster. Perhaps I am a trifle decadent, but I cannot help believing in the splendid word; "sacrifice," for example, is surely far finer than "murder." '

'I am all in the dark,' said Phillipps. 'I cannot even imagine by what track you are moving in this labyrinth.'

'I think that before very long the whole matter will be a good deal clearer for us both, but I doubt whether you will like hearing the story.'

Dyson lit his pipe afresh and leant back, not relaxing, however, in his scrutiny of the street. After a somewhat lengthy pause, he startled Phillipps by a loud breath of relief as he rose from the chair by the window and began to pace the floor.

'It's over for the day,' he said, 'and, after all, one gets a little tired.'

Phillipps looked with inquiry into the street. The evening was darkening, and the pile of the Museum was beginning to loom indistinct before the lighting of the lamps, but the pavements were thronged and busy. The artist in chalks across the way was gathering together his materials, and blurring all the brilliance of his designs, and a little lower down there was the clang of shutters being placed in position. Phillipps could see nothing to justify Mr. Dyson's sudden abandonment of his attitude of surveillance, and grew a little irritated by all these thorny enigmas.

'Do you know, Phillipps,' said Dyson, as he strolled at ease up and down the room, 'I will tell you how I work. I go upon the theory of improbability. The theory is unknown to you? I will explain. Suppose I stand on the steps of St. Paul's and look out for a blind man lame of the left leg to pass me, it is evidently highly improbable that I shall see such a person by waiting for an hour. If I wait two hours the improbability is diminished, but it still enormous, and a watch of a whole day would give little expectation of success. But suppose I take up the same position day after day, and week after week, don't you perceive that the improbability is lessening constantly —growing smaller day after day? Don't you see that two lines which are not parallel are gradually approaching one another, drawing nearer and nearer to a point of meeting, till at last they do meet, and improbability has vanished altogether? That is how I found the black tablet: I acted on the theory of improbability. It is the only scientific principle I know of which can enable one to pick out an unknown man from amongst five million.'

'And you expect to find the interpreter of the black tablet by this method?'

'Certainly.'

'And the murderer of Sir Thomas Vivian also?'

'Yes, I expect to lay my hands on the person concerned in the death of Sir Thomas Vivian in exactly the same way.'

The rest of the evening, after Phillipps had left, was devoted by Dyson to sauntering in the streets, and afterwards, when the night grew late, to his literary labours, or the chase of the phrase, as he called it. The next morning the station by the window was again resumed. His meals were brought to him at the table, and he ate with his eyes on the street. With briefest intervals, snatched reluctantly from time to time, he persisted in his survey throughout the day, and only at dusk, when the shutters were put up and the 'screever' ruthlessly deleted all his labour of the day, just before the gas-lamps began to star the shadows, did he feel at liberty to quit his post. Day after day this ceaseless glance upon the street continued, till the landlady grew puzzled and aghast at such a profitless pertinacity.

But at last, one evening, when the play of lights and shadows was scarce beginning, and the clear cloudless air left all distinct and shining, there came the moment. A man of middle age, bearded and bowed, with a touch of grey about the ears, was strolling slowly along the northern pavement of Great Russell Street from the eastern end. He looked up at the Museum as he went by, and then glanced involuntarily at the art of the 'screever,' and at the artist himself, who sat beside his pictures, hat in hand. The man with the beard stood still an instant, swaying slightly to and fro as if in thought, and Dyson saw his fists shut tight, and his back quivering, and the one side of his face in view twitched and grew contorted with the indescribable torment of approaching epilepsy. Dyson drew a soft hat from his pocket, and dashed the door open, taking the stair with a run.

When he reached the street the person he had seen so agitated had turned about, and, regardless of observation, was racing wildly towards Bloomsbury Square, with his back to his former course.

Mr. Dyson went up to the artist of the pavement, and gave him some money, observing quietly, 'You needn't trouble to draw that thing again.' Then he too turned about, and strolled idly down the street in the opposite direction to that taken by the fugitive. So the distance between Dyson and the man with the bowed head grew steadily greater.

Story of the
Treasure House

'There are many reasons why I chose your rooms for the meeting in preference to my own. Chiefly, perhaps, because I thought the man would be more at his ease on neutral ground.'

'I confess, Dyson,' said Phillipps, 'that I feel both impatient and uneasy. You know my standpoint: hard matter of fact, materialism if you like, in its crudest form. But there is something about all this affair of Vivian that makes me a little restless. And how did you induce the man to come?'

'He has an exaggerated opinion of my powers. You remember what I said about the doctrine of improbability? When it does work out, it gives results which seem very amazing to a person who is not in the secret. That is eight striking, isn't it? And there goes the bell.'

They heard footsteps on the stair, and presently the door opened, and a middle-aged-man, with a bowed head, bearded, and with a good deal of grizzling hair about his ears, came into the room. Phillipps glanced at his features, and recognized the lineaments of terror.

'Come in, Mr. Selby,' said Dyson. 'This is Mr. Phillipps, my intimate friend and our host for this evening. Will you take anything? Then perhaps we had better hear your story—a very singular one, I am sure.'

The man spoke in a voice hollow and a little quavering, and a fixed stare that never left his eyes seemed directed to something awful that was to remain before him by day and night for the rest of his life.

'You will, I am sure, excuse preliminaries,' he began; 'What I have to tell is best told quickly. I will say, then, that I was born in a remote part of the west of England, where the very outlines of the woods and hills, and the winding of the streams in the valleys, are apt to suggest the mystical to any one strongly gifted with imagination. When I was quite a boy there were certain huge and rounded hills, certain depths of hanging wood, and secret valleys bastioned round on every side that filled me with fancies beyond the bourne of rational expression, and as I grew older and began to dip into my father's books, I went by instinct, like the bee, to all that would nourish fantasy. Thus, from a course of obsolete and occult reading, and from listening to certain wild legends in which the older people still secretly believe, I grew firmly convinced of the existence of treasure, the hoard of a race extinct for ages, still hidden beneath the hills, and my every thought was directed to the discovery of the golden heaps that lay, as I fancied, within a few feet of the green turf. To one spot, in especial, I was drawn as if by enchantment; it was a tumulus, the doomed memorial of some forgotten people, crowning the crest of a vast mountain range; and I have often lingered there on summer evenings, sitting on the great block of limestone at the summit, and looking out far over the yellow sea towards the Devonshire coast. One day as I dug heedlessly with the ferrule of my stick at the mosses and lichens which grew rank over the stone, my eye was caught by what seemed a pattern beneath the growth of green; there was a curving line, and marks that did not look altogether the work of nature. At first I thought I had bared some rare fossil, and I took out my knife and scraped away at the moss till a square foot was uncovered. Then I saw two signs which startled me; first, a closed hand, pointing downwards, the thumb protruding between the fingers, and beneath the hand a whorl or spiral, traced with exquisite accuracy in the hard surface of the rock. Here, I persuaded myself, was an index to the great secret, but I chilled at the recollection of the fact that some antiquarians had tunnelled the tumulus through and through, and had been a good deal surprised at not finding so much as an arrowhead within. Clearly, then, the signs of the limestone had no local significance; and I made up my mind that I must search abroad. By sheer accident I was in a measure successful in my quest. Strolling by a cottage, I saw some children playing by the roadside; one was holding up some object in his hand, and the rest were going through one of the many forms of elaborate pretence which make up a great part of the mystery of a child's life. Something in the object held by the little boy attracted me, and I asked him to let me see it. The plaything of these children consisted of an oblong tablet of black stone; and on it was inscribed the hand pointing downwards, just as I had seen it on the rock, while beneath, spaced over the tablet, were a number of whorls and spirals, cut, as it seemed to me, with the utmost care and nicety. I bought the toy for a couple of shillings; the woman of the house told me it had been lying about for years; she thought her husband had found it one day in the brook which ran in front of the cottage; it was a very hot summer, and the stream was almost dry, and he saw it amongst the stones. That day I tracked the brook to a well of water gushing up cold and clear at the head of a lonely glen in the mountains. That was twenty years ago, and I only succeeded in deciphering the mysterious inscription last August. I must not trouble you with irrelevant details of my life; it is enough for me to say that I was forced, like many another man, to leave my old home and come to London. Of money I had very little, and I was glad to find a cheap room in a squalid street off the Gray's Inn Road. The late Sir Thomas Vivian, then far poorer and more wretched than myself, had a garret in the same house, and before many months we became intimate friends, and I had confided to him the object of my life. I had at first great difficulty in persuading him that I was not giving my days and my nights to an inquiry altogether hopeless and chimerical; but when he was convinced he grew keener than myself, and glowed at the thought of the riches which were to be the prize of some ingenuity and patience. I liked the man intensely, and pitied his case; he had a strong desire to enter the medical profession, but he lacked the means to pay the smallest fees, and indeed he was, not once or twice, but often reduced to the very verge of starvation. I freely and solemnly promised that, under whatever chances, he should share in my heaped fortune when it came, and this promise to one who had always been poor, and yet thirsted for wealth and pleasure in a manner unknown to me, was the strongest incentive. He threw himself into the task with eager interest, and applied a very acute intellect and unwearied patience to the solution of the characters on the tablet. I, like other ingenious young men, was curious in the matter of handwriting, and I had invented or adapted a fantastic script which I used occasionally, and which took Vivian so strongly that he was at the pains to imitate it. It was arranged between us that if we were ever parted, and had occasion to write on the affair that was so close to our hearts, this queer hand of my invention was to be used, and we also contrived a semi-cypher for the same purpose. Meanwhile we exhausted ourselves in efforts to get at the heart of the mystery, and after a couple of years had gone by I could see that Vivian began to sicken a little of the adventure, and one night he told me with some emotion that he feared both our lives were being passed away in idle and hopeless endeavor. Not many months afterwards he was so happy as to receive a considerable legacy from an aged and distant relative whose very existence had been almost forgotten by him; and with money at the bank, he became at once a stranger to me. He had passed his preliminary examination many years before, and he forthwith decided to enter at St. Thomas's Hospital, and he told me that he must look out for a more convenient lodging. As we said good-bye, I reminded him of the promise I had given, and solemnly renewed it; but Vivian laughed with something between pity and contempt in his voice and expression as he thanked me. I need not dwell on the long struggle and misery of my existence, now doubly lonely; I never wearied or despaired of final success, and every day saw me at work, the tablet before me, and only at dusk would I go out and take my daily walk along Oxford Street, which attracted me I think by the noise and motion and glitter of lamps.

This walk grew with me to a habit; every night, and in all weathers, I crossed the Gray's Inn Road and struck westward, sometimes choosing a northern track, by the Euston Road and Tottenham Court Road, sometimes I went by Holborn, and sometimes by the way of Great Russell Street. Every night I walked for an hour to and fro on the northern pavement of Oxford Street, and the tale of De Quincey and his name for the Street, "Stony-hearted step-mother," often recurred to my memory. Then I would return to my grimy den and spend hours more in endless analysis of the riddle before me.

'The answer came to me one night a few weeks ago; it flashed into my brain in a moment, and I read the inscription, and saw that after all I had not wasted my days.' "The place of the treasure house of them that dwell below," were the first words, I read, and then followed minute indications of the spot in my own country where the great works of gold were to be kept for ever. Such a track was to be followed, such a pitfall avoided; here the way narrowed almost to a fox's hole, and there it broadened, and so at last the chamber would be reached. I determined to lose no time in verifying my discovery—not that I doubted at that great moment, but I would not risk even the smallest chance of disappointing my old friend Vivian, now a rich and prosperous man. I took the train for the West, and one night, with chart in hand, traced out the passage of the hills, and went so far that I saw the gleam of gold before me. I would not go on; I resolved that Vivian must be with me; and I only brought away a strange knife of flint which lay on the path, as confirmation of what I had to tell. I returned to London, and was a good deal vexed to find the stone tablet had disappeared from my rooms. My landlady, an inveterate drunkard, denied all knowledge of the fact, but I have little doubt she had stolen the thing for the sake of the glass of whiskey it might fetch. However, I knew what was written on the tablet by heart, and I had also made an exact facsimile of the characters, so the loss was not severe. Only one thing annoyed me: when I first came into possession of the stone, I had pasted a piece of paper on the back and had written down the date and place of finding, and later on I had scribbled a word or two, a trivial sentiment, the name of my street, and such-like idle pencillings on the paper; and these memories of days that had seemed so hopeless were dear to me: I had thought they would help to remind me in the future of the hours when I had hoped against despair. However, I wrote at once to Sir Thomas Vivian, using the handwriting I have mentioned and also the quasi-cypher. I told him of my success, and after mentioning the loss of the tablet and the fact that I had a copy of the inscription, I reminded him once more of my promise, and asked him either to write or call. He replied that he would see me in a certain obscure passage in Clerkenwell well known to us both in the old days, and at seven o'clock one evening I went to meet him. At the corner of this by-way, as I was walking to and fro, I noticed the blurred pictures of some street artist, and I picked up a piece of chalk he had left behind him, not much thinking what I was doing. I paced up and down the passage, wondering a good deal, as you may imagine, as to what manner of man I was to meet after so many years of parting, and the thoughts of the buried time coming thick upon me, I walked mechanically without raising my eyes from the ground. I was startled out of my reverie by an angry voice and a rough inquiry why I didn't keep to the right side of the pavement, and looking up I found I had confronted a prosperous and important gentleman, who eyed my poor appearance with a look of great dislike and contempt. I knew directly it was my old comrade, and when I recalled myself to him, he apologized with some show of regret, and began to thank me for my kindness, doubtfully, as if he hesitated to commit himself, and, as I could see, with the hint of a suspicion as to my sanity. I would have engaged him at first in reminiscences of our friendship, but I found Sir Thomas viewed those days with a good deal of distaste, and replying politely to my remarks, continually edged in "business matters," as he called them. I changed my topics, and told him in greater detail what I have told you. Then I saw his manner suddenly change; as I pulled out the flint knife to prove my journey "to the other side of the moon," as we called it in our jargon, there came over him a kind of choking eagerness, his features were somewhat discomposed, and I thought I detected a shuddering horror, a clenched resolution, and the efforts to keep quiet succeed one another in a manner that puzzled me. I had occasion to be a little precise in my particulars, and it being still light enough, I remembered the red chalk in my pocket, and drew the hand on the wall. "Here, you see, is the hand," I said, as I explained its true meaning, "note where the thumb issues from between the first and second fingers," and I would have gone on, and had applied the chalk to the wall to continue my diagram, when he struck my hand down, much to my surprise. "No, no," he said, "I do not want all that. And this place is not retired enough; let us walk on, and do you explain everything to me minutely." I complied readily enough, and he led me away, choosing the most unfrequented by-ways, while I drove in the plan of the hidden house word by word. Once or twice as I raised my eyes I caught Vivian looking strangely about him; he seemed to give a quick glint up and down, and glance at the houses; and there was a furtive and anxious air about him that displeased me. "Let us walk on to the north," he said at length, "we shall come to some pleasant lanes where we can discuss these matters, quietly; my night's rest is at your service." I declined, on the pretext that I could not dispense with my visit to Oxford Street, and went on till he understood every turning and winding and the minutest detail as well as myself. We had returned on our footsteps, and stood again in the dark passage, just where I had drawn the red hand on the wall, for I recognized the vague shape of the trees whose branches hung above us. "We have come back to our starting-point," I said; "I almost think I could put my finger on the wall where I drew the hand. And I am sure you could put your finger on the mystic hand in the hills as well as I. Remember between stream and stone."

'I was bending down, peering at what I thought must be my drawing, when I heard a sharp hiss of breath, and started up, and saw Vivian with his arm uplifted and a bare blade in his hand, and death threatening in his eyes. In sheer self-defence I caught at the flint weapon in my pocket, and dashed at him in blind fear of my life, and the next instant he lay dead upon the stones.

'I think that is all,' Mr. Selby continued after a pause, 'and it only remains for me to say to you, Mr. Dyson, that I cannot conceive what means enabled you to run me down.'

'I followed many indications,' and Dyson, 'and I am bound to disclaim all credit for acuteness, as I have made several gross blunders. Your celestial cypher did not, I confess, give me much trouble; I saw at once that terms of astronomy were substituted for common words and phrases. You had lost something black, or something black had been stolen from you; a celestial globe is a copy of the heavens, so I knew you meant you had a copy of what you had lost. Obviously, then, I came to the conclusion that you had lost a black object with characters or symbols written or inscribed on it, since the object in question certainly contained valuable information, and all information must be written or pictured. "Our old orbit remains unchanged"; evidently our old course or arrangement. "The number of my sign" must mean the number of my house, the allusion being to the signs of the zodiac. I need not say that "the other side of the moon" can stand for nothing but some place where no one else has been; and "some other house" is some other place of meeting, the "house" being the old term "house of the heavens." Then my next step was to find the "black heaven" that had been stolen, and by a process of exhaustion I did so.'

'You have got the tablet?'

'Certainly. And on the back of it, on the slip of paper you have mentioned, I read "inroad," which puzzled me a good deal, till I thought of Gray's Inn Road; you forgot the second *n*. "Stony-hearted step——" immediately suggested the phrase of De Quincey you have alluded to; and I made the wild but correct shot, that you were a man who lived in or near the Gray's Inn Road, and had the habit of walking in Oxford Street, for you remember how the opium eater dwells on his wearying promenades along that thoroughfare? On the theory of improbability, which I have explained to my friend here, I concluded that occasionally, at all events, you would choose the way Guilford Street, Russel Square, and Great Russell Street, and I knew that if I watched long enough I should see you. But how was I to recognize my man? I noticed the screever opposite my rooms, and got him to draw every day a large hand, in the gesture so familiar to us all, upon the wall behind him. I thought that when the unknown person did pass he would certainly betray some emotion at the sudden vision of the sign, to him the most terrible of symbols. You know the rest. Ah, as to catching you an hour later, that was, I confess, a refinement. From the fact of your having occupied the same rooms for so many years, in a neighbourhood moreover where lodgers are migratory to excess, I drew the conclusion that you were a man of fixed habit, and I was sure that after you had got over your fright you would return for the walk down Oxford Street. You did, by way of New Oxford Street, and I was waiting at the corner.'

'Your conclusions are admirable,' said Mr. Selby. 'I may tell you that I had my stroll down Oxford Street the night Sir Thomas Vivian died. And I think that is all I have to say.'

'Scarcely,' said Dyson. 'How about the treasure?'

'I had rather we did not speak of that,' said Mr. Selby, with a whitening of the skin about the temples.

'Oh, nonsense, sir, we are not blackmailers. Besides, you know you are in our power.'

'Then, as you put it like that, Mr. Dyson, I must tell you I returned to the place. I went on a little farther than before.'

The man stopped short; his mouth began to twitch, his lips moved apart, and he drew in quick breaths, sobbing.

"Well, well,' said Dyson, 'I dare say you have done comfortably.'

'Comfortably,' Selby went on, constraining himself with

an effort, 'yes, so comfortably that hell burns hot within me for ever. I only brought one thing away from that awful house within the hills; it was lying just beyond the spot where I found the flint knife.'

'Why did you not bring more?'

The whole bodily frame of the wretched man visibly shrank and wasted; his face grew yellow as tallow, and the sweat dropped from his brows. The spectacle was both revolting and terrible, and when the voice came, it sounded like the hissing of a snake.

'Because the keepers are still there, and I saw them, and because of this,' and he pulled out a small piece of curious gold-work and held it up.

'There,' he said, 'that is the Pain of the Goat.'

Phillipps and Dyson cried out together in horror at the revolting obscenity of the thing.

'Put it away, man; hide it, for Heaven's sake, hide it!'

'I brought that with me; that is all,' he said. 'You do not wonder that I did not stay long in a place where those who live are a little higher than the beasts, and where what you have seen is surpassed a thousandfold?'

'Take this,' said Dyson, 'I brought it with me in case it might be useful'; and he drew out the black tablet, and handed it to the shaking, horrible man.

'And now,' said Dyson, 'Will you go out?'

The two friends sat silent a little while, facing one another with restless eyes and lips that quivered.

'I wish to say that I believe him,' said Phillipps.

'My dear Phillipps,' said Dyson as he threw the windows wide open, 'I do not know that, after all, my blunders in this queer case were so very absurd.'